"I wanted.

"I have a right"

"Dena and I" Jane felt the pinching around her heart. "Do you think I would have loved her more if we had been born in the same family?"

"It's not the same. You have your whole family. All I have is that baby. How can you be so selfish?"

"I'm not being selfish. I'm following Dena's wishes. Has it ever occurred to you that maybe *my family is one of the reasons Dena wanted Angie with me?*"

Cash shoved his hands into his pockets and stared down at the ground.

"Don't you see? Dena loved you, but she turned to my family for what she lacked." Jane wanted to add, *Dena wanted Angie to love God, too, Cash,* but she knew this would shatter the tentative link she was trying to forge. Cash had never understood Dena's love for the Lord.

Instead she said, "Cash, you've decided to live your life solo, but I think Dena preferred Angie to be part of a choir...."

be a real help.

LYN COTE

Born in Texas, raised in Illinois on the shore of Lake Michigan, Lyn now lives in Iowa with her real-life hero, Steve, and their son and daughter—both teens. Lyn has spent her adult life as a teacher, then a full-time mom, now a writer.

When she married Steve over twenty years ago, she "married" the north woods of Wisconsin, too. Recently she and her husband bought a fixer-upper cabin on a lake there. Lyn spends most of each summer sitting by that lake, writing. As she writes, her Siamese cat, Shadow, likes to curl up on Lyn's lap to keep her company. By the way, Lyn's last name is pronounced "Coty."

Never Alone
Lyn Cote

Published by Steeple Hill Books™

STEEPLE HILL BOOKS

Steeple
Hill™

ISBN 0-373-87030-2

NEVER ALONE

Printed in U.S.A.

It is not good for man to live alone.
—*Genesis* 2:18

For my friend Angie

Prologue

The icy January wind roared around the gray mausoleum, assaulting the group of mourners huddled several yards away, at the double graveside. Jane felt as though the piercing wind whistled right through her. Her heart had been shattered—just as Dena's and John's bodies had been shattered by a car out of control on an icy street. Only baby Angie, strapped in her car seat, had survived.

The forest green canvas canopy flapped wildly overhead. Glacial winds moaned and buffeted Jane. She shivered while tears streamed down her face.

Cash stood ramrod straight beside her at his only sister's grave. Tears blurred her sidelong view of his face, but his chin, his whole face, looked like it had been carved from stone. A sob shuddered through her. How could Cash hold in his grief? He'd adored Dena.

Standing at the head of the graves, the pastor, wrapped in a heavy black overcoat, gave her a sympathetic look. He went on, "We know John and Dena's faith was deep. We know they have claimed the promise—'To be absent in the body is to be present with the Lord.'"

*But I want Dena here with me! She was my best friend.
We've spent our whole lives together!* She felt a touch on
her sleeve as Cash handed her his handkerchief. She wept
harder. She had her family. Now Cash had only Angie.

She silently endured the graveside parting to its end. The
pastor said the final prayer, then walked to Cash and offered
his hand. "Please accept my sincerest sympathy. Losing
both of them so young is a terrible loss."

Cash shook hands. "Thank you for handling the service."

"I only wish I could do more. Grieving is a long process.
If you need someone to talk to—"

"I'll handle it myself."

Knowing how much Cash hated any show of sympathy,
she nodded to the minister, then slipped her hands into the
crook of Cash's elbow and pulled him back a step. "Cash,
Grandmother wants you to come home with us."

He looked down at her. "That's kind of her. But I have
things to take care of."

Folding up the side of her collar against the wind, she
knew she should insist, but her own sorrow robbed her of
the strength to argue. If only they had the closeness she'd
always longed for, they could comfort each other. She imagined turning to Cash, opening the front of his coat and bury-
ing her face into his starched white shirt. In wordless sympathy, he would bend and kiss her hair. She shook her head.
This won't help.

"When are you going to pick up Angie?" she asked. The
worrying wind swirled around her legs and flared her skirt.

"Tomorrow. After I see Tom about the will."

"Would you like me to come over and help you—"

"No."

She shivered again. She'd known he would say no, but
she'd had to offer. For Dena's sake, for her own sake.
"You'll call if you need help?"

He nodded, but she knew he would never call. When had

he ever called her? All those years she had dreamed he
would notice what she felt for him....

He turned away from her to accept another mourner's
condolences. She wanted to stay beside him, but she forced
herself to walk away. Icy snow suddenly flew from the gray
felt sky. Each particle stung her wet, wind-chafed cheeks
like a pinprick. She joined her grief-stricken parents and
grandmother, who were still standing beside the graveside.

As she followed her family into their large sedan, Tom
Dawson, another old friend, stepped close. He'd pulled up
the collar of his steel gray overcoat. With his face framed
by these two flaps, he bent forward to keep his words more
private. "Jane, I need you to stop by my law office tomorrow afternoon."

"Why? Tom, I—"

"It has to do with Dena's estate."

The bleak sky, vicious cold and her ragged sorrow twisted
together and wrapped around her like a wet, raw rope—
dragging her down. She couldn't bear much more. "Cash
can take care of all that."

"Wills are never as simple as one anticipates, Jane. You
have to be there."

Chapter One

"This is going to be a shock for both of you."

His lawyer's unexpected words jerked Cash's thoughts from his deadening grief. More than the words themselves, it was the way Tom said them—painstakingly—like a man connecting a detonator wire to a bomb.

What could be more of a shock than losing my only sister? Numb with sorrow, Cash glanced toward Jane, who sat beside him. Petite, dressed in a somber brown, she was looking down at her hands folded in her lap. Her chin-length red hair fell forward, concealing her face from him. "Red" and his baby sister had been best friends from the cradle. Images of Dena and Jane together as children had haunted him all morning. An impulse to smooth Red's hair behind her ear where it usually lay, touched him, but he couldn't. She wasn't a child anymore.

"I hope you'll take this calmly," Tom went on.

Tensing, Cash sat up straighter. Jane, looking delicate and vulnerable, gripped the arms of her wide leather chair. Silence welled up in the room. The mantel clock ticked a stolid counterpoint to the uncertainty, which expanded moment by moment.

"What is it?" Cash rasped at last.

Tom breathed in deeply. "Dena and her husband didn't leave guardianship of Angie to you, Cash."

Cash lunged to his feet. "I'm Dena's only remaining blood relative. Her daughter has to come to me. She's all I have left!"

Tom hesitated, then looked up into Cash's eyes. "That would be true *if* Dena and her husband hadn't specified guardianship of their daughter."

A spear of betrayal plunged through Cash's heart. *Dena, I helped raise you. How could you give Angie to someone else?* Cash took the will from Tom's hands, but couldn't focus on the print.

"Who?" Cash demanded, "Who was appointed?"

Tom averted his gaze. "Dena and her husband gave Jane full custody."

Jane gasped.

Cash struggled to mask his anguish. After losing Dena in a senseless auto accident, assuming the care of his little Angie had been his only consolation. He wanted to roar with pain and outrage.

Tom read the awful words aloud, "If we should die before our daughter, Angela Jane Johnson, is of age, we name Jane Lucinda Everett as her guardian and give her full physical custody."

"Dena left Angie to *me?*" Jane echoed in disbelief.

"You didn't know about this?" Cash picked up the document and waved it toward her.

She shook her head, tears slipping down her pale cheeks. "If I'd known, I would have insisted on taking her home with me after the accident. Not leave her in foster care for three days."

Cash watched her cry, despair surging through him. With

great effort, he tightened his resolve. Control brought decision. He faced Jane. "You'll have to sign Angie over to me."

"What?" Jane stared at him. "We're talking about a *baby,* not a two-party check."

Cash tossed the document on the mahogany desk. "Jane, you don't want Angie. You're a career woman. You've never shown any interest in marriage and children."

She turned his words back on him. "What about you? You're a career man. You've never shown any interest in marriage and children, either. Does that mean you don't want Angie?"

Cash clenched his jaw. "Angie belongs to me."

"Angie doesn't *belong* to anyone."

"I'm ten years older than Dena and you. I'm better able to provide for Angie. I've already hired a nanny."

Jane leaned forward. "Obviously Dena wanted a mother for her baby, not a nanny."

He ignored her. "She's a highly experienced nanny. I have nothing against you as a person, but you've never taken care of an infant."

"That's not true. I stayed with Dena the first two weeks after she had Angie—"

"And that's the extent of your experience. Except for your visit home at Christmas, you've been in northern Wisconsin—"

"That's where I live—"

"I've visited Angie, at least once a week since her birth," he said. "Angie won't even know you."

"She's only five months old."

"Her age is unimportant. I don't know what my sister was thinking—"

"She was thinking she wanted *me* to have Angie, not you." Jane halted and colored as if with shame. "I'm sorry."

Cash looked past her. Her apology meant nothing. Anger and betrayal still churned inside him. To maintain control, he focused on the rows of legal books on well-spaced shelves lining the wall. The deep shades of burgundy, black, coffee brown, and forest green dragged his mind back to Dena's funeral. They were the colors of funeral-home carpet, casket lining, coffin finish and graveside greenery. His grief threatened to crush him. *No escape.*

He turned back to Tom. "This is legal? Jane really has been given full custody of my niece?"

"Yes. I'm sure you and Jane can come to some visitation arrangement—"

"I live in Chicago, remember? Jane lives three hundred miles northwest. I'll be a seven-hour drive away."

Tom looked at him steadily. "I am aware of the distance, and so were Dena and John."

Cash jutted his chin forward. "If Jane won't cede custody to me, I'll fight for it."

"A court challenge?" Tom questioned.

Jane stood up, knocking her purse to the floor. "You can't mean that."

Cash crossed his arms over his chest. "You leave me no other choice."

"Hold it there, both of you," Tom ordered. "Sit down."

Cash said, "Angie belongs with me. I—"

"Sit down." Tom's tone left no room for argument.

Jane took her seat. Cash didn't want to stop until he'd convinced them Angie must be with him. But after struggling with himself briefly, his respect for Tom made him follow suit.

"We've all been friends since we were kids. Otherwise, I'd let you two fight this out in court. But Dena was my friend, too. I feel obligated to protect her little girl."

"*Protect* her child?" Cash asked. "You're not making sense."

"Yes, I am. Just listen. Later today the Department of Children and Family Services will turn Angie over to Jane—"

"No!"

Tom continued, "Cash, stop interrupting. This is too crucial to ignore. They'll turn Angie over to Jane as the specified guardian—unless you contest it. If you contest Jane's guardianship, they'll likely keep Angie."

"Oh, no," Jane breathed.

"Keep Angie? I don't understand what you're saying." Cash's disgruntled gaze pierced Tom.

Tom looked at Cash grimly. "There have been a lot of spectacular custody battles lately. Social workers have gotten gun-shy. If this looks like it could become a case of contested custody, the state of Illinois might decide it's in Angie's best interest to keep her in foster care—until the custody battle is settled by the court. Do you know how long these battles can last?"

"Years," Jane murmured.

"That's right. Years," Tom said, giving Cash a pointed look.

"It would be awful," Jane said.

"Worse than awful," Tom continued. "Angie might stay with the same family, or she could be shifted to a dozen different foster homes—"

Cash sat stonelike.

"She could be hurt emotionally." Jane pressed her fingertips to her temples.

"She could be scarred for life," Tom reiterated. "Is that what you want for Dena's child, Cash?"

"No," Jane almost moaned it.

Tom stared at Cash. "And I warn you, the DCFS already realized that a blood relative has been passed over. I got a call from them, asking me if I thought this would run smoothly."

"I can't believe this is happening," Cash said.

Jane echoed his words softly.

"The child welfare system comes with endless possibilities for delay and frustration," Tom said. "I can't let you take any chances with that little baby girl."

Cash stood up and began pacing. Dena, how could you keep Angie from me? I love her as much as I loved you. Did you doubt that? He asked Tom sharply, "Did Dena tell you why she named Jane guardian?"

"No, when I asked her and her husband, they refused to tell me."

"They must have had a reason," Jane said, her voice showing her own uncertainty. She searched Tom's face, then Cash's.

"There is none." Cash's mouth tightened into a stubborn line.

Jane sat up straighter. "No one chooses a guardian for their baby daughter without a reason."

Cash ignored her. "What if Jane just turns Angie over to me?"

Tom steepled his fingers. "I don't know—"

"I wouldn't," Jane said quietly.

"What?" Still standing, Cash leaned forward over his chair, rested both palms on its arm and pinned her with his intense gaze.

"An Everett never contests a will. My family would be very upset—"

"You wouldn't be contesting a will," Cash interrupted. "You'd be doing the right thing."

Jane cleared her throat. "Dena adored you, Cash. Giving me Angie goes against what *both* of us expected. That means Dena must have had a powerful motive. I don't know what it is yet, but I won't violate Dena's will."

"Dena couldn't have wanted this to happen," Cash countered. "Her husband and I never quite hit it off. *He* must have—"

"No." Tom cut him off. "Dena made it clear that wasn't the motivation. The only thing that has occurred to me is the fact Jane would have family to back her up, whereas you, Cash, are alone."

Cash slumped into his chair. *Alone.* The word hung over his head. He muttered, "I'm capable of providing good care for my only niece."

"That's not the question here," Tom said. "Frankly I've allowed you two to stray from the main point. It comes down to this. Do you want Angie in Jane's care while you two settle this? Or do you want your niece in the tender care of the state of Illinois?"

Cash looked up. "Those are my only choices?" His voice broke on the final word.

"For now…yes," Tom replied.

"What if I let Jane take Angie now, but later I decide to contest it in court? What happens in that case?"

"Then Angie might have a good chance to be left in Jane's care while the case is settled," Tom replied.

Cash gave his words a twist of sarcasm. "You mean it's a case of the lesser of two evils?"

"You can put it that way if you wish." Tom leaned forward, folded his hands on his desk and stared at Cash.

Cash glanced at Jane, but the sympathy in her steady eyes made him look back to Tom. "So what do you want me to do?"

Tom took a deep breath. "I want you to go with Jane to pick up Angie."

"*I* have to go? Why?" Cash didn't think he could bear watching someone else claim Angie. The walls of the room pressed closer than they had at the beginning of the meeting.

"I don't want any delay. If you show up with Jane to

pick up Angie and appear to favor it, there shouldn't be a hitch.''

''I'm not an actor, Tom.'' Cash found it difficult to speak. A knot clogged his throat.

''You're a businessman. A successful businessman knows how to start negotiations. Always start in a position of strength.''

''Giving *in* is a position of strength?'' Cash asked.

''In this case, yes. If you let guardianship go as the will dictates, you and Jane will stay in the driver's seat. If you quarrel at this point, the state of Illinois will take the steering wheel. In that case, none of you will ever be the same.''

A tense silence mushroomed until it dominated the room.

Like a man slowly freezing to death, Cash felt himself slipping into numbness. His gaze fastened on Jane's bright hair. While everything else in the room had dulled, it still gleamed like a lamp through a thickening haze.

''Cash?'' Tom prompted.

''Angie can go with Jane.'' Even to himself his voice sounded rough with emotion.

Jane closed her eyes.

Cash felt one last surge of energy. ''For now.''

Jane stepped into Cash's black Lincoln and felt the whoosh of cold air as Cash closed the door beside her. He entered the driver's side, started the car and pulled out of the parking lot of Tom's office.

This morning, because Jane hadn't trusted her emotions enough to drive herself to Tom's Chicago office, she had ridden in on the commuter train. So now Cash and she sat in his sleek car on their way to a Department of Child and Family Services office to take custody of Dena's five-month-old daughter.

I will be taking Angie home with me. The words held no reality for her. Suddenly images of diapers, bottles, formula crowded her mind. *Thank You, Lord, for Mother and Grandmother. What would I do without them?* Being named Angie's guardian had never crossed her mind. Dena, why did you do this?

Flashes of the cold, dreary city passed by the car window, red brick apartment buildings and offices, city snow in shades of dirty white to black, people bundled in down jackets with hoods in winter colors: navy, gray, brown.

She glanced at Cash's profile. He drove smoothly as though this were any drive, but his calm outward appearance didn't deceive her. Riding alone with him was like sitting in a lion's cage.

Deep below his unruffled surface, even the overwhelming shock and sorrow he suffered hadn't blunted his dominating presence. No matter how she fought it, no matter what the circumstances, Cash Langley could always touch her heart, make her long to press her hand against his hard, chiseled jaw.

She was suffering, too. Six days ago Dena had called her full of news about Angie sitting up by herself for the first time. If I'd only known it was our last call, Jane thought. Pain gripped her heart, nearly forcing a gasp from her.

Her own anguish made her yearn to comfort the solemn man so near but so distant. He was a handsome man with fine, straight features, steel blue eyes and black hair combed back from his face like folded wings. His profile always put her in mind of a medieval king. Today he was a brooding king, dark emotion making the determined line of his jaw even more grim than usual.

She ached to pull him close, to murmur words of solace. But it was impossible, had always been, would always be. Cash didn't want comfort, now or ever.

"Here it is," Cash ground out the three words. He parked on the street. Shivering in the mid-January wind, she preceded him to the door. He opened it and held it for her. They walked side by side to the desk.

Jane cleared her dry throat. "I'm Jane Everett. I'm here to pick up Angie Johnson." She and Cash were asked to take seats. They sat silent, miserable, separated by an invisible wall of Cash's making. Jane tried to pray, but the overheated room and the grieving man beside her sapped her energy. She could only pray within. *Dear God, Dear God.*

Several minutes later a woman in a dark suit asked them into her office. She said, "Good day," without the slightest touch of warmth.

A chill shivered through Jane. All of Tom's warnings played through her head once more. She forced herself not to give Cash a sideways glance and tried to behave as though picking up a baby were an everyday occurrence in her life.

"May I see a picture ID, Ms. Everett?"

Jane fumbled in her purse, dropping tissues and her lipstick, but she managed to bring out her wallet.

While Jane retrieved the items she had dropped, the woman read her driver's license thoroughly.

"You live in Wisconsin, Ms. Everett?"

"Yes," Jane croaked, then moistened her dry lips.

"Mmm," the social worker said. "That might not be advisable—"

"Why?" Cash snapped.

The woman widened her eyes and stared at him. "And you are, sir?"

"Cash Langley, the child's uncle."

"I see." She pursed her lips. "I would feel better if the child weren't going to be moved such a great distance so quickly."

Jane cleared her throat. "I'll be staying with my parents in Lake Forest for a while."

"Lake Forest?"

"Yes," Jane said, holding tightly to her budding panic.

The woman eyed Cash momentarily, then changed subjects. "I have some papers for you to sign."

The woman explained each document as she placed it before Jane on the desk. The small printing on the documents wavered in front of Jane's tired eyes. She could barely focus on where to sign her name. Document followed document. Jane lost count.

Finally the woman gathered up all the papers, tapped them neatly into one stack and slid them into a pocket folder. "I'll see if the child has arrived yet."

Jane and Cash waited silently in the small, crowded office. Though she kept her attention forward, she noted the tenseness of his face. She couldn't let him suspect she yearned to kiss away the crease etched across his forehead and the small tight lines around his mouth. He would never return her feelings.

"Here she is, Ms. Everett." The social worker held the squirming baby like a sack of potatoes across one arm.

Jane jumped up to take Angie from her. The baby whined and rubbed her eyes fretfully. "Are you tired, sweetheart?" Jane murmured. Love for this child and sorrow nearly choked her with their force, but she held on to her self-control grimly. Then she recognized the white snowsuit with a bunny tail and ears Angie wore.

Tears rushed up in Jane's eyes and a sob caught in her throat. Helplessly she felt her composure give way within. "Cash," she gasped.

Before she finished speaking, he was next to her, lifting the baby from her trembling arms and leading her back to a chair.

"Is there some problem?" the social worker asked.

"I gave Dena...this snowsuit...as a shower gift for Angie," Jane gasped between sobs.

"Ms. Everett, are you sure you are able to take custody of the child today? Perhaps you aren't up to—"

"Jane will be fine," Cash insisted. Angie fussed louder.

Jane fought down her sorrow. She subdued the sobs, but was unable to staunch her tears. "My...my mother and grandmother are waiting at home."

"I'm driving," Cash added. "Are there any more formalities?"

"No, but do you have a legal car seat in your vehicle? It is against state—"

"A brand-new one from Marshall Field's is waiting for Angie in my back seat." Cash didn't bother to look at the woman.

Angie began howling in earnest, and the social worker quickly ushered them out of her office.

Jane, tears still washing down her face, stinging her skin in the biting cold, stood outside the car while Cash placed a screaming Angie into the new car seat. Feeling overwhelmed once more by the reality of Dena's death, Jane slipped by Cash into the passenger seat. Then Cash, behind the wheel, glanced at the city traffic and pulled out at his first opportunity.

Angie screeched with frustration from the back seat. Jane wept. With each passing vehicle, gray slush splattered the windshield. Though the car's heater blew full blast into her face, Jane still trembled, feeling like a frozen maple leaf fluttering on a bare tree.

At last they left the congested Chicago streets behind. After a few minutes of smoother highway driving, the baby shuddered with several more loud sobs, then dropped off to sleep slumped to the side in her car seat.

Jane laid her head back against the headrest and took a calming breath. "I'm sorry I fell apart like that. Somehow seeing the snowsuit—"

"I understand," he cut her off.

Jane bit her lower lip. Guilt clutched her. "I'm sorry about this, Cash. I didn't know—"

"Are you willing to give Angie to me now?"

Jane looked down, avoiding eye contact. "It's not that easy."

"Why not? I'm Dena's brother."

"And I was Dena's best friend. I need time to think—"

"Think about what? Angie's mine!"

"Cash, there must be more to this."

Cash made a sound filled with irritation.

"In my whole life, I never told one secret of Dena's or broke one promise to her. She has given me Angie. I will not betray her trust."

Jane watched the self-sufficient mask Cash had lowered for just a few moments snap back into place. Jane felt him withdraw from her. The distance between them grew until she felt cramped by its presence.

The man beside her drove expertly down the interstate toward Lake Forest. He finally pulled into her parents' driveway. Jane looked at the house next door where he and Dena had grown up. Though Jane couldn't have stopped herself from looking toward the house if she tried, Cash never glanced in its direction.

He lifted Angie out of the car seat, handed her to Jane, then unhooked the car seat and set it on the recently shoveled sidewalk to the house. "You might need it." He turned back to the car.

"Cash." Jane grabbed for his arm. Angie woke up and began to squall. "Come in with me. My parents—"

"I need to go." He walked around the rear of the car.

"Where? Come in. I don't want you to leave this way."

"Then give me Angie." Over the top of the car between them, he stared at her.

"Come in. You'll be better among friends."

"No." He shook his head and got into the car.

"Cash, please come in. I don't want you to be alone."
Jane barely heard his response over Angie's wails.

He said, "I'll be better off alone."

"When will I see you again?" she called after him.

Holding a squirming, whining Angie, Jane watched as he drove away. Then her parents, their coats thrown over their shoulders, helped her into the house, where Jane struggled and won the battle against more tears. Cash might not need her, but Angie did.

Cash stared at the deep blue door of Jane's parents' house. It had taken him over a week to gather the strength to face once more Dena's giving Angie to someone other than himself. If Angie weren't on the other side of this door, he wouldn't be here. But Angie was. Pressing all his anger into a tight ball of resistance, he knocked firmly.

"I was just thinking of you." Jane's grandmother, Lucy, peered around the door.

"Am I that popular here?" Cash asked gruffly and stepped inside.

"Well, why haven't you listened to your answering machine?" Petite, frail with age, Lucy stood on tiptoe to kiss his cheek.

Momentarily he stood still, then leaned down and returned the kiss. "How are you, Lucy?"

"Heartbroken. The same as you." Lucy pulled him into the foyer. "You arrived just in time to say goodbye. Phil is in the garage loading my suitcases into the car."

Cash wanted to thank her for flying home from wintering in Florida for his sister's funeral, but he couldn't bring the words to his lips. How could he put into words his gratitude for her years of putting Band-Aids on his scrapes, her gentle way of brushing his childhood bangs out of his eyes before she bent to kiss his forehead? Past images of the loving matriarch of this house threatened to drown him in sorrow

over all he'd lost. First his mother, then his father, now
Dena…and Angie. Instead he cleared his throat. "Headed
for O'Hare?"

She nodded and led him into the living room, urging him
down beside her on the beige sofa. She took his hand in
hers and searched his eyes. "I won't waste words on sympathy. You and I know each other too well. If you need me
for anything, you have my Florida phone number."

"There's only one person I need—Angie."

"I know, but Dena must have had her reasons."

"Of course you think I should leave Angie with Jane."

"Don't say 'of course' like that. You know if I thought
Jane were wrong to keep Angie, I wouldn't mince words."

Her militant tone brought a slight smile to his lips. "I
know," he murmured. "I just don't agree."

"How could you?" she asked. "If I were you, I'd do
anything to be near my niece."

"But?" He lifted one eyebrow.

"But it's an Everett family law. We never contest wills.
It's disrespectful to the departed and only makes lawyers
rich and a family poor."

"Don't you think this is—"

Cash was interrupted by the appearance of Lucy's daugh-
ter-in-law, Marge. He stood and let her embrace him.

Marge murmured, "Lucy, we must leave now." Cash
helped Lucy into her vintage tweed coat, and the two
women hurried toward the kitchen.

Lucy turned back briefly. "Jane is upstairs with Angie."
She motioned him to go up, then called over her shoulder,
"God bless you, Cash. He would, you know, if you'd only
let Him."

In the stillness of Lucy's wake, Cash stood at the bottom
of the familiar staircase. He knew this house as well as he
knew the one next door. Looking up, he pictured Jane and
Dena, as young girls in matching white terry cloth robes,

standing at the top of the stairs. *Good night, Cash,* they called down to him.

Gathering his strength against these memories, which might weaken his resolve to reclaim Angie, he walked up the steps and followed the sound of a baby's sudden wail. He stopped in the doorway of Jane's childhood room. She was lifting Angie, dressed in fuzzy pink pj's, out of a crib.

Jane turned and gave him a startled, then a questioning look.

Cash's chest tightened. Jane had never looked so feminine. With a child in her arms, she no longer struck him as his kid sister's pal. But Angie belonged within his arms. He stretched himself to his full height. "I've come for Angie."

Chapter Two

"Oh?" Jane's tone was calm, but her heart pounded so loudly in her ears its drumming drowned out the baby's crying. Cash's unflinching power washed through her senses, calling her as always to draw near him. But panic, so like what she'd experienced that awful day in the social worker's office, snaked through her and threatened to immobilize her.

"Is she hungry?" Cash asked.

"She just finished ten ounces of formula after a bowl of rice cereal." Outwardly calm, but reeling inside, Jane fell back on the routine she had devised to deal with Angie's frantic crying every time she needed sleep. Feeling like a windup toy, she carried Angie to the white-flounced changing table.

"What's making her cry?"

"I'm checking her diaper." Jane slid a finger between two pj buttons. "She's dry." Fighting for control with each measured motion, she reached back and pulled a pink baby blanket off the side of the crib. "Where have you been for eight days, Cash?"

"To the ends of the earth and back again. You don't look too happy to see me tonight." He still stood propped against the doorjamb.

"My grandmother was worried." *I was worried.*

"I want Angie."

Her stomach twisted, but without showing the effect of his words on her, she finished tightly bundling up the crying baby and sat in the rocker.

"What's wrong with her?" he asked sharply, peering through the shadows at Angie.

Jane felt like shouting the question back at him, What's wrong with her? But she forced herself to reply mildly, "My grandmother says that's what Angie's asking us. This is the only way we've found to get her to sleep, day or night." With that, Jane began rocking vigorously, firmly patting the baby's rump through the wrapping of the blanket. Under Cash's scrutiny, Angie's wails and Jane's fear mounted in intensity.

"Cash, this is hard enough without you glaring at me," she said with bravado.

"I'm not leaving. I want my niece."

As Jane met the challenge of caring for Angie in spite of the stress, she gained more control. She held her index finger up to her lips, motioning him to speak more softly. "Why did Dena give your niece to me, then?"

"I can't explain it." He stopped, then lowered his voice. "People make decisions. They change their minds." He held up his palms in a gesture of not knowing. "Maybe my sister made this decision after we disagreed about something."

Angie hiccuped between her sobs. Jane rocked and patted, not missing a beat, though inwardly the urge to flee the small room and Cash's moody regard still tempted her.

"That doesn't seem to be working."

"It takes time." Jane warned him away with a shake of her head. Am I afraid of Cash?

"Why aren't you back in Wisconsin? How long can you leave your dress shop closed?"

"My shop isn't closed. I have two trusted employees taking care of things." Still pushing down tremors of alarm, she made herself continue to concentrate on her physical movements.

"How are you going to take the stress of this when you have to get up the next morning and go to work?"

"The same way you would," she spoke in time to her rocking.

"I would have help—"

"I'll have help. I've got friends and my Uncle Henry, Aunt Claire and their daughter, Tish. I'll arrange day care just like you would."

"Family help won't last. People say they'll help—"

"Everetts help Everetts," Jane said tightly. She noticed she had forgotten one of the elements needed to calm Angie. She nodded toward the wall next to him. "See that mobile of lambs? Wind its knob, will you?"

After he complied, the tinny, music-box melody of "Rock-a-bye Baby" competed with Angie's shrieks.

"Don't you see that single parenthood is going to be too much for you?" he insisted.

"I only see that this baby needs me." Her rocking now kept time with the tune.

"I don't understand why you can't see reason. Angie is not your responsibility—"

"Dena made her my responsibility." She held on to Angie like a lifeline. Cash's shadowed eyes spoke volumes about the sorrow he'd suffered over the past week.

Over the past decade, he had isolated himself from everyone but Dena and Angie. Now there was only Angie, and Angie belonged to her. Jane bowed her head. If only he would let her show him some kindness, show him the love which abounded in her life.

Cash raked his fingers through his already-tousled hair. He pushed away from the doorjamb and strode forward, his arms out to take the baby. "This isn't working—"

Angie gave one loud gasp. With a shudder, the baby's last sob broke and her tension released.

Gently Jane reduced the tempo of her rocking, then slipped a pink pacifier into Angie's quivering lips. When the music box ran down, Jane hummed, still uneasy under Cash's gaze. At last, she stood up and laid the sleeping baby on her side in the crib.

Cash moved closer. Together they looked down at the now-peaceful child. Despite the conflict between them and her new-sprung fear, Jane still felt drawn to everything about him, the scents of his soap and his leather jacket, the quickness of his breathing and the force of the man, which nothing diminished. When Jane couldn't bear his nearness and the anxiety anymore, she tugged at his sleeve. They stepped out into the dimly lit upstairs hall.

Jane, concealing her roiling emotions, looked up into Cash's face. "So?"

The stubborn anger in his eyes troubled Jane. She shivered in the warm hallway.

"Angie is mine. Why won't you be reasonable?"

Jane folded her arms. "Dena had a reason for giving me Angie. I don't know what it was, but until I can understand her motivations, I see no room to alter her wishes."

He flung himself away from her and hustled down the stairs.

Hugging herself, she leaned over the rail of the landing. "What are you going to do?"

"I'm going to do what Lucy said she'd do!"

"What's that?"

"Whatever it takes to be near Angie." He slammed the front door behind him.

Jane held her breath, listening for Angie to stir, but the baby slept on.

Feeling suddenly drained, Jane sat down on the highest step and propped her elbows on her knees. Dena must have had a reason. *Lord, help me understand. Am I doing Your will by following Dena's wishes? All I know for sure is Angie needs me and for the first time Cash frightens me. Would he really take Angie from me? I can't believe that.* But recalling Cash's parting words sent a stark shiver through her.

"Hi, Jane!" Rona Vitelli blew into Jane's Dress Shop on a gust of a glacial, late-February wind. "I heard you were back!"

Jane grinned. It was Monday morning. After driving Jane home on Friday, her parents had spent the past weekend helping Jane settle Angie into her house. They had just left a half hour ago to drive home.

Of course, Rona, the town's "ears" would appear bright and early on Jane's first day back at her shop. Rona liked her news served up fresh. "Hi, Rona, you're just in time to help me."

"Is this little Angie?" Rona bent over the new playpen Jane had just set up near the shop's front window.

Jane nodded, her arms full of skirts on hangers.

"She's a little doll! Such dark hair! She'd fit right in with the Vitelli clan!"

"Help me, Rona." Jane's arms sagged with the weight of her burden.

Rona swung around and reached out to lift the clothing in Jane's arms. "No." Jane stepped back and nodded toward the playpen. "Pick up Angie and follow me."

"Oh." Rona scooped Angie up and trailed Jane to a six-foot-long clothes rack at the back. When Rona first picked Angie up, the baby fussed, but when she realized Rona was her means to keeping Jane within sight, Angie calmed down and gurgled sociably.

"You have to be in sight all the time?" Rona guessed.

Quickly hanging the skirts by size on the bar, Jane nodded.

Rona entertained Angie by gently twirling right, then left. "Well, she's at that age. About seven to eight months they start wanting Mom or *else!* Do you think it has to do with losing her parents?"

"Yes, some. She's sleeping a lot better now." Jane hung and smoothed the last skirt in place. "But she is very demanding."

"You're just going to keep her here at the shop with you?" Rona gave the baby an Eskimo kiss and Angie giggled in appreciation.

"Now, while it's quiet, yes. When the resort season starts in May, I'll have to hire a baby-sitter and slowly wean her—wean both of us—from having only me on call twenty-four hours a day."

"Well, she looks happy now."

Jane took Angie back into her arms.

"Tell me, Jane…"

Jane grinned at her friend's conspiratorial tone. "Tell you *what?*"

"Are your only two employees really both pregnant and due June fifteenth?"

"No." Jane carried Angie back to the playpen and set her in it. "One is due June fifteenth and the other is due June twenty-fifth. How did you find out I was losing both of them for the whole summer? They just told me!"

"My cousin works at the hospital, you know—"

"So anything you don't hear at the restaurant, she hears there?"

"Exactly. Which brings me to my point—you're going to need to hire—"

The front door swung open sharply, jangling a small bell attached to it. "Hi, Jane!" Carmella, Rona's daughter, walked in. "What did she say, Mom? Am I hired?"

The word, *hire,* shocked Jane's stomach with the instant sensation of disaster-about-to-happen.

"Carmella, I was just about to introduce that topic—"

The door opened a second time and the little bell jingled politely this time. It was Jane's Aunt Claire, followed by Tish, her daughter.

Aunt Claire greeted everyone, looking at them over her half glasses. "Jane, I couldn't wait any longer. I had to run over on my break from the library. Is this our little Angie?"

Jane stood, sandwiched between the two mother-and-teenage-daughter pairs. On her right were Rona and Carmella, both petite, curvaceous, with dark hair and nutmeg eyes. On her left were her Aunt Claire and cousin Tish, both tall, willowy, with fair skin and strawberry blond hair. They bent over the side of the playpen. Tish's thick hair cascaded artfully down the back of her short leather jacket to the belt of her tight, designer jeans.

Angie looked up and giggled at Aunt Claire.

"So you think your aunty Claire is amusing, do you?" Aunt Claire chuckled and touched the end of the baby's nose. "What do you think of this?" From her tan wool coat pocket, Claire pulled out a soft rubber duck squeeze toy. Angie grabbed it and shrilled her joy at the honking sound it made in her hand.

Jane eyed the two teenagers. "Is school off today?"

"Teacher conferences—" Rona replied.

"Well, Mom?" Carmella asked.

Rona sighed. "Jane, I was wondering if you'd consider trying Carmella out as a salesclerk this June. She says she's tired of busing tables and doesn't want to waitress."

"Not with my dad and uncle standing over me every minute," Rona's daughter muttered.

Jane's stomach twisted itself into a curly Q. This was one of the disadvantages of small-town life. Only one answer could be given, "Sure. Can you come after school some afternoons in May to train?"

"Great!" Carmella gave a little hop. "Just name the day."

"What about me, Jane?" Tish had lifted Angie from the playpen. Angie giggled each time Tish kissed the sensitive skin behind the little girl's ear. "I was going to ask you for a job this summer, too."

Jane's stomach dropped to her toes. *Carmella Vitelli and my cousin, Tish, too? Even their grandmother, Lucy, called Tish a spoiled brat.*

"This isn't at all the way one inquires about employment," Claire chided Tish. "Besides, aren't they expecting you back at DQ this summer?"

"Mom, two summers at DQ is enough. I'll be sixteen June first. Besides if I work here, I get twenty percent off on clothes instead of ice cream!"

"Oh!" Aunt Claire opened her eyes wider. "I hadn't thought of that." She stopped to kiss the hand Angie offered her.

Jane mentally swallowed the bitter pill labeled "Keeping Peace in the Family." "Well, I guess I won't have to advertise for replacements." She smiled bravely while Carmella and Tish exchanged glares. *Oh, great!* she thought.

Within minutes Rona and her daughter departed. Aunt Claire started to go, too.

"Mom, I'll stay here," Tish said. "I'll watch Angie while Jane catches up on her work."

Claire turned to Jane with a questioning look.

The offer surprised Jane. "Thank you, Tish. That would be a real help."

Claire touched her daughter's arm with affection. "I'll bring lunch later and we'll celebrate Angie's first day at Jane's Dress Shop." Claire walked to the door. "Remember, Jane, never hesitate to call us—day or night. Your uncle Henry, Tish or me."

Tish followed Jane as she went to the counter to start to sort through the receipts for the past three weeks.

"I'm really sorry you lost your friend."

Jane looked up. "Thank you, Tish."

"I always envied you having a friend like her."

Jane struggled with the pall which fell like a shadow across her mood.

"And her brother is *so* handsome." Tish jiggled the baby in her arms. "Wouldn't it be romantic if you two ended up getting married, sort of like in an old movie?"

Jane bent her head to hide the pain she felt contort her face. "Cash never acts very romantic, Tish."

The echoing clap of the brass knocker on her front door reverberated through Jane's head. As she walked into the small entry hall, she put a hand to her pounding forehead.

Seven-month-old Angie was teething, and the nighttime hours were... She couldn't think of a word to describe the stress and exhaustion of endless dark hours spent rocking and pacing with a fussy, inconsolable baby.

Jane straightened her spine and looked down at Angie, who sat on her right hip. Knowing that Cash would be quick to criticize, Jane had spent the last hour bathing the baby and dressing her in a pink corduroy overall and a ruffled, candy-striped blouse.

Angie smiled, and Jane's heart melted. "You little doll." She kissed Angie's forehead.

The brass knocker banged twice more. Jane's smile faded. She turned the doorknob, icy cold against her palm.

Cash stepped over her threshold, and a frigid March gust

rushed in with him. Making it obvious he wanted contact only with Angie, his head bent immediately to be at eye level with the baby. "Hi, Angie."

"Hurry up and get this door shut. She just got out of the bath." Jane immediately regretted her harsh tone, but after weeks apart, Cash's presence struck Jane sharper than the winter wind against her face. Over his shoulder, she glimpsed an older blue Jeep Wrangler at the curb. "What happened to your Lincoln?" she asked. As she spoke, the dread that had marred his last visit to her parents' home ignited inside her.

He eyed her crossly, but closed the door behind him. He held out his arms to take Angie.

Reaction to his reluctance to look at her, and her own growing uneasiness, caused Jane to turn her back to him and say sternly, "Come in by the fire and get that coat off. Handing this baby to you now would be like sitting her in an icebox."

Cash gritted his teeth, but he trailed behind Jane into the cozy living room. He hung his heavy, beige camel coat on the coatrack at the room's entrance. A lively fire burned behind a brass, fan-shaped screen. The fire's warmth drew him, and with his back to the fireplace, he clasped his hands behind and surveyed the room to give himself time to get his rancor under control.

He watched as Jane settled into a wing chair covered in a green, flowered print. Momentarily her shining, light auburn hair against the dark background snagged his attention. Her pale, peach-tinged skin glowed, making him think of the coming spring. Then his eyes slid to Angie, who sat in her lap.

Jane had positioned the baby with her back to him. He watched Angie squirm onto her knees and push herself around. When she faced him, she smiled with satisfaction. His gaze lifted to meet Jane's. Her melancholy eyes arrested his attention and softened his heart. He wanted to gather her into his arms to comfort her, but he shook off this unexpected reaction. After she heard his news, their fragile truce would be shattered. Had her grandmother told her yet? He couldn't tell.

He scanned the room again, trying to get a feel for Angie's home. *Angie's home,* the words filled him with discontent. Angie belonged with him. But in Angie's best interest he'd been forced to accept the dictates of Dena's will—even though everything within had urged him not to. Tom's counsel about arranging joint custody without the meddling of social workers and judges had been wise, and he would heed it—as long as Jane cooperated fully. He knew what he wanted and he would get it.

With approval he noted Jane had installed a wooden gate at the base of the steps to the upstairs. A paperback book by a pediatrician lay open, facedown on the coffee table. He watched Jane lift the book off the table and guiltily tuck it between the sofa cushions. So Jane didn't know everything about babies, after all.

Other than the book, the room appeared nearly bare of ornaments, out of character for an Everett. Everetts decorated their homes with style and grace. Each piece chosen both to beautify and to recall memories.

Jane gave him a tart glance. "You didn't answer my question. Didn't you drive up in your Lincoln?"

Vanilla-scented candles flickered on top of the mantel. Mellowing in the cozy room, he fought being enmeshed in the gracious presence of Jane Everett. "Sold it. Didn't drive. Flew up with my instructor." He stepped forward and, without asking permission, lifted Angie off her lap.

The news startled Jane so much she let the baby go without a word. "Instructor? You're learning how to fly?"

He carried Angie to the overstuffed white sofa and sat down. "I should be licensed before summer."

Jane felt her breast tighten, making it hard to draw a breath. "You'll be flying up, not driving?"

He nodded. "I'll cut my travel time in half. I'll leave the Jeep at the airport here and fly up from Midway."

"Oh." Jane's spirits plummeted, leaving her mind whirling.

"Hi, Angel," he murmured, close to Angie's ear. The baby girl eyed him curiously, then fingered his sparkling tie tack.

"Why did you wear a suit today?"

"I was trying to keep up with Jane of Jane's Dress Shop." He gestured at her baggy, gray sweats.

Jane flushed. Dressing Angie had taken all her time and what had been left of her energy, but she wouldn't admit that to him.

"I had a business meeting in town earlier," he said with a touch of apology in his voice.

She bit her lower lip. His contracting firm was located in Chicago. What business would he have up here? Her panic thrummed to life. *Something is happening.*

Angie pulled on Cash's tie tack again. Rising abruptly, Jane felt a pain like a mallet striking her right temple. She crossed to Cash and reached for his tie.

He gripped both her hands in one of his. "What are you doing?"

"I'm going to take off that tie tack. She might put it in her mouth."

"*I'll* do it." He stopped her hands, undid the tie tack and slipped it into an inner pocket.

From a steady, pounding mallet, the ache in Jane's head switched to the surge and ebb of a crazy tide. She straightened up slowly, feeling a little woozy. Then she recalled she hadn't eaten since breakfast—a 5:00 a.m. breakfast.

From his suit pocket, Cash produced a stuffed toy—a

black-and-white cocker spaniel. Angie squealed and reached for it.

The squeal zigzagged through Jane. Her headache level soared. She mumbled, "I'll make tea." She walked through the arched door into the kitchen. Once there, she pressed her head against the cool door of her small, rounded, white refrigerator.

Her pulse beat a rapid rhythm in her ears. Weeks of erratic sleep, bizarre meals like baby prunes with zwieback teething biscuits and adjusting her work schedule at her shop had taken their toll.

Why today of all days? The tension in Cash's visit had tipped the scales of her physical misery. This visit wasn't going as she had planned. She'd wanted to be cool, in charge, unruffled. Instead she felt like a ball of yarn unraveling under the batting paws of a determined cat. Somehow, some way she had to toughen herself, make her nerves impervious to both the charm and intimidating essence of Cash Langley.

Flying lessons? What next?

Turning to the stove, she picked up her blue-and-white enamel kettle and carried it to the sink. As she filled it, Jane gazed wearily at her kitchen. Dirty dishes with hard, dried scraps and smears filled both sides of the sink. Breakfast and lunch remains still littered the floor around Angie's high chair. Jane set the kettle on the burner and switched it on. The flames sputtered under the kettle, burning away the moisture on the bottom.

The phone jangled. Jane lifted the receiver off the black wall phone. The welcome voice of her grandmother instantly made her relax and smile.

"I wanted you to hear this directly from me, Jane," Lucy said without preamble. "Is Cash there yet?"

"You're all right, aren't you?" Jane asked anxiously. Her grandmother would be seventy-six on her next birthday.

"I'm fine. I just wanted you to know that I've sold the land on Lake Elizabeth."

"What?"

"I'm using the money to establish endowments for needy art students at several Christian universities."

"But…I…" Jane stammered.

"I sold it to Cash."

"Cash! But Cash builds condos in Chicago—"

"Not anymore," Cash's cool voice interrupted. He lounged in the arched doorway with Angie in his arms. The baby busily patted his nose with her small, pudgy hand.

Without thinking, Jane hung up the phone and turned. "You! Why didn't you tell me?"

"Lucy wanted to tell you."

"How did you get her to agree to this!" Jane braced her hands on her hips.

"She called me. It was *her* idea."

"I don't believe that for a minute. This is your doing, Cash Langley, and you know it. Why would you suddenly decide to move here after ten years of contracting in Chicago?"

"I didn't tell you where to sell dresses. Why should you care where I build houses, Red?"

"This has nothing to do with business. You're trying to take Angie away from me." Her words were irrational, but she couldn't help herself.

"You're the one who took Angie away from me. You thought you could keep me a *convenient* seven-hour drive away."

He went on. "Soon I can fly to Chicago, take care of business and be back in the same day—easy. Next month I'll be starting Eagle Shores, a new subdivision just five miles from here. As long as Angie is here, I'm here to stay."

Jane forced down tears. Cash had annihilated all her plans for limiting his involvement with Angie, with her.

Sensing tension, Angie whimpered.

"Give her to me. She needs me." Jane held out her arms. Cash released the baby reluctantly.

The kettle whistle pierced the angry silence. Angie shrieked. Jane quickly removed the kettle from the stove. The baby rubbed her eyes and whimpered again.

"Angie needs her bottle and nap." Jane couldn't keep the brittle snap out of her voice.

"All right, but I'll be back tomorrow. And get this into your red head. Next month I'll be moving into my family's lake cottage permanently and you'll be seeing me—daily." He turned from her. In less than a minute, she heard her front door slam. Angie flinched and pressed her baby-soft cheek against Jane's neck.

Only then did Jane realize she'd hung up on her grandmother. The distance between Eagle Lake and Chicago had been the only protection between Cash's presence and her own peace of mind. How could her grandmother have erased the three-hundred-mile barrier?

Worse yet, Cash had made it plain he understood she hadn't wanted him near. Guilt hit her hard. What's happening inside me? Keeping Cash away from Angie is an awful thing to want. But she couldn't deny the alarm she felt. Angie rocked herself forcefully in Jane's arms and began to howl. It was Angie's way of announcing, "I need a nap now!"

While Jane performed the tricky maneuver of filling a bottle with formula and putting it to warm on the stove, she pressed the baby to her shoulder. She sang "This Little Light of Mine" to soothe Angie, but her own mind struggled with the implications of Cash's move. Caught between the blades of attraction and panic, Jane was being sliced in two.

She didn't want to feel this way, frightened and defensive. Cash was Dena's brother, after all. She was not showing him even a hint of God's love, the love that should shine through her. Surely in His wisdom, God would show her how to deal with her grief over losing Dena and the conflict over Angie. And only God knew how she would handle Cash's move to town, where he could drop in at will and break her heart every day of the year.

Chapter Three

Jane looked up as her shop bell rang. Rona started talking as the door closed behind her. "Jane, I'm so glad you're here." As usual, Rona allowed Jane no chance to greet her. "I came in to see if you were coming to the Jaycee's dinner tonight at our restaurant—"

"Mom...I told you." Carmella had followed in her mother's wake. "I already made out the name cards. She's made her donation and reservation—"

Rona stopped her daughter's words with a look that sizzled like hot grease in a skillet.

Jane closed the cash register and eyed Rona with suspicion. "Okay. I'll bite, Rona. What's his name?"

Rona pouted. "I don't know how you always know—"

"We should elect you town matchmaker and pay you a salary. Who is he?" With an unhappy premonition, Jane lowered her voice, "I hope it isn't Roger Hallawell?"

"Mom," Carmella whined. "We're going to be late for our dentist appointments. That's why I took today off, remember?"

"This was my day to work, Mel," Tish said to Carmella

as she came from the back of the store. The two girls glared at each other.

"So what, Le-ti-ci-a?" Mel demanded, emphasizing each syllable of the other girl's full name.

Tish retorted, "Car-smell-a, this is my day to work."

"Tish, go down in the basement and price those new skirts please," Jane said smoothly. Tish turned with a toss of her blond mane and Mel made a face at her back. After playing referee between these two for almost a month, Jane wanted to scream with frustration.

"Carmella, wait outside please," Rona requested in a saccharine tone. Though obviously put out, the girl obeyed without comment.

"Jane, you know what her father said, if she tries to get away with any of her tricks here, fire her. If she acts up, she deserves to bus tables another year. Anyway, you *will* be sitting next to Roger Hallawell. He's the best catch around. I won't rest till I'm throwing rice at you!"

Standing outside, Carmella tapped on the window. Rona looked down at her watch. "I've got to go!"

As she watched Rona and Mel rush down the street, Jane shook her head over her friend's unwanted meddling. Romance with Roger Hallawell was the last thing on Jane's agenda.

Bing. Bing. The sound from the activity center attached to the inside of Angie's playpen caught Jane's attention. She walked over and beamed down at the baby. "Did you wake up, sweetheart?"

Jane bent and lifted Angie out. "You're such a good girl to take your nap while all the ladies come in and gab about dresses. Do you want to go to Grandmother's?"

Angie clapped her hands. Jane kissed Angie's chubby cheeks and carried her to the rear of the store where a changing table sat. Just as Jane finished changing Angie's diaper, Tish came up from the basement. "Are the skirts done?"

"Yes, the skirts are done," Tish answered in a voice laced with ill temper.

"Tish, you may get away with your moodiness at home, but I won't tolerate it here. Your parents told me that if you weren't ready to work in a shop, not to hesitate to tell them. If I fire you, you'll be back at DQ for the summer."

Her cousin's face blushed hot pink.

Both of them knew that while Tish's parents doted on her, they insisted she work each summer to learn responsibility. And Jane knew it must be difficult for her cousin to attend high school where her own father taught, but Tish had to learn not to take her problems out on others, especially in a place of business.

"I'm going to Grandmother's for about two hours." Jane went on breezily, "Then I'll be back. If you need any help, call me. Keep the cash drawer locked. Here's the key."

Tish slipped on the wrist key chain. Angie's pudgy little arms reached for Tish, who often baby-sat her. Tish smiled and kissed Angie's forehead. "Bye-bye, Angie." Tish waved like a baby and Angie giggled at her.

Outside, Jane hooked Angie into the car seat. In Jane's red Blazer, they drove out of town onto the highway amid tall, green-leafed maples, pines and birches. Up the progressively steep rises and around the final curve, she approached Lucy's white cottage. Farther up the same steep hill on the left sat her parents' summer cottage. Their house perched on a modest cliff over Lake Tomahawk, making it necessary to park cars below to the rear of the house.

As she stepped down from the Blazer with Angie in her arms, the sighing of the wind through the high pines greeted her. Even in the shade of these statuesque pines, the heat and humidity of the summer day weighed her down, but her mood lifted, anyway. "We're here, Angie."

Angie grinned in reply. Jane climbed the long flight of steps to her parents' back door. As arranged, Lucy waited for them just inside. "Hello, sweethearts." Lucy kissed Angie behind her right ear.

Angie grinned and patty-caked.

"Jane, help me with these." Lucy turned and Jane tied the strings at the back of her grandmother's favorite paint-flecked smock. Jane smiled in appreciation of the bright yellow cotton gauze sundress under the smock. No old-lady colors for her grandmother.

Lucy led them inside. "I have everything ready here in your parents' air-conditioned living room. I can't believe we need air-conditioning! I've summered in northern Wisconsin all my life, and I've never seen anything like this year's ninety-plus temperatures every day. And the storms!" She paused dramatically for emphasis. "I'd like to paint your portrait outside or in my cottage, but we'd just be miserable."

Jane nodded. "It was already seventy-eight degrees at 6:00 a.m."

"Hot or not, we've got a busy summer ahead of us, don't we?"

Jane grinned ruefully. "My summers are always busy."

"And profitable. You deal in living art! If a woman doesn't leave your dress shop looking and feeling more lovely, more feminine, it's her own fault."

"Some people don't think that's very important."

"Nonsense! A woman who feels good about herself is a woman who is kinder to others. All art should add to the joy of living."

"Thank you, ma'am." Jane gave a mock curtsy. Praise from her grandmother, a long successful portrait artist, felt good.

"You're welcome. But we have two August deadlines—"

"Two?"

"Yes, in addition to the portrait of you for your parents' anniversary, I've decided to paint a miniature of Angie for Cash to celebrate her first birthday."

Envy leaped into Jane's emotions. Setting Angie's diaper bag in the corner, Jane gently released the baby onto the polished oak floor. The child crawled toward a box of blocks beside a tweed chair. With a block in each chubby fist, Angie banged them against the floor, then against each other.

"You would make a very poor poker player, Jane."

"What?" Jane looked to Lucy.

"You're still upset with me for selling my land to Cash."

An avalanche of the recurring panic, which even the mention of Cash now created in her, landed in the pit of Jane's stomach. She lifted her chin and said evenly, "It was your property. I had nothing to say either way."

"That's very true, but I know you're unhappy about it. If you want to express your opinion, feel free."

"It's done. I accept it." Jane, avoiding Lucy, kept her eyes on Angie.

"But you don't accept having Cash so close, do you?"

The thread of anxiety over Cash's intentions concerning Angie made Jane wince inside. "I've adjusted."

"Do you think it's right to keep Cash away from his niece?"

"No, of course not," Jane said.

"You've been avoiding Cash a long time, you know."

Jane felt another internal jab. *Why are you asking me about this, Grandmother?* "We've just not been involved in the same pursuits."

Lucy came a step closer. "Are you still in love with him?"

Thunderstruck, Jane couldn't speak. Shock undulated through her in wave after wave.

"Did you think you'd fooled everyone?" Lucy folded her arms in front of her.

"How?" Jane gasped.

"It began the night of your sweet-sixteen birthday party. After nearly everyone had left, Cash arrived. He was wear-

ing a tux because he'd just come from some big charity 'do'
downtown. The delicious way he looked I could have fallen
in love with him myself. He gave you a pearl ring—which
you never wear—and then he kissed you. I saw your face
and I knew he'd be the one in your heart.''

''It was just a schoolgirl crush,'' Jane stammered. Lucy's
poignant description of the night Jane had lost her heart to
Cash brought sights, sounds of that long-ago night cascading
through her. That night, for the first time, she had experienced love, love so new, so innocent...so doomed to dis-
appointment. To Cash, she would always be ''Red,'' Dena's
pal.

''You're telling me you don't have those feelings for him
any longer?'' Lucy appraised Jane with her steady gaze.

''Why didn't you ever say anything?'' The now-familiar
tightness in her breast when coping with Cash's new prom-
inence in her life left Jane breathless.

''It wasn't the right time. You were still so young, it was
merely a promise for the future.''

Jane shook her head and turned away. ''You're talking
about ancient history.''

''All I know is—as a family—we fall in love and stay
that way. Look at Tish's mother. Claire met Henry here the
summer of her fortieth year. Never showed any serious interest in any other man. Six weeks later they eloped! Everetts never love moderately.'' Lucy smiled.

Jane took a deep breath. ''I'm not in love with Cash
Langley.'' *Not if I can help it.*

''Well, I wish you were.''

''What?'' Jane turned to face Lucy. ''Haven't you always
told me not to become unequally yoked?''

''I believe if Cash could break out of his icy shell by
falling in love with you, a love of God would not lag far
behind. He's not a bitter man, just a man with a frozen
heart.''

As she went on, Lucy's voice softened. "Cash deserves someone special. He's been through so much."

"Cash doesn't want anyone—special or not."

"Yes, and the one time he broke out of his reserve and he fell in love—"

"You don't have to tell me. Anyone could have told him she was a disaster looking for a victim."

"Don't sound so hard, dear. It's not like you. You know it's hard for him to trust women after his mother abandoned his family."

"That's just an excuse. Dena fell in love, married and was very happy." Talking about Cash made her angry, but talking about Dena choked Jane. She couldn't go on.

"I'm sorry, dear, I didn't mean to upset you. But we must talk about Dena as naturally as we can, for Angie's sake. Dena and John are at peace with God. Until we see them again, we must make them live on through our memories."

Jane nodded, held back tears by forcing herself to breathe normally.

"When I have a chance, I'm going to make that point to Cash. He must start talking to Angie about her mother. Until he moved up last week, Cash was only able to visit you and Angie on weekends. There just hasn't been time, but there are a few other things I might mention, too."

Lucy leaned forward and returned to her original question. "Jane, you're not still trying to avoid him, are you?"

Lost amid painful images of her lost friend, Jane asked, "What?"

"Are you avoiding Cash?"

"No," Jane heard herself lie and felt guilt stain her cheeks. Grandmother, don't go on asking questions I don't want to answer!

"Well, good. I'm glad that's settled. It's nice to know everything's running so smoothly for you."

The tinge of irony in Lucy's voice, and Jane's own conscience, made her glance quickly into her grandmother's face.

Lucy glanced at her Mickey Mouse watch. "Let's get started." They checked on Angie, who rolled cheerfully onto her stomach and crawled to an oak basket near the stone fireplace. The baby girl puckered her forehead as she began to take one pinecone out of the basket at a time.

"That'll keep her busy," Jane murmured. Finding out Grandmother knew, had known for years, about her secret feelings for Cash made Jane feel exposed. Her deepest secret had never been a secret to her perceptive grandmother. Had anyone else guessed? Cash must never know. It would give him another weapon against her.

Lucy gestured for Jane to sit down on a white wicker chair near the picture window overlooking the lake. Switching on several recessed lights and a few pole lamps, Lucy directed them toward Jane. Back at her easel, Lucy hummed softly and took up her palette.

At Lucy's request, Jane wore her favorite pair of blue jeans and peach, short-sleeved blouse with white collar and cuffs. She knew better than to question her grandmother's choice, but still she didn't feel right posing in faded jeans for her very feminine mother, who still preferred wearing skirts to slacks. "Did I wear what you wanted?"

Lucy halted her preparations. "Look at yourself against the background. You have an artist's eye." She stepped behind the easel.

Jane scanned herself and her surroundings. Peach and white to emphasize her redheaded coloring. Denim against the white wicker, the faded flowered-print cushions, and natural birch paneling created a casual, homey effect. Lucy held her palette in her right hand and her palette knife in her left and began to mix colors.

Still tense, Jane sat down on the chair. In the peace punctuated by the sounds of Angie's contented play, Jane concentrated on the swish of the brush in paint and the frequent clack of the palette knife striking wood. The scent of paint and turpentine, forever linked with Lucy in Jane's mind, permeated the room. The familiar, tastefully decorated, but homey living room wrapped around Jane like a comfy shawl on a cool evening. In an uneven rhythm, Angie banged wooden blocks together with gusto.

Jane relaxed. "I'm glad you thought of painting my portrait for my parents' anniversary. When I say they've been married thirty-five years, it makes them sound old, but they never seem that way to me."

Her grandmother smiled vaguely in reply.

Then Jane remembered what she wanted to ask her grandmother. "There's something else I wanted to talk to you—"

The back door opened and shut briskly. "Lucy!" Cash strode into the living room.

In her bright yellow dress, Lucy turned to him like a daffodil following the sun. He leaned over and kissed Lucy's lined cheek. Angie dropped her blocks and crawled madly toward him. He bent and captured Angie, swinging her up slightly in the air, making her squeal with delight.

Jane stiffened. Dressed in work jeans and a light khaki shirt, Cash gazed across at Jane. With his face and neck tanned by days of working in the sun, he looked rugged. He looked glorious. Jane drank in the sight of him, while at the same time an impulse to grab Angie and run made her grip the arms of the wicker chair.

"Jane, how did Angie do with her second set of shots on Monday?" he asked.

"I told you I'd call if there was any problem."

"That means she had no reaction?"

"Just a little fussy." Jane stared up at him, daring him to go on.

Lucy patted his arm, then turned back to the easel. "I'm

so glad you'll be nearby all summer. I'll be able to walk over anytime.''

"Please call first to see if I'm home, because I'll usually be busy at the site. I'm doing a lot more hands-on with this development. But I'll look forward to sitting on my pier with you, watching the sun set. I wanted to ask you if you know someone reliable who could clean house for me once a week.''

"Jane, could your friend Kathy work Cash into her schedule?''

"I'll give him her number.'' Jane cleared her throat. "What brings you here, Cash?''

"Cash volunteered to entertain Angie during our sittings, so we can make the most of our time,'' Lucy replied. "Isn't that nice?''

Many words, none of them nice, went through Jane's mind. Now she understood Lucy's question about whether she was avoiding Cash. Had Grandmother, always frank and without subterfuge, set her up? What is going on here? Jane struggled to keep her composure.

Cash, Angie in his arms, stared directly at Jane as though sending his message loud and clear. I'm here to stay. Get used to it.

Jane's awareness of Cash made her stomach feel full of fluttering butterflies, big ones with soft feathery wings. Trying to ignore him, she swung her feet up, letting herself lounge sideways in the chair. "Is this the pose you want?''

"We started without you, Cash,'' Lucy said. "What do you think?'' Lucy rested her chin on the back of her hand that held the brush.

"Is that what you want her to wear?'' Cash moved to Jane's father's favorite recliner and perched Angie on his lap.

"It's her favorite outfit. Don't you like the contrasts in color and texture?''

Jane stared at both of them in shock. Lucy never let anyone question her artistic judgment! It was the one thing she
wouldn't stand for!

"I see what you mean," Cash mused. "But personally,
for a portrait for Marge and Phil's living room, I see her in
a flowered dress like the one you wore that afternoon when
we went to the Chicago Historical Society Museum."

"You're right," Lucy agreed. "Marge would prefer
something more feminine on her only daughter. As a matter
of fact, I have the dress with me. You remember it, don't
you, Jane? I bought it on my last trip to Paris with your
grandfather?"

"I prefer jeans." Jane tightened her mouth.

"But don't you think your mother would prefer a dress?"
Lucy coaxed.

Jane's mouth became a straight line. "I suppose. But
shouldn't it be a dress of mine?"

"No, your mother would recognize the dress. She knows
how special it is to me. I think it would make the portrait
dearer to her."

How could she argue with that? Grimacing inwardly, Jane
nodded.

Lucy smiled at Cash. "I can always count on your sense
of style." She turned back to Jane. "For today, just sit as
though you have a dress with a wide skirt flared out on each
side of you." Lucy made spreading motions with her hands.

Cash pushed back in the recliner and played patty-cake
with a grinning Angie. He had seen surprise, argument and
reluctant agreement play across Red's expressive face. He
glanced at Jane now sitting in her prim pose. Her shining
cap of wavy copper hair caught his eye, as usual. Then he
looked into her stormy eyes. The emerald fire in them captured his attention. Why hadn't he ever noticed how deep
and true a green they were?

With only a fraction of his thoughts on the baby, Cash

began a game of peekaboo with Angie. Using Angie as cover, he continued his observation of Jane. She sat still, but did not appear relaxed. Her hand touched her hair, next her copper-flecked nose. She squirmed in her seat. His gaze fastened on her narrow waist and the soft, round curve of her hip. His mind halted there. Why would he be thinking like that about Red?

Moments passed. Angie's noises and Lucy's painting sounds filled the large room.

Finally Jane said discontentedly, "I don't know how much longer I can sit still like this."

"Talk to me, dear. It will take your mind off posing," Lucy said.

"What about?"

"What did you want to discuss with me just before Cash arrived?" Lucy peered around the easel.

When Jane remained silent and frowned, Cash wondered if he had been the topic of discussion.

"It's a problem I'm having at the shop," Jane began grudgingly. "Maybe you can help me solve a mini-mystery?"

"I'm intrigued already. Go on." Lucy began stroking the canvas with short, exact strokes.

"When I was closing the shop two nights ago, I went through all the racks, checking sizes like I always do. When I went through the tennis outfits, one size eight was missing. You know how small the shop is and how carefully I choose my inventory—"

"It wasn't sold or hung on a different rack under a jacket or left in a dressing room?" Lucy stared at Jane with almost comical concentration.

"None of the above." With her lips still held in a half smile for the portrait, Jane's nose wrinkled. "That was Tuesday. The next day I searched discreetly for it."

"So?" Cash pushed up to a sitting position in the recliner. The problem snagged his attention in spite of himself.

Jane continued, "So this morning it was back on the correct rack."

"Ah." Lucy stepped back from the canvas, scrutinized Jane and frowned.

"Ah, what?" Jane asked, her tone rising.

"Sounds to me like someone took it, got cold feet and brought it back," Lucy said.

"My thoughts exactly." Cash kissed the tip of Angie's nose.

"But I hate to think that of either Mel or Tish." Jane sounded troubled.

"It could have been a customer who made a mistake or regretted shoplifting," Cash added.

"Could be." A narrow line appeared between Jane's eyebrows. "I don't like it—period. It gives me a funny feeling to suspect people."

"I can understand that, but it shouldn't happen again. You know some people only learn by doing," Lucy said.

"What do you mean?" Jane asked.

"I mean someone's conscience taught her honesty is the best policy." Lucy turned toward Cash. "Didn't you mention pilfering at your building site?"

It was a topic he didn't really want to discuss, but Lucy had made it unavoidable. "Yes. I thought up here I wouldn't have to hire a security guard for my site like I did in Chicago—"

"You're missing things?" Jane asked, sounding unconvinced.

"Not much, but it's odd." Cash's voice became edged with irritation. "Either the thieves are stupid or clever. I can't decide which."

"What do you mean?" Lucy selected a new brush.

"It means either the crook is too stupid to try to cover his tracks or it's the opening volley of trouble—"

"Trouble? Up here?" Jane said.

"A north woods version of turf wars. This is a limited market. Maybe some contractor doesn't want new competition."

"That's foolish," Jane began.

"Foolish is right. I play fair, but I always play to win." Cash stared into Jane's eyes. He easily read her resistance to him.

You'd better get used to my being around, Red. I'm in Eagle Lake full-time and you'll be seeing a whole lot more of me. Count on it. But he couldn't take his eyes from the afternoon sunlight glinting on Jane's burnished hair.

Chapter Four

Dreading the evening already, Jane parked her red Blazer outside Vitelli's Villa. As she walked beside her grandmother toward the restaurant, Jane stared down at reflections of streetlights on the wet asphalt. About an hour before, black rain clouds had opened for a brief, intense storm.

"Besides this dreadful humidity—what's bothering you?" Lucy asked.

Jane sighed. "Oh, sitting next to Roger Hallawell and being away from Angie all evening."

Lucy slipped her arm into Jane's. "You'll handle Mr. Hallawell. And whatever other failings she has, Tish is wonderful with Angie. In fact, it's been a revelation to me."

"Me, too. When I see her with Angie, it makes me forget what a pill she can be. Aunt Claire and Uncle Henry love her so much—"

"Don't worry. God will bring her through."

"How do you know that?"

"Because I remember myself at sixteen. The acorn never falls far from the tree."

Jane wanted to pursue this comment, but they had reached

the entrance of the dimly lit restaurant. A couple coming out of Vitelli's held the door for them.

"It's back in the banquet room," Jane murmured.

"Lead the way. I hate these dark dungeon restaurants. An old lady with the start of cataracts has enough trouble as it is."

"I didn't know you had cataracts," Jane said.

"It's not a fact I tell someone whose portrait I've just started."

Jane shook her head ruefully. "Grandmother!"

Carmine Vitelli had decorated his restaurant to resemble a café in a vineyard—trellises with bunches of plastic grapes, colorful hanging lanterns, red-and-white-checked tablecloths topped with candles. Jane had never been able to decide if Carmine Vitelli thought this was the only way to decorate an Italian restaurant or if it was high camp and he was having a good laugh on everyone. Regardless of the interior, Vitelli's was known for miles around as the best in Italian food, so neither Jane nor anyone else had ever questioned the decor.

They entered the banquet room. Carmine stood behind the podium welcoming everyone to the dinner. Lucy and Jane slipped quietly into their seats at the table where Rona sat with Jane's Uncle Henry and Aunt Claire. In the chair beside Jane's sat Roger Hallawell. He had risen politely to acknowledge Lucy and Jane's arrival.

"Good evening, Jane. You're looking lovely as usual." Hallawell was a large man in his early forties.

Jane respected Roger. He had built a successful contracting firm with his own sweat. She could admire that, but what she couldn't accept was his blatant, unwelcome pursuit of her. She had no intention of becoming his second wife. Across the table, Jane saw the matchmaker's sparkle in Rona's eye. Jane promised herself a long chat with Rona very soon.

The waitresses began serving one of Carmine's specialties, a salad topped with minced black olives, Parmesan and a sweet red-wine-and-vinegar dressing. Jane's stomach rumbled in happy anticipation. Carmine sat down.

Jane bent to draw a tissue from her purse when an unexpected voice said, "Good evening, everyone." Jane looked up, and her spirits fell. Cash. Why hadn't she considered he might attend the banquet tonight?

Cash, dressed in a casual sport jacket in a flattering shade of dark gray, stood behind Lucy. He gazed across at Jane. His black hair was swept away from his face and brushed the back of his collar. Tieless, he'd left the top button of his white shirt open. An unwelcome shimmering coursed down Jane's arms and legs. His blue eyes taunted her. Sitting up straighter, she attempted to take firm control of herself.

"Hello, Langley." Carmine rose to shake hands. "I think you're over there with the Bannings and the Martins."

"Oh, the Bannings!" Lucy popped up from her seat. "Cash, let me trade places with you. I wanted to see them about getting our summer bridge group organized."

"Whatever you say, Lucy." Cash's attention remained fixed on Jane. Lucy left, and Cash sat down across from Jane.

"So you're Langley?" Roger barely concealed the challenge in his voice.

Cash glanced at the man, then ignoring him, opened his napkin and began to eat his salad.

"You garnered quite a plum securing that land on Lake Elizabeth. Must be nice to have the right friends," Roger went on in a derisive tone.

Cash's buying Lucy's property still rankled in Jane's own mind. Obviously she wasn't alone.

"I am privileged to call Lucy Everett my friend," Cash said stiffly.

Like a shift in the wind, Jane felt the rest of the people

at the table become uneasy. What was Lucy's reason in placing two competing contractors face-to-face? Did she think putting the two of them together socially would temper their competition?

"Cash, I'm so glad you were able to come on such short notice." Rona smiled. "We don't usually get to see you this often."

Cash nodded toward Rona. "I'm happy to dine at Vitelli's anytime."

Though Jane had lost interest in eating, she took a bite of a tomato wedge and tried to look like she enjoyed it.

"Where's Angie?" Cash asked Jane pointedly.

Instantly Jane felt herself bristle, but she kept her tone nonchalant. "Oh, I had an offer to sell her to a band of passing gypsies—"

"Tish is—" Uncle Henry began.

"Happy to sit with Angie. She is a beautiful child," Aunt Claire finished.

"That jumper looks good on you, Claire," Rona said.

Claire grinned and blushed. A rust-colored bandanna tied around her neck accented the denim jumper and blue chambray blouse. "I like it myself. I have this niece who keeps me in style."

"Keeps us all in style," Rona agreed.

"Keeps us all broke," Carmine complained good-naturedly.

"Or employed. I—" Henry said.

This began one of Aunt Claire's and Uncle Henry's famous verbal duets.

"Jane, we really appreciate your hiring our Leticia so young—" Claire cut in on her husband.

Henry took over, "We explained what an opportunity it was for her. Most sophomores are lucky—"

"To be serving hamburgers somewhere," Claire added.

By now everyone at the table followed the conversation like a Ping-Pong game.

"The job at your shop exposes her to so many job skills—" Henry went on.

"And she can buy such nice clothes—"

"At employee discount," Henry finished for them.

Jane glanced around the table to gauge the others' reactions to her aunt and uncle. Often during one of their "duets," Jane wondered how it would feel to be so close to someone, you could finish the other person's sentences.

In the conversational vacuum after Claire and Henry finished speaking, Carmine and Hallawell started talking sports. Jane nibbled at her salad and looked across the table. The stark beauty of Cash's blue eyes and his thick black lashes snared Jane's gaze. She couldn't take her eyes from him. Suddenly she realized he was aware she was studying his face. He arched an eyebrow, and she felt her cheeks warm. She looked away.

Rona announced, "Jane, I volunteered you yesterday."

"For what?" Jane asked.

"Art in the Park."

"Me?"

"I'm performing in the puppet show this year," Rona went on.

"I'm doing finger painting—" Claire began.

"With Jell-O," Henry finished.

"But," Jane said, slightly exasperated, "I'm not artsy—"

"We have a new tent—perfect for you," Rona said. "The Dress-Up Tent, filled with old clothes, high heels, you know!"

"I planned to take Angie this year," Jane said in desperation.

"I'll be glad to take her through the exhibits while you work," Cash said, delivering the coup de grâce.

Jane's spirits sank. For seven years, she'd avoided Art in

the Park. Now, the year she planned to take Angie, she would be stuck at a workstation.

"My crew volunteered to help put up and break down the exhibits. In a small town, everyone takes part in civic activities." Roger directed his attention at Cash.

Instant silence ensued. Jane wished she could slip out and go home to Angie. Why couldn't Hallawell just leave things alone? What did he think he would gain by goading Cash? Or did the man think at all before speaking?

Cash sent the contractor a frigid glare. The waitress who placed bubbling lasagna in front of him interrupted the confrontation. The rich aroma of the lasagna wafted around the table.

With a defiant glance toward Cash, Roger leaned close to Jane's ear and said, "Did I tell you I just dropped a bundle on a new Sea Nautique?"

Jane shook her head.

"Do you still water-ski?"

"I don't have much time—"

"You've got to make time for yourself. Now why don't I pick you up tomorrow afternoon? We'll take my boat out and see what she can do."

"I don't think so."

"Oh, now come on, honey."

Cash cut in, sounding bored, "She doesn't want to go water-skiing with you. I can't blame her."

Hallawell's face turned scarlet, but he went on talking about the new speedboat to Carmine.

Cash tried to rid himself of the pique this man seemed to relish causing. Hallawell's presence had somehow intensified Cash's awareness of Jane. Cash couldn't stop resenting the way Hallawell hovered next to her. He didn't like any man who acted as though a woman should be grateful for his attention. On the contrary, Jane was a woman who could command any man's attention. She deserved only the best.

No matter which way Cash turned, Jane's warm, bright hair caught his eye. When she nodded and talked to her aunt, her copper waves bounced and caught the candlelight. He almost shifted restlessly in his seat, but realizing that this would send a signal of discomfort to the smug competitor across from him, he stilled his body.

Then he caught the last of a sentence Hallawell was saying to Jane. "Bigger contractors cut corners."

"By bigger contractors, do you mean me?" Cash asked. He didn't let the antagonism he felt touch his tone. Expressions stiffened visibly on the faces of the people within earshot. Suddenly their table became a silent island, surrounded by groups where friendly chatter, the clinking sound of ice in glasses continued.

"I was only speaking generally." Hallawell's conciliatory words didn't match his abrasive tone.

Around the table everyone waited for the immediate outbreak of verbal hostilities. But after exchanging looks rife with challenge, Cash and Hallawell both let it drop, and Carmine started telling a joke.

Just as the scoops of lemon and lime Italian ice were being served, a waitress told Cash he was wanted on the phone in the lounge. When he returned, the sociable atmosphere at the table quieted. "It was the sheriff." His tone was harsh. "Trespassers have been caught at my site. They were armed with cans of spray paint. Evidently they planned to *decorate* my model home, but were caught before they had a chance." Everyone except Hallawell voiced sympathy. Cash nodded in reply, then left, walking quickly.

In the semidarkness of the parking lot, Cash fumbled in his pocket, separating his keys from the loose change. He felt a touch on his arm. Whirling around, he caught Jane by her bare arms. "You!" The restaurant lights lit her face clearly. Surprise had widened her eyes.

"Me. Let go."

Against his calloused palms, her skin was smooth, soft. Resisting the urge to slide his hands farther up her sleek skin, he released her abruptly. "Sorry. But you shouldn't sneak up on people. Did I forget something?"

"I didn't sneak up on you. If you'd been listening, you'd have heard me. I'm going with you." She slipped her thumbs into the front belt loops of her denim skirt. The cream silk blouse she wore shimmered in the low light.

"What?" He lifted his gaze to her face.

"I came to keep you company while you inspect the damage to your site."

He filled his lungs with the hot, humid air. "I don't need your help—"

"I insist." Her pale skin glowed in the light from the restaurant. She fidgeted with her collar.

He grimaced. Her very feminine presence distracted him already. "That isn't necessary."

"If the tables were turned and it was my shop, wouldn't you insist on going along?"

"That's different."

"Because I'm a small, weak woman?" Her head tilted as her chin lifted to him in argument.

"Don't start that. Thank you for offering, but it isn't—"

"Necessary," she finished for him. "But now it is."

"Why?" He felt his ire rising. Not only because of her insistence, but because of the provocative pose she flaunted in his face.

"Because I'll look like an idiot. Everyone in town saw me follow you. I don't want to have to explain—"

He sighed in resignation. "Get in." He clicked open the lock, and she slipped in. He caught a breath of her cinnamon-scented cologne. It brought to mind the richness of her auburn hair in the candlelight at their table. If he ran his fingers through it, would it feel as silky as it looked?

He slid behind the steering wheel. The suffocating heat

made him flip on the air-conditioning. "I'm going out to the site first." Smoothly he shifted into reverse, backed out of the space and shifted into first.

"Oh, I thought you'd go directly to the sheriff. There wasn't any damage done."

"That's right. But I want to see if the sheriff's deputy missed anything. Also I've found that letting a vandal sit in 'the tank' and count the minutes till someone comes to press charges can be very effective."

"You mean this has happened before?" Her soft voice sounded like velvet in the darkened Jeep. It caused a shiver to slither up his neck.

"In Chicago. A construction site irresistibly draws trespassers, thieves and vandals."

"I'd never thought about that before."

"That's not surprising. It's like your little mystery of the missing size eight. I wouldn't have thought that one up on my own." As she nodded, her fine golden loop earrings swayed in the low light. Her earlobes looked pale pink, soft....

With determination, he turned his eyes forward. This reoccurring awareness of Red as a woman was getting to be irritating. It must be all the pressure of the new project and all this Hallawell garbage. In silence, Cash drove trying to keep his eyes on the road, trying to ignore the tantalizing woman beside him.

The large sign lit up the entrance of the Eagle Shores subdivision while the remainder of the site sat in darkness. Cash drove directly to his model home. "I'll leave the air-conditioning on."

"I'm coming with you." Jane pulled on her door handle and jumped out.

He followed suit. Outside the Jeep the sultry night air wrapped around Cash like a cocoon. "Is this Louisiana or

Wisconsin?'' He swept his hand over the fine perspiration on his forehead.

He met Jane in front of the Jeep. Pointing skyward, he said, ''There's the real culprit, the full moon.''

Jane followed his glance, then turned back to his face. ''The moon?''

''If it hadn't been light enough to see, our 'spray-paint commandos' wouldn't have been out tonight. I think I'll have to invest in some motion-activated floodlights and hire a watchman.''

Crickets serenaded the night in endless crescendos. He snapped on his flashlight. ''I'm going to check the door and window locks, then we'll head over to the sheriff.'' He glanced into her face and bowed slightly. ''Shall we take our moonlight tour?''

She slipped her hand in the crook of his elbow. This simple act of trust hit him unexpectedly. It was dark, she was in heels, the ground was uneven. He knew it was practicality that motivated her touch, but her touch unlocked a deep sadness inside of him. How many times had he given his arm or hand to his sister, to lead her, to steady her? His younger sister no longer needed his protection. His eyes smarted with unshed tears, making him relieved they were in the shadows.

Breathing as evenly as he could, he concentrated on the routine he had performed so many times on other sites, and his sadness ebbed. He flashed the beam of light up and down the outer walls and directed the beam to the latch of every ground-floor window. He tested the back door and ended their circuit with a check of the front door.

''That does it.'' He turned back to his Jeep, but Jane's hand stayed on his arm. He wanted to thank her for touching him. It had stirred hurtful memories, but only at the start. Her touch had connected them in a way he hadn't realized he'd needed.

They settled themselves in the Jeep's interior. Cash flipped on the air-conditioning. He made a wide turn and headed for the county road. "How about a picnic Saturday?" he asked, surprising himself.

"A picnic?" Jane asked. "My, you're optimistic. It'll probably be ninety-eight in the shade and pour buckets two minutes after I put all the food out on the picnic table."

He loved the wry twist of her humor and he knew why. It was one of the many traits she had inherited from Lucy. He grinned to himself, but kept his tone even. "Why don't I pick you two up at eleven. We'll drive north to Sandy Lake Beach."

"Very well," she said.

The atmosphere in the Jeep had mellowed. They rode in companionable silence. He pulled into the parking space outside the local sheriff's office. He shut the car door behind Jane, and without a word they walked toward the entrance. Cash held the door for her, and she slipped past him.

"Langley?" The sheriff stood up at his desk and came to the counter.

Cash held out his hand. Momentarily the sheriff's eyes lingered on Jane as though questioning her presence. She nodded toward Cash and sat down.

"How did you manage to get the vandals before they had done any damage?" Cash asked.

"After I heard about things disappearing from your place—"

"How did you hear that?" Cash demanded.

The sheriff grinned. "Small town. Anyway, I decided to have a man patrol the site every hour. The deputy was already behind them when they turned into the entrance. He lagged behind, parked and trailed them on foot to your model home. They had just pulled the spray-paint cans out of paper bags and were aiming when he switched on his flashlight. It doesn't usually happen that neatly."

Cash nodded and folded his arms across his chest. "How old are they?"

"Eighteen. Shirt-tail relation to some of Hallawell's crew."

"Not minors?"

"They'll be charged as adults. But it will only be trespassing with intent to commit malicious mischief. If my deputy hadn't stopped them—"

"No. I'd rather not clean up a mess—or charge anyone with anything. I don't think this was their own idea."

The sheriff leaned back with his arms lapped over each other on his chest. "What did you have in mind?"

"A good scare."

The sheriff nodded slowly. "I'll bring them out of the detention room in cuffs. That tends to drop a man's confidence."

Trying to keep a low profile, so that no action of hers would change or hinder what was happening, Jane moved farther back into the shadows and sat down on a vinyl, straight-backed chair. The scene unfolding before her was more interesting a character study than she would have predicted.

Cash, the hard-headed, success-is-everything businessman, was surprisingly willing to overlook youthful indiscretions. Why hadn't she realized the love he'd always shown Dena denoted a compassionate heart? Her memory recited, "Blessed are the merciful for they shall obtain mercy."

She heard the sheriff's voice, now strident and loud. Two teens, both with identical, "buzzed" hairstyles came into view from behind the counter. One teen already bowed his head in defeat, but the other's chin lifted in defiance.

"Mr. Langley," the sheriff announced in a gruff, combative tone, "these are the two perpetrators."

Cash, his hands still across his chest, said nothing, but eyed the two as he would have looked at a piece of chewing gum stuck to the bottom of his shoe. Jane was glad he wasn't looking at her that way. "I told you I didn't want to see them." Cash's voice was cutting, and the scorn he applied to the words was chilling.

The bowed head dropped fractionally lower. The defiant chin lifted another inch.

Cash went on, "I just wanted to press charges and leave the rest to the county prosecutor."

"You certain you want to go ahead and charge them?" The sheriff wheedled. "Isn't this case too minor—"

"Malicious mischief isn't minor," Cash said sharply. "I doubt that if I went out to their car and spray-painted it, they would hesitate to charge me."

"They're both first-time offenders—"

"That isn't the point...."

The defiant one spoke up, looking at the sheriff, "Why are you bothering to talk to him. We didn't ask—"

"Quiet," Cash snapped. "You're in big trouble, haven't you realized that? This isn't the high school dean's office. You're eighteen, an adult. This fiasco will earn you a permanent record."

The defiant chin lifted only fractionally this time. "So?"

Cash's voice lowered and his tone became venomous. "How about this? How is it going to feel when you have to call your parents to post bail for you?"

Silence. The young man's mouth opened. His chin dropped in an uncontrolled free fall. The other offender uttered a slight moan.

"Mr. Langley," the sheriff wheedled, "won't you consider an apology and some sort of restitution? No actual damage was done."

As the rest of the scene was played out, Jane watched avidly. Both teens apologized to Cash, promised to steer clear of the Shores and agreed to perform twenty hours of community service during the remainder of the summer. As the boys were finishing up the details, Cash and Jane left.

During the drive back, both of them sat in a tired silence. Cash drove her back to her Blazer, then he followed her home. There he insisted on walking her to her door, and she was too fatigued to protest her independence. It was nearly midnight, the start of the stillest time of the night.

She stopped on her back step, turned toward him and paused. His compassion to the two young men tugged at her emotions once more. She longed to rest her hand along his hard jaw. Verses she had learned about kindness, "Be kind one to another…" "Love is kind…" ran through her mind.

Suddenly and completely, Cash felt the shift in Jane's mood. He could read the change in the way she leaned close to him, the inviting tilt of her head, the barely perceptible parting of her lips. All evening her presence had enticed him. Now she softened to him, invited him.

Her cinnamon cologne still sent out its faint fragrance. Her full bottom lip captured his senses. If he leaned down to skim it with his tongue, he wondered what it would taste of. His chin dropped closer to hers. She didn't move. He felt her breath against his cheek. His lips parted.

The call of a loon on the nearby lake made them both gasp. He froze. Standing up straighter, he took a deep breath with difficulty. His lungs felt constricted.

She touched her fingers to her lips. "Good night," she said and stepped inside.

After he heard her lock turn, he stood a few more seconds on her top step. He wanted to call her back, to thank her for going with him. And had that unexpected softening of Jane really happened? Would he have kissed her? Or was it just his imagination and the moonlight?

Chapter Five

Despite the uncomfortably hot, muggy evening wind, Jane walked languidly toward her shop. She disliked equally the heat outside and the air-conditioned isolation inside her shop. In spite of her dawdling, she finally arrived at the shop door and stepped in. Oh, well, only a little over two hours to closing for another busy Friday night.

"Jane, Lucy called." Tish said, "You're not supposed to drive out to Lucy's after work. Angie will be at your house."

Jane frowned at Tish's disrespectful use of their grandmother's given name. "That's peculiar. Grandmother doesn't drive at night anymore."

Tish shrugged. Several tourists browsed through the racks. Tish stood outside the fitting rooms, conferring with a customer through the closed door.

"May I help you or do you just want to browse?" Jane asked a woman near her.

"Just browsing," the woman replied quickly.

"Fine. Let me know if I can help. I'm Jane."

She politely canvassed the remaining strangers, then went

to stand by the counter. Finally the first woman she'd spoken to asked to try on a black challis skirt. Jane led her to the available fitting room. "Let me know if you need anything else," Jane murmured as she shut the door.

Within minutes the woman peeked out around the door. "Do you have this in size eight? My pre-vacation diet worked!"

"Of course," Jane said mechanically.

But as she shuffled through the rack of skirts, a cold weight dropped to the pit of her stomach. Though she knew she had another black challis skirt in size eight in her inventory, none hung where it should. Is one hanging in the dressing rooms? Tish had just cleaned out the dressing rooms and returned everything left in them to the correct racks. Jane drew the dreadful conclusion that another piece of merchandise was missing. The size-eight culprit is still with me.

She felt like stamping her foot in frustration, but she went ahead and chose an alternate skirt she thought would be equally flattering to the customer. Along the way she added a complementary blouse, cardigan and scarf.

"I'm sorry," she told the woman. "I didn't have that exact skirt in size eight. As long as you are in the dressing room, would you care to try these on?"

The woman glanced unhappily at the clothing Jane offered her. "I suppose so."

Jane handed her the hangers. This was her usual initiation to a new client, a hand-picked ensemble suited to a woman's coloring and style.

Within minutes Jane watched another woman step out of the dressing room like an emerging butterfly from a cocoon. The customer timidly walked over to view herself in the three-way mirror. "This is lovely," she said in awed surprise. Jane smiled. The ritual of helping another woman discover how good she could look in clothes meant for her usually exhilarated Jane, but the disappearance of the size-eight had blunted her pleasure.

The customer smiled shyly at her attractive reflection. She ran her hand down the lapel of the sweater's collar. "I've never seen a sweater quite like this."

"It was hand knitted in Italy."

"For a shop way up here?"

Jane smiled at the ingenuous question. "Many of my customers find it convenient to shop here on their vacation. They make it a part of their yearly routine. I've just brought out more fall items. Is there anything else I could show you?"

The customer gave Jane a shrewd look. "I can see that you know what you're doing. I'd like a few everyday outfits for the fall. I do quite a bit of volunteering, and I work in my husband's law office part-time...."

After listening intently to the woman's information about herself, Jane went through the racks expertly pulling together skirts, slacks, blouses, sweaters and blazers. At the mirror, Jane held them in front of the woman, demonstrating all the flattering combinations they created. An hour later Tish helped the woman carry out a myriad of Jane's signature gold-and-teal bags and boxes to her car.

"How did you do it?" Tish declared as she walked back into the quiet shop. "She bought everything you showed her!"

Jane smiled. "I will share my secret with you in hopes you'll learn how to do it. Most women want to dress well, but they don't know how to do it for themselves. This customer was a woman in search of quality and individuality. Until now, she's been afraid some pushy saleswoman—with only a commission in mind—would intimidate her into buying something expensive that she doesn't like. So she shops at very large, impersonal department stores, instead of a small shop like mine. When she realized I knew how to help her dress the way she had always longed to, she ceased to be afraid."

"Wow!"

"When the former owner decided to retire and sell this shop, I was able to buy it because after working for six summers here, I had already established a strong clientele. That's why my parents backed me and helped me buy it."

"Gee, I didn't know that. How did you learn how to match customers to the right clothes?"

"Well, that's a longer story, and we don't have time for it now, but in the future—if you really want to learn—I'll take time to teach you."

"Okay!"

Jane smiled broadly. Helping a woman find her distinctive style was always a heady experience for her. Tish's unexpected, uncharacteristic enthusiasm and approval also pleased her. But recalling the disappearance of the size eight skirt still took some of the glow off the evening.

Jane sighed. "It's time to close. Let's shut her down." The two of them went through the nightly routine and parted for home.

When Jane finally walked into her house, it was dark, after 10:00 p.m. Inside, she heard Angie's muffled crying. As she hurried upstairs, the back of her neck tensed. She had hoped Angie's teething pain would take a break. She didn't want to wear Lucy out. The crying stopped, and Jane held back the greeting she had been just about to voice.

She topped the staircase, then halted at the sight of Cash's broad shoulders and dark head held high. Her stomach fluttered wildly. *Cash.* She strained to bring his name to her lips. He turned. Angie lay propped with her face against his shoulder. At the sight of Angie in his arms, a second shock wave vibrated through her, changing quickly into temper. What is he doing here with Angie?

While Cash patted Angie's back, he stared at her, then he

began bouncing the baby slightly by taking exaggerated steps. He turned his back and walked away from Jane.

She pursued him. Tapping Cash on his shoulder, she whispered, "Give her to me."

She held out her arms.

He began humming, blotting out the sound of Jane's whisper. He shook his head and turned away from her again.

Breathing fast, she trailed behind him. She whispered again. "Why are you here?"

He shook his head at her. "Not now," he mouthed. "She's almost asleep. Leave me alone."

Jane flushed with anger. Cash had no right, appropriating Angie here in her house. But she didn't dare upset the infant, who was now so close to settling down for the night.

She tapped Cash's shoulder again. She mouthed to him, "Did she take her last bottle?"

He nodded.

"Does she have a night diaper on?"

He nodded curtly, then waved the back of his hand motioning her to go away.

Seething, Jane left him in the hallway, went into her room and shut the door firmly but soundlessly. There she vented her agitation by shedding her white linen suit, pitching it piece by piece into the heaping basket of clothing in her closet. She jerked on a yellow cotton knit T-shirt and matching shorts. Standing before the mirror, she raked her comb through her mussed hair.

Without any effort, she could put together the explanation for Cash's appropriation of her home, of Angie: he'd stopped by Lucy's cottage and suggested he take Angie home, so Jane wouldn't have to drive out to Lucy's after work. Jane slapped the comb down on her vanity. How could Lucy resist him? Cash Langley, the good neighbor.

A faint tap sounded on her door. She opened it.

Cash whispered, "Downstairs."

She led him down to the kitchen, the point in the house farthest from Angie's room. Standing with the kitchen table between them, Jane crossed her arms and opened her mouth.

Cash cut her off. "First thing in the morning, I'm buying an air conditioner for Angie's room."

"Air conditioner?" The word took her by surprise.

"Why haven't you realized that Angie would sleep better if she weren't so uncomfortable in this heat?"

"I...I don't like air-conditioning," she stammered.

"You have it in your shop."

"That's for the customers."

"Does Angie rate less than your customers?"

"Of course not, but I've never needed air-conditioning before." Jane felt as though she were being buffeted by wave after wave of disapproval. "Cash, why—"

"I don't care about what you've needed in the past. Angie can't sleep well in that small upstairs room without air-conditioning."

"Stop!" Jane held up both hands. "This isn't about air-conditioning! What are you doing here?"

"Didn't you get my message? Lucy looked tired to me, so I told her I would take care of Angie and let her get to bed early."

"Lucy looked tired?" Jane asked, feeling a tug of guilt.

"Yes, she hasn't been sleeping well in this heat."

"She never said anything about that to me."

"I had to worm it out of her." Cash crossed his arms in front of his chest.

"You did?"

"Yes, I did. I persuaded her to start sleeping over at your parents' air-conditioned cottage till this heat breaks. I walked her there, then brought Angie here."

Jane felt deflated, guilty. But she wouldn't let him divert her. "I'm glad you did that for Lucy, but I still want you to understand you can't just walk in and take over Angie and my house."

Cash drew himself up straighter. "Taking good care of Angie—"

"Angie is *my* responsibility. Maybe you're right. Air-conditioning might be a good idea. This has been such an unusual summer. But I'll be the one to decide—"

"How do you think it makes me feel, knowing Angie needs something and I have to argue *with you* about whether she gets it or not? I won't be pushed aside!"

"I'm not pushing you aside...."

"Yes, you are. You do it every time I try to get close to Angie."

"That's not so." Jane spoke, then realized Cash's words were true.

"Yes, it is."

Jane blushed. *Dear Lord, I didn't mean to lie. I know I'm handling this badly. Help me.*

Cash leaned forward and put his hands flat on the kitchen table. "I've had it with your possessive attitude. In the past six months, I've been busy moving here and getting the Shores off the ground, so I've let matters over Angie float. But I haven't folded. You may be in possession of my niece, but she still belongs with me—whether you're in the picture or not."

Jane's throat tightened.

"Tomorrow is our Saturday picnic. I will come early and install an air conditioner in Angie's room, then we'll talk about joint custody." He left her.

Jane slumped into the nearest chair and rested her head on her hand. She sat there a long while until she was able to think clearly again.

What is wrong with me? I started fighting with Cash— without waiting for the facts. He hadn't done anything I wouldn't have done myself. Why had she been tempted to snatch Angie out of his arms and run? She was attracted to Cash, but terrified by what he might do next. Her heart twisted painfully.

For a split second she saw Dena's face in her mind. She folded her arms on the tabletop and buried her face in them. "Oh, Dena," she whispered to the empty room, "I thought we had years and years ahead of us. Now all I have left of you is Angie." A moan worked its way up from deep inside her. Would the pain of Dena's loss ever lessen? Would the panic she felt whenever Cash held Angie in his arms ever cease?

"That should hold it in place." Cash turned the screwdriver one more time, then stepped back to look at the new air conditioner, perched in Jane's east window.

"Are you sure you want it in my room?" Jane asked guardedly.

"Yes, having Angie sleep in here, I'll be sure you can hear her. If I left her in her own room with the door closed, you might not hear her over the air conditioner."

Jane wanted to tell him, in no uncertain terms, that she would hear Angie's cry through ten doors, but she still reeled from his threat of last night. What exactly about joint custody *did* he plan for discussion today? Her heart froze. She couldn't even begin a prayer.

While she watched him rearrange the antique furniture in her room to fit in Angie's crib and changing table, she bounced Angie on her hip and worried.

The phone rang. Without a word, Cash lifted Angie from Jane's arms. When he closed the door behind him, Jane sat down and picked up the receiver of her bedside phone.

"Jane," Lucy said, "are you angry with me about last night?"

"No, Grandmother. I'm so sorry. Why didn't you tell me you were too tired to watch Angie?"

"Because I wasn't, until about 7:00 p.m. Then all my energy just drained away. If I could have persuaded Angie to settle down, it wouldn't have mattered, but she didn't have that in mind."

"I feel terrible. I won't let it happen again."

"Don't fuss, dearest. I feel much better this morning. Did Cash tell you he bullied me into sleeping at your parents' last night?"

"Yes, and this morning he's bullied me into letting him put in a window air conditioner in my room." She couldn't keep the ire from her voice.

"This morning!" Lucy chuckled. "He certainly didn't waste time, did he?"

"Oh, Grandmother, he said he still wants Angie." A quaver shook Jane's voice.

"Did that surprise you?"

"Yes! He hasn't said anything—"

"Jane, Cash isn't easily turned away from a goal. Of course he still wants Angie."

Jane bit her lower lip. "How can I stop him?"

"My only advice is not to let him roll over you like a tank. You're an Everett. Stand up to him."

"How?"

"God will provide the answer when you need it. Just ask Him. Now, your parents called. They're due in tonight."

"Tonight? Already?"

"Yes, dear, it's the end of June. They're driving up to spend Fourth of July at the lake."

"Oh, yes."

"I'll see you tomorrow morning—when you aren't so distracted." Lucy hung up.

Jane sat holding the phone. Closing her eyes, she tried to still her anxiety and draw on God's strength. But God seemed too far from her. Fear had walled her in. She put down the phone and went downstairs.

Cash was waiting for her. "Ready?" he asked.

She nodded and picked up the diaper bag on the bottom step. As she walked through the house, shutting off lights and locking doors, she reminded herself that she was an Everett. She could handle any situation.

They stowed the picnic gear behind the rear seat of Cash's blue Jeep, then took off. Cash set out down the highway till he turned down an old county road.

Jane sat back, trying to relax.

"Well, do you want to make a bet on whether or not we'll be all alone at the park?" he asked.

"I'd say yes, we'll be on our own, and I wouldn't want to take your money." Jane glanced back at Angie.

"Did Lucy ever ask the county board why there's this big beautiful park here that only we seem to use?"

"No, she was afraid that they'd put up bigger signs and soon we'd—"

"Be overrun with tourists." He nodded.

Jane smiled as Angie slapped her hands on the padded bar of her car seat.

"Having fun, Angel?" Cash asked over his shoulder.

Angie cooed.

Jane frowned.

Cash glanced at Jane. "Tom called me yesterday. You haven't drawn out any money from Angie's trust."

"I haven't really needed anything."

"The fund is ample. You're supposed to use it for Angie's expenses."

"I don't want to. I'm able to support Angie on my own."

"So am I." Cash's tone became gritty. "But the fund—"

"I want that to be a large part of her inheritance."

"She will receive an ample inheritance from me."

"But when you marry, Cash, that inheritance would have to be spread thinner."

"I'm not going to marry—"

"I think that's unlikely." Jane turned to look at him.

"I'm not going to marry," Cash insisted, leaving no room for argument. The topic of marrying hit him unexpectedly. What if Jane married? The thought of Jane marrying a stranger appalled him. Why hadn't he considered this possibility before? Why hadn't Dena? An unknown man taking part in Angie's life? *No!*

A small, weathered sign announced, "Sandy Lake Beach—Two Miles." He drove on, feeling grim.

As they turned a tree-lined corner, the park appeared before them. A small, but beautiful space with a well-groomed lawn, pristine dark green picnic tables and a wide sandy beach, all completely unpeopled, waited for their use.

"Six and a half miles south the beaches are packed," Jane said. "Every time I come here I expect to find—"

"A horde of tourists. So do I." He turned to Angie. "We're here, Angel."

Before Jane could undo her seat belt, Cash had unhooked his and Angie's and had swept the baby out of the Jeep. He swung her high, seating her behind his head, across his shoulders, with his hands gripping the baby's pale, chubby ones. Carrying the diaper bag, Jane hurried ahead of him.

Cash frowned as he watched her. In spite of himself, he was fascinated by the motion of her hips under her pale yellow sundress. The dress hung straight from the sleeveless shoulders down to the hips where it was gathered beneath the swell of her bottom. He clenched his teeth momentarily. Red had walked in front of him a thousand times. Why was he noticing the seductive sway of her hips now?

In the shade of the two large oaks, Jane shook out the quilt and laid it over the green grass and pine needles. Out of direct sunlight and cooled by the lake breeze, the temperature was warm yet comfortable. Jane reached for Angie, but Cash ignored her and swung the child down onto the quilt.

Angie crawled swiftly to Jane. Lifting the child's hands, she helped the baby to stand up. Angie giggled. Then Jane coaxed Angie down onto the soft, cotton quilt and proceeded to change the baby's wet diaper. Jane looked up and found Cash frowning down on her.

"I thought you were going to take her to the doctor about her diaper rash."

"I haven't had time," she replied defensively. "I'll make the appointment Monday."

"You know I'd take her anytime she needs to go. Just call me."

"I'm quite capable of—"

"Let's not argue. I can take a baby to the doctor, too. And next time I won't wait for you. I'll take her myself."

"You can't." Looking up at him defiantly, Jane let Angie roll onto her knees. "Only a parent or guardian can seek medical services for a minor." Jane scattered a few toys from the diaper bag in front of Angie.

Frustration laced with anger zigzagged through Cash. He felt close to his breaking point. He breathed deeply, trying to rein in his anger.

Cash swung Angie up into his arms and walked toward the baby swings. Jane hurried to keep up with him. He slipped Angie into the black rubber seat, hooked the safety belt around her middle and gave her a gentle push from behind. Angie squealed.

All the months of pushing down his own feelings and making changes in his life to suit Jane rose in his throat and choked him. She'd had her way for the past six months. Now he'd have his. Jane stood in front of Angie, just beyond the range of the swing. He looked into her face. "I want Angie."

Jane fidgeted with her gold loop earrings and then smoothed her hair back over her ear. "You've made that clear before today. Do you intend to sue for custody?'' She faced him directly, though her chin trembled.

He read the storm of fear in the green depths of her eyes. ''I have a right to claim my only family—''

''Dena and I were like sisters.'' Jane felt a pinching around her heart. ''Do you think I would have loved her more if we had been born in the same family?''

''It's not the same. Angie is my blood,'' Cash insisted.

''Dena was my sister, too. Blood or not.''

''You have your whole family. All I have is Angie! How can you be so selfish—''

''I'm not being selfish. I'm following Dena's wishes. Haven't you spent any time thinking about *why* Dena chose me as guardian?'' Again she winced inwardly.

''It was obviously just a foolish decision that Dena would have changed if she'd had time to think it over.''

''That's emotionally and intellectually dishonest and you know it.''

Cash frowned.

''Has it ever occurred to you that maybe my family is one of the reasons Dena wanted Angie with me?'' What had begun as a pang each time she said Dena's name, now became a full-scale tightness in her chest which made it hard for her to breathe.

''What?'' He gave the baby girl another gentle push.

''Don't you realize how Dena hated being so alone?''

''She wasn't alone. She had our father and me.''

''Your father traveled constantly while Dena was growing up. And you were ten years older than we were. Didn't you ever notice how she was always next door at my house or with Lucy?''

''What are you saying? Are we going to have a contest over who loved Dena more?''

''No! You're not listening to me!'' Her heart pounded while the heaviness in her breast increased.

"What am I missing?"

"When you were growing up, your parents were still together—"

"I don't want to go into that."

"Just listen. After your mother left, you no longer were a complete family. Your father traveled. You were busy at school, busy with a different stage of life than Dena. You weren't a kid when she was."

"Are you making this up or did Dena really feel this way—that she didn't have a family?"

Jane nodded, controlling her reactions to her inner distress. "We talked about it a lot when we were teens together. You were away at school, and then you went to Chicago to start your business."

"If Dena resented this, why didn't she say something?"

"She didn't resent it. It wasn't your fault! She wasn't crippled by it. She was just glad she had me and Lucy and my parents." Though filled with her own suffering, Jane watched Cash. She had to make him understand the part of Dena's reasoning she had surmised. Dena hadn't given her Angie in order to wound her brother.

Cash shoved his hands into the pockets of his jeans and stared at the ground.

"Don't you see? Dena wanted to share my family with Angie. Dena loved you, but she turned to my family for what she lacked." Jane longed to add, *Dena wanted Angie to love God, too, Cash,* but she knew too well this would shatter the tentative link she was trying to forge. Cash had never understood Dena's love for the Lord.

"I never knew she felt that way," he muttered.

"Cash, you've decided to live your life solo, but I think Dena preferred Angie to be part of a choir."

"What you've said really changes nothing."

"Changes nothing?" Jane's voice shrilled, "What do you mean?"

"I mean, why do I always have to share *my* time with Angie, with you? I'd like to have her to myself."

Though she had never feared that Cash would steal Angie, her panic accelerated.

"Why do you cling so tightly to Angie? Every time I come near it's as though you're pushing me away."

"I don't push you away," Jane denied weakly.

"Yes, you do. I want to know why, and I want you to stop it."

"But Angie is so little yet." Jane quivered.

"What has that got to do with anything?"

"She still needs me to be with her."

He shrugged his shoulders in a show of irritation. "You leave her with baby-sitters on and off every week."

"Just my aunt, uncle, Tish and Lucy." She felt herself crumbling inside.

"Why not me, then?"

"It's not the same." She looked down at the open toes of her sandals.

"Yes, it is. Why won't you let me take charge of Angie some evenings?"

Her head snapped back up to face him. "Because that's what you'd do—*take charge of Angie,* just like you did last night."

"What do you mean by that?" His deep voice began to rise in volume. "Am I supposed to be in the wrong, because Angie and Lucy needed air-conditioning?"

"No, but don't you see, you didn't talk the matter over with me." Her voice and body shook. "You just came in and took over. 'You need this, so I'll do that.' No discussion. Just issuing orders." She hugged herself, trying to mask her trembling.

"Why do you have to be so touchy?"

"Why do you have to be so bossy?"

"Bossy. Touchy. It comes down to this, Red. I've turned

my life upside down to accommodate my sister's twisted will and your lifestyle. I reorganized my business. I learned to fly. I moved north and started a whole new branch of my firm. Now I'm going to have Angie by myself one day a week or *else.*"

Jane felt her self-control disintegrate, just as it had that January day in the social worker's office. Just the way it had over the past six months during private moments whenever she thought of Dena. To hide her tears, she rushed a few yards away into the forest of fir trees.

Casting a glance at the peacefully swinging baby, Cash pursued Jane. "Come back here," he called through tightly clenched teeth.

He caught up with Jane easily and spun her around to face him. "Why are you crying like this? Do you think I'll let you have your way if you cry hard enough?" He gripped her by the shoulders. "I won't be manipulated by tears."

"I can't help it," she spoke between sobs. She pressed her hands over her face. "I miss Dena so much."

"We weren't talking about Dena. Why did you bring her up? Is this some kind of emotional blackmail? Do you think if you can upset me, I'll let this drop?"

"No, but whenever I think about being away from Angie, my grief over losing Dena bubbles up and I can't stop it."

"I can't help that. I lost Dena, too."

"I know, but in some way inside me, Angie and Dena are linked. Losing Angie feels like losing Dena."

"Of course they're linked. Why else would I want Angie? If you don't let me have Angie one day a week, you'll force me to take you to court."

"No." Tears rolled down her cheeks. Cash's grip braced her, keeping her standing straight, bolstering her with his strength. A glance up into his pained face slowed her tears. She brushed away her tears with her fingertips. "I'm sorry.

I didn't mean to hurt you." She looked up at him, her eyes pleading for understanding. "Truly, Cash."

"I miss Dena, too," he said gruffly, tugging her back to where Angie still swung.

"I know." She wiped away her tears. "It's still so hard to accept. I keep telling myself Dena is with God, beyond pain and sorrow. But that doesn't ease away the hurt of loss." For a moment Jane let herself imagine the comfort of resting her head on Cash's broad shoulder.

They were silent awhile. Then Cash raised his chin. "When can I have Angie to myself?"

Jane made herself think. She had lost Dena, but in spite of her grief, she was bound by her faith to do what was right for Angie and Cash. Though she didn't feel it right now, she knew God would provide the extra strength she would need to overcome her fears. "All right." Saying the words turned her insides to quivering jelly again, but she looked up into Cash's face resolutely.

"When?" he demanded.

"In two months, Angie will be a year old."

"I can have her on her birthday?"

"No, I'm planning a big party on that day. You can have her on the twenty-fourth?"

"The twenty-fourth." He wanted to press her to move the date forward, but perhaps it was better to accept this hard-won concession. He'd just hold her to it. Reluctantly, he nodded.

Jane tugged at his arm and he followed her back to Angie, who was kicking her chubby legs and cooing skyward at the large white clouds overhead. At the sight of Jane, the baby gave one quick cry. "Want your bottle, sweetie?" Jane asked.

Cash carried the baby back to the quilt and laid her down. Jane rummaged through the denim bag and brought out a bottle of formula. With the bottle finally clutched between her chubby hands, Angie relaxed and sucked loudly.

"I feel like I've run a ten-mile race," Jane murmured. "Before we have lunch, would you mind if I stretched out for a few minutes?"

"Go ahead. I'll watch Angie."

Jane lay down beside the baby and closed her eyes. When Angie's eyes also drifted shut as she sucked contentedly, Cash lay down, too. He stared up into the blue sky for a long time, then glanced at Jane beside him. The lake breeze played with wisps of red hair around her tranquil face. One of her arms was extended and curved around Angie. The tiny freckles, flecks of gold, on Jane's arm fascinated him. The blue-tinged shadows beneath her eyes touched his heart. Jane hadn't begrudged any of the lost sleep and worry it had cost her to care for his niece.

He stirred inside and resented it. Why had he started noticing Red as an attractive woman? This afternoon when she'd wept, he'd fought the urge to pull her into his arms. In all the years he'd known her, she had never meant more to him than his kid sister's best friend.

Now every time he saw her—even when they argued—he imagined what her lips would taste like and how soft her skin would feel.

Chapter Six

"'He hideth my life in the depths of His love, and covers me there with His hand,'" Jane sang the final phrase of the chorus, then sat down along with the rest of the congregation. The gentle words of faith, penned by Fanny Crosby nearly a century before, soothed Jane's heart like warm water bathing chilled fingers. During the showdown with Cash the day before, so many memories and so much sorrow had been stirred, she needed comfort.

On the wall to her right hung a wood panel on which the Beatitudes had been carved. "Blessed are they that mourn for they shall be comforted" caught her eye. Quieting her spirit, she opened herself, asking for God's comfort. The peace of the church settled around her like a cozy blanket.

The pastor began his sermon. The summer sunshine glowed through the stained-glass window behind him, highlighting the dove of peace flying above the jewellike blue Jordan River. The quiet of church, broken only by a few throats clearing and the turning of pages, soothed Jane. Then Lucy patted Jane's hand. The gentle touch filled with affection nearly brought tears to Jane's eyes.

As usual, Jane, with Angie in her arms, sat in the middle of the pew between Lucy and Tish. On the other side of Tish sat Aunt Claire and Uncle Henry. Beside Lucy were Jane's parents. Never before had Jane comprehended the significance of her family's placement along the church pew. The youngest, the most frail, nestled in the midst of loved ones.

When Dena and she had been children, Jane had thought they had been placed in the midst of parents so they could be watched for misbehavior. Now she wondered what it would feel like to sit all alone. No doubt Cash would insist on sitting alone. Jane shook her head a fraction. Cash's armor had always been impenetrable. Once she had dreamed of piercing it and making him love her. Now she knew it was an impossible hope.

Restless in the quiet church, Angie left Jane and climbed onto Tish's lap. Tish leaned forward and rubbed noses with the baby. Angie squealed her pleasure. When Jane automatically shook her head at Tish, she noticed a flash of white through Angie's parted lips. She slid her index finger into the baby's mouth.

"Ouch!" Jane gasped as Angie bit down.

Instant silence. The pastor stopped speaking and turned toward the Everett family. The small congregation imitated him.

Crimson with embarrassment, Jane spoke up, "I just discovered Angie's first tooth."

Laughter, then spontaneous applause rippled through the church. The pastor grinned, cleared his throat and began again. When the service ended, a throng of grandmothers cooed and crooned over Angie.

Finally Jane joined her family, who were gathered in the shade of an old maple. Henry and Phil discussed the possible places to have lunch. Lucy turned to Jane. "I want you to invite Cash to our Fourth of July picnic."

"Oh?" Jane tried to sound unconcerned.

"Yes, Marge or I could extend the invitation, but I think it should come from you."

"Why?" The warm wind fluttered around them, catching Jane's full white skirt.

"So he'll know he's really welcome." Lucy stared into her granddaughter's eyes significantly.

"Very well. I'll call him from the shop later today." *And I'll remind myself that Dena would want me to invite her brother to spend time with Angie.* She stiffened her will. Though her human feelings fought against it, she would do what was right, with God's help.

With Angie on her hip, Jane waited inside the back door of her parents' summer cottage. In the background Jane heard her mother and grandmother teasing each other in the large country kitchen where they were making a "vat" of potato salad for the annual Fourth of July picnic. From a few cottages away, firecrackers burst in rapid pops like popcorn. Angie twisted in Jane's arms, trying to see where this unusual noise came from.

"Those are firecrackers. It's Independence Day, Angie," Jane said soothingly. "We're going to have fun. Uncle Cash is coming." Jane kissed Angie's soft, downy cheek. "But look. Here comes Aunty Claire, Uncle Henry and our lovely but spoiled cousin, Tish." The baby gave serious attention to the threesome walking up the steps. Jane opened the door for them. A hot wind blew against Jane's cheeks warming her unpleasantly.

"Hello——" Uncle Henry started.

"Jane," her aunt finished. They both kissed Angie and Jane lightly on the cheek and then went in, calling greetings to Lucy and Jane's mother.

Tish paused beside Angie. "Hello, sweety." As was her custom, Tish gave Angie an Eskimo kiss.

Angie leaned toward Tish, asking to be taken. Jane tried to hold on to Angie, but the little girl pushed and grunted till Jane gave in. Triumphantly Tish hugged the baby to herself and walked toward the kitchen door.

Jane stepped outside. The lake wind wafted around her, doing its best to stir the humidity-laden heat. Cash's Jeep swooped around the bend, making Jane's stomach flutter wildly. "Don't get edgy," she whispered to herself. "I must share Angie and not let my grief spoil everything." She tried to make herself decide how to handle Cash today. What if being with him stirred her ill-fated infatuation with him? Would she do or say something that would reveal this to Cash? The thought shook her to her toes.

Cash bounded up the steps. When he came abreast of Jane, a tantalizing excitement shivered through her. Pushing aside her reaction to him, she shaped her mouth into a welcoming smile.

"Where's Angie?" he asked.

"Hello, Jane," Jane said formally, trying to teach him manners. "Happy Independence Day."

Cash paused. "Sorry. Happy Independence Day. Where's Angie?"

Beckoning him ruefully with her hand, she turned. "Come on in. All the action's in the kitchen." The nonchalance in her tone pleased her.

She led him through the house into the large country kitchen. A sudden pride in her family filled Jane with joy. Her grandmother and mother stood side by side, tapping hard-boiled eggs against the sides of the stainless steel sink. The two women were a study in contrasts. Marge, a brunette with an ivory complexion, was fashionably thin and taller than fair Lucy. Marge wore a sporty pair of navy cotton slacks and a white blouse while Lucy wore a floral sundress in shades of peach and yellow.

Her aunt and uncle sat at the table with her father, Phil,

who with his fair coloring, looked a great deal like his mother and daughter. For a moment Jane felt like saying something stupid like, This is my family!

"Cash!" Phil stood up. "Great to see you. Happy Independence Day!" Henry stood, also, and shook Cash's hand warmly.

"Come here, Cash," Marge instructed. Cash obeyed. When he was beside her, she turned and gave his cheek an affectionate peck. "We're so glad you've joined us today."

"We'll see if he can put up with us for a whole picnic," Lucy put in saucily. Cash grinned and leaned over to kiss Lucy's cheek.

At the far end of the room near the pantry, Tish was dancing a sort of waltz with Angie in her arms. When Angie caught sight of Cash, she squealed.

"Cash, this is my cousin, Tish." Jane motioned toward Tish who blushed as though embarrassed. Angie's continued squealing forced Tish to bring her to Cash. At Phil's invitation, Cash sat down beside Henry.

"Janie," Phil ordered, "break out the new deck."

From a kitchen shelf, Jane took down an unopened pack of ornate blue-and-white cards. She tossed it to her father.

Phil broke the seal and opened the box. "Hope you're in the mood for Crazy Eights, Cash."

"Haven't played in a long time," Cash admitted. "Why don't I just watch—"

"No shirkers allowed in this family," Henry said with a cheerful flourish. "In this world of constant change, there is one constant—on the Fourth of July, the men in this house play Crazy Eights. Now we don't play for money, but we do play for honor. And I plan to defend my championship again this year."

Aunt Claire beamed at her husband.

"Claire," Phil chided, "I always told you, you married a card shark." Phil began to deal three hands efficiently.

Tish sat down beside Cash. "I'll help you remember the rules." With her head tilted coquettishly, she smiled.

On the other side of Tish, Jane found herself squelching the urge to shake her cousin. Jane took a deep breath and went to her mother's side. "Are all your eggs cracked?"

"Yes, all the Humpty-Dumpties have taken their great falls," Lucy replied mournfully.

"Why don't you finish the relish tray?" Marge motioned toward a large platter, piled high with fresh vegetables.

Jane nodded and brought out the cow-shaped, wooden cutting board. She began peeling carrots. Her eyes were on her task, but her ears monitored the banter of the card game.

Cash held Angie in his lap and glanced down once more at his cards. The little girl was in one of her serious moods when—either due to fatigue or a personality quirk—she became relaxed. He held his cards in both hands in front of him, and Angie, though drooling onto her terry cloth teething bib, almost looked as though she were studying his cards, too.

He heard Lucy and Marge, talking in easy tones about discarding the eggs that had green around the yolks and trying to fix blame for this blight. The sounds that Jane was making as she peeled and sliced the vegetables were rhythmic, assured, soothing.

He picked up a card and mentally recalled the suit he was trying for with this hand. He smiled to himself. He had drawn a wild card, a joker. He only had to play one other card and he would win this hand. His next turn gave him his chance. He laid down his cards and won.

The chagrin of the other two players was loud, but good-natured. The next hand was dealt, but this time Claire and Tish changed places with Lucy and Jane. Lucy claimed Angie from Cash. Again the women watched the card play, urging on their favorites enthusiastically.

Cash glanced at the cheerful group around the table. He

hadn't really thought about what it would be like spending the Fourth with Jane's family. Knowing Lucy as he did, he wondered why he had not guessed the day would be casual and lighthearted.

When it had been just his own family: Dena, Dad, and himself, there had never been much fanfare on any occasion. After their father's death, Dena had chosen to spend most of her holidays with the Everetts. Now he could see why, but at the time he had been too busy with business to make much attempt at creating holiday cheer. He himself hadn't needed other people to celebrate every special day. But Dena had loved being with the Everetts. Maybe Red had been right. Maybe Dena had wanted Angie to be part of this.

The fierce competition of Crazy Eights raged till the final hand and to Cash's surprise, Henry won again.

"Hurray!" Claire exclaimed. Grinning, Henry received his champion's kiss from her.

"Now on to phase two!" Lucy declared.

Both Phil and Henry stood up with military straightness. At their encouragement, Cash followed their example. Out of the refrigerator, Claire and Jane brought a huge platter of marinated beef back ribs. The pungent aroma of garlic, spices and tomato sauce went right to Cash's taste buds. His mouth watered. "Ribs?"

Marge chuckled. "Didn't Jane tell you we always have barbecued ribs for Independence Day?"

"No, if she had, I would have skipped breakfast," he said honestly.

"Oh, dear," Marge moaned as she wrung her hands in mock anguish, "I hope the extra ten pounds I bought will be enough!"

Laughter broke out among the Everetts. Cash looked around the kitchen. Only Tish was trying to behave non-chalantly, as if she felt embarrassed for his sake. All this dreadful year, every change of season, every holiday, even an unsentimental one like the Fourth of July, had brought bittersweet memories not only of Dena, but also their father and mother, as though the loss of Dena had reinforced all his bereavements. But he hadn't been left completely alone. He still had Angie. She was all he needed.

"Be off with you!" Lucy ordered.

Ceremoniously, Phil and Henry took charge of the platter, a long-handled pair of tongs, a pot holder mitt and a spray bottle of water.

"You don't have to go out if you don't want to," Tish said softly beside Cash.

"I wouldn't want to shirk my duty. I want to earn that extra ten pounds of ribs."

Without showing any response, Jane listened to this exchange between Cash and Tish. Was it just Tish's way of separating herself from the zany humor that her family favored? Or was her young cousin falling for Cash's potent charm?

Angie began to fuss. As the door closed behind the three men, Jane turned to the refrigerator to bring out a bottle to warm. Going through the mundane routine helped quiet her nerves.

After the ribs had been grilled to Phil and Henry's standard of perfection, Cash watched as the Everetts took their places around the long redwood picnic table on the screened-in porch. The hot ninety-two-degree wind still blew, but an inside picnic was obviously impossible for the Everetts to consider.

In pleasant amazement, Cash viewed the feast laid out on the long table. The huge platter of aromatic ribs occupied the center. American potato salad with its pale mustard color had been decorated with a "sunrise" of egg slices. In addition, yellow corn on the cob with melted golden butter nestled beside the greens and reds of fresh vegetables on their tray. Pink-red chunks of watermelon filled a huge, green glass bowl and next to each place setting stood a tall, amber tumbler of iced tea, each with a generous wedge of lemon on the rim.

All around him, the easy banter continued. Unexpectedly he felt a thaw around his heart. He hadn't realized he had been so frozen inside since Dena's death till this day of warmth.

At the head of the table, Phil bowed his head. Everyone else became still with anticipation. Cash waited to see what Phil would pray. "God bless this food. God bless this family. God bless this land. Amen." Then, as though a switch had been thrown, the chatter began again, and the bowls started their journey from hand to hand.

When the eating was complete, Cash felt unusually full and unusually satisfied. The food had tasted as delicious as it had looked. Glancing down he saw Angie at the foot of the picnic table, seated in her high chair. She had a little bit of the whole menu on her face, hair, hands, bib and tray. She was grinning widely and cooing.

Marge also caught sight of Angie. "Look at our beautiful grandchild, Phil!" Marge sprang out of her chair. "She looks good enough to eat!" She hurried to Angie and un-hooked her from the chair. As Marge hugged her and kissed her on the nose, Angie beamed. "You sweet baby, we are so lucky to have you. Yes, we are. Our first grandbaby. Can you giggle for your old Grandma?" She tickled Angie once on the belly and Angie obligingly giggled.

"Should we give Grandpa a messy kiss?" Marge asked Angie, carrying her over to Phil. Angie reached out with her chubby, gooey hands and, chuckling, Phil kissed them. When he tried to take the child from his wife, Marge pulled away. "You'll get your turn later, Grandpa!"

Aunt Claire said, "Henry, I think it's time we—"

"Gave Phil and Marge their gifts," Henry finished and

went into the house, returning with a large paper bag. Grinning, he drew out two white hats. "This one's for Marge."

"And this one's for Phil."

The two baseball-style caps were white except for the red lettering embroidered on the fronts. One read "Grandma". The other read "Grandpa". Obviously delighted, Phil and Marge both immediately put them on.

"Oh, Henry, they're wonderful," Lucy declared. "Where's my camera?"

Jane went in, returning with Lucy's old 35mm. Lucy quickly posed the beaming Marge and Phil as they held Angie between them.

While all this took place in front of him, Cash sat immobile. He fought the urge to break down into tears. Except for Lucy, he had never considered how Jane's parents and family would react to Angie in their midst. That Phil and Marge would accept Angie as their first grandchild with pride and love had never entered his mind. Probably because he had never known his own grandparents. For so long there had only been just Dena and him.

He stood up abruptly and hurried outside, the screened door banging shut behind him. Shoving his hands into his pockets, he walked quickly down the wide steps to the Everetts' pier and halted at the end of the wooden dock. Then he let the tears come while the hot, bold wind lashed him, drying the tears as quickly as they fell.

"Cash?"

Turning slowly, he saw Jane tentatively approaching him. It was as though he was seeing her for the first time. Her full lips the color of summer peaches were parted slightly. She glowed with life, vibrant and generous.

"Cash?" She repeated, pausing only a step from him.

Her concerned expression caused a spasm around his heart. "You didn't need to come after me. I'm all right."

His mouth felt suddenly dry, and his voice sounded hoarse to his ears.

"Mom is concerned about you. She's afraid we did something that upset—"

"I'm fine. Let's go back. This wind feels like the Santa Ana in California."

He watched Jane give him one more worried glance. Then she led him back up the steps to the house.

Later, when the hot wind that had blown all day finally stilled, and darkness tinted the high clouds the color of slate, Phil announced it was time for the sparklers.

They all trooped outside to the grassy lawn overlooking the lake. Phil sat on the back porch steps, Angie reclining royally on his lap. Nearby on an old canvas-and-wood lawn chair, armed with a butane lighter and a coffee can half-filled with water, sat Henry, the "lighter" and the "extinguisher." Marge, Lucy, Claire and Jane swirled with the sparklers, twisting and exclaiming over the variety of the sparklers' fire: some traditional red and gold, and others startling green and blue.

Cash leaned against the house, watching the ladies and Angie's captivated expression as she took in her first sight of sparklers. At the display of the dancing, sputtering sparks, the little girl's mouth and eyes opened wide in absolute wonderment.

The ladies laughed and teased each other while painting bright, but vanishing, patterns against the darkening sky. The sparklers' sizzling sound punctuated the wash of waves against the nearby sandy beach. In the distance, while boats already chugged by toward town, more firecrackers and bottle rockets popped and exploded.

Cash felt a warmth that had nothing to do with the heat of this long day. The Everett family Independence Day celebration captivated him as much as Angie was captivated by the sparklers' shining colors.

Only one person did not seem to be enjoying this part of the celebration: Tish. With her waist-length golden hair reflecting the flash of sparklers, Tish walked toward him in an obviously planned-to-be-sexy walk. She leaned back against the house and assumed a seductive pose; one knee bent, her arms back. Cash smiled to himself as the young girl practiced her feminine wiles. Obviously Tish was at the age where she would not enjoy lighting sparklers. She wanted to distance herself from childish things.

The first words from Tish's mouth proved his thought true. "This is so childish." Tish grimaced. "I don't know why they do this every year."

"Angie seems to be enchanted by the show."

"Sparklers are for kids. I mean, my family must seem really weird to you."

Cash chuckled softly. "Every family should be this weird."

Jane, from behind the dazzling light of her long, red Oriental sparkler, observed her cousin's pose and the fact that Tish and Cash were talking privately. Jane felt the unmistakable nip of jealousy. At the beginning of the evening she had experienced a touch of that unreasoning fear of losing Angie to Cash. Now was she jealous of Tish? Why wouldn't her emotions make sense? Cash was not going to take Angie, and he wasn't interested in Tish. As the sparkler burned down to Jane's fingertips, she yelped in pain.

By the time the sparklers had all been beautifully burned, Cash had allowed himself to be persuaded to go by boat to Eagle Lake's fireworks display. With Angie riding on his shoulders, he walked in the midst of the Everetts as they all trooped down to the pier and boarded a large pontoon boat. On board, they settled onto lawn chairs and Marge passed out soft drinks.

Angie snuggled deep in Cash's arms. He felt mellow for the first time since Dena's death. For a moment he pictured his sister among them, smiling. For once, thinking of Dena brought no pain.

The boat slowly moved across the lake and through the narrows toward town. The distant reflections of lights from the houses they passed flickered like candle flames on the water. He imagined Dena's joy over the beauty of the night.

Within sight of town, Phil cut the motor and dropped anchor near several other boats. Friendly greetings from boat to boat were exchanged by acquaintances and strangers alike. Phil left on only the small boat lights, red and green on the front and white on the rear. They bobbed on the gentle waves. Cash leaned back in his chair, savoring the contentedness of this day, letting it spread through him.

On a hillside behind them, Jane caught glimpses of spirals from sparklers in the darkness and enjoyed the excited shrill laughter of the children, waving and twirling them. She glanced at Angie who was sound asleep in Cash's lap. For once, no warring emotion tugged at her. Cash and Angie appeared so peaceful, she could not help but smile at them. Then her father murmured that the fireworks were about to start, and everyone focused on the sky over the city park. They all waited.

Letting herself relax to the soothing rhythm of the waves beneath them, Jane closed her eyes briefly. The day had not been strained as she had feared...except for her own short attack of jealousy over Tish's attention to Cash. The spot on her fingertips where she had burned herself still felt as though it were on fire.

Boom! Jane jerked upright in her seat. She must have dozed off for a few seconds. As the town's Fourth of July pyrotechnic show got off the ground, the sky above was sprinkled with golden sparks. She quickly looked to see if the sudden noise had wakened the baby, but obviously it would take more than fireworks exploding to disturb Angie tonight.

"Do you think she'll sleep through all of this?" Cash murmured close to her ear. The flashes from the fireworks glistened in his eyes. She tried to take her gaze from him, but couldn't. Reaching out, she lightly smoothed back Angie's dark, wispy bangs.

Wap! The second projectile shot into the air, bursting into long magenta streamers. Wap! Wap! Two more escaped gravity—a huge yellow-gold chrysanthemum formation blossomed and disintegrated above them. Inside Jane, fireworks went off, too. Cash had taken her hand in one of his. She was afraid to look at him. Her breathing became shallow.

"This is the way to see fireworks," Cash said.

"Haven't you been to Chicago's extravaganza at Buckingham Fountain?" She could barely speak. She was careful not to move her hand. Why didn't he let go?

"Sure, but that's what makes this so different. No crowds. No traffic."

The display caught Jane's attention in spite of herself. "Ooh," she heard herself and all the others in the boat voice appreciation.

Wap! Wap! Boom! Boom! BOOM! The series of thundering explosions unleashed cascading bursts of shimmering gold, red, white, and blue on the breeze. That breeze also carried the oohs and ahs from the audience in town, but the dominant factor in Jane's mind was her hand in Cash's.

A full half hour of fireworks artistry dominated their attention. Cash relaxed his hold on her hand, but didn't release her. The inner turmoil his touch caused echoed the riotous display of color and sound. Then came the grand finale. The sky was overtaken with a massive bouquet of scarlet, magenta, royal blue, gold. The booms and cracks echoed deafeningly, joined by shouts of approval and applause.

Silence. Jane looked over at Cash and smiled timidly. In the shadows cast only by the boat's two small lights, she caught him studying her intently. Their eyes met. Jane's senses zipped to an even higher level of consciousness. Then he let go of her hand. He leaned down and kissed the top of Angie's sleeping head, and Jane felt as though his lips had touched her also.

"Oh, is it over already?" Lucy's complaint broke into Jane's thoughts.

"Yes, Mother. You'll have to wait till next year," Marge said not unsympathetically. There were other similar sentiments made while Phil turned on the motor and they chugged toward home.

The rapid beating of Jane's heart quieted very gradually on the long ride back. The now-cool lake breeze fluttered over Jane's face and lifted her hair around her ears. Angie slept on beatifically in Cash's arms.

Sometime later, after Jane hadn't been able to find her car keys, she found herself being driven home by Cash. He escorted her and Angie inside, a picnic hamper and the diaper bag in his hands. All the bustle of the day had ended, and Jane felt as if they were the only people left in town.

Once inside the house, Jane went directly upstairs. A little Bo-Peep lamp on the high dresser softly illuminated the baby's room. Being alone with Cash after a day together made Jane intensely aware of her movements. Feeling Cash's eyes on her felt like the touch of his hand on hers earlier.

From the doorway Cash watched Jane's hands as they changed a soggy diaper and snapped Angie into a lightweight pink sleeper. Finally, when the baby was dressed comfortably and rolled to her back, Jane laid a thin white blanket over the sleeping child. Drawn to Jane as well as Angie, Cash quietly stepped closer to the crib.

Standing beside Jane, Cash caught the last fragrance of Jane's cinnamon cologne and Angie's baby powder. It was a compelling mix of scents: woman and child. The soft light in the room highlighted the bronze of Jane's hair. The quiet buzz of the air conditioner and Angie's contented breathing were the only sounds in the cozy room.

Cash couldn't take his eyes off Jane's profile. Her gleaming, warm copper hair, creamy skin glowing in the low light, her full lower lip. He observed her shiver and wondered if it was due to her awareness of him. Because he was certainly very aware of her.

That lower lip of hers drew his eyes down. He leaned forward...and touched his lips to hers. A breathless moment passed between them. Then as his lips played across hers, she gasped, fanning her warm breath against his mouth.

"Jane." He pressed his lips to her again. They felt like satin and tasted spicy and warm. As she stepped nearer into his embrace, he felt her hands claim his shoulders.

"Jane," he whispered again. His arms went around her. She fit against him so neatly.

The phone rang, and they fell apart as though a stranger had walked into the room. Jane hurried to answer it. Angie whimpered in her sleep. Cash stroked the child's back till she quieted.

Then he walked out into the dark hall. He heard Jane's voice and then the receiver being put back into its cradle. Still mulling over what he and Red had just experienced, he took a controlling breath.

Jane came out to meet him in the hall. "It was Mother." Her voice was just above a whisper. "They found my keys behind the bread box in the kitchen. I put my purse there when I first arrived. My car keys must have fallen out. That was why we couldn't find them."

He nodded. "I'll bring them in with me in the morning."

"That's not necessary. My parents will deliver the keys and my Blazer tomorrow."

He nodded. She moved ahead of him and paused at the

top of the staircase. "I'll go down and lock up after you leave."

He followed her, trying to think of what to say to her about the kiss he hadn't meant to take. Matters over Angie had just begun to ease. He had guessed the invitation to spend the Fourth with her family had been Jane's way of reaffirming her commitment to share Angie with him. So why had he kissed her? He wasn't a kid with uncontrollable hormones. Had he upset the delicate balance between them?

At the back door he cleared his throat. "I didn't— I hope I didn't offend you. I never—"

"That's okay. It's been a long day for all of us. Good night." Jane smiled tightly and let him out. He waited for her to lock the door, then walked toward the alley where his Jeep was.

With her back pressed against the door, Jane felt herself weighted down with emotion. What she had feared had happened. After all these years, Cash had finally kissed her. And then apologized. How was she going to keep a healthy distance from him now? He was evidently feeling the pull of their situation just as she was. Otherwise why would he have kissed her?

It had been devastating to know how easily he could sweep past her defenses and make her recall those first few childish years after her sixteenth birthday, those days when she had been foolish enough to think she might find a way to win Cash. Since then, it had been hard, painful work to put up walls to guard her heart against her own vulnerability to Cash.

Now her walls would have to be higher and stronger or she ran the risk of becoming even more hurt.

Chapter Seven

Jane, seated at her desk in the shop's brightly lit basement, checked invoices and a balance sheet. From upstairs she heard the scraping of clothes hangers on racks and the steady rhythm of the manual carpet sweeper. Tish was making sure all the sizes were in the right places, and Mel was doing a once-over with the sweeper on the aisles and dressing room floors. Both girls were supposed to be keeping an eye on Angie, who was in her playpen near the cash register. Occasionally Jane heard a bell ring as Angie played with her activity center.

The shop would open in fifteen minutes. Even in the basement, Jane heard the steady gush and swish of the rain over the pavement. A sharp thunderstorm which had begun an hour after dawn still washed over them. Rain would make for a busy day. Tourists, unable to boat and swim, would come in to browse.

Though deep in her figures, Jane became gradually aware that the two reassuring sounds above had been replaced by hushed, but heated, voices. Suddenly the long day ahead of sitting for the portrait and working at the shop stretched out even longer before her. The rivals are at it again. *God, give me patience. And I need it right now.* With a labored sigh, she closed her paperwork and trudged up the steps. In one hand she carried the working cash to start the day.

"You dumb blonde," Mel said, nose to nose, with Tish. "He's just using you to make Nancy Ledbetter jealous."

"Who's jealous? You are! That's who's jealous!" Tish tossed back. "Tony says it's all over between him and Nancy—"

"Girls," Jane cut in, "we open in ten minutes." Both heads swung to her reluctantly. Each of their faces wore a mulish expression.

"Okay," Mel said grudgingly, and went back to her sweeping.

Tish maintained her defiant stance a moment longer and then, with a swish of her golden mane, turned back to the rack nearest her.

After stopping at the side of the playpen to encourage Angie at her attempt to turn the dial and ring another bell, Jane walked over to the cash register drawer and unlocked it. Methodically she counted the money from her hand into each compartment: ones, fives, tens and twenties, letting the mundane task soothe her ruffled nerves.

From behind, Jane heard a sharp tapping on the front window. All three of them turned to see Cash, wearing a khaki slicker, peering into the shop. Tish, closest to the door, started forward.

"I'll get it," Jane said. Tish halted, and in a huff went to the rear of the shop. She began shoving hangers along a rack there. Scrape! Scrape!

Jane strode to the door and opened it. "What brings you to town?"

His rain-dotted face lifted into a hesitant smile. "Thought I'd offer you and Angie breakfast, then drive you both out to Lucy's for your sitting. I won't be able to get anything else done this morning.''

He sounded ill at ease. She looked up into his eyes and saw the uncertainty there. He was testing her, seeing if she would continue to resist sharing Angie with him.

The carpet sweeper nipped Jane's heels.

"Oh! Sorry, Miss Everett,'' Mel said from behind her.

Jane rotated and found both girls staring at Cash. "That's all right, Mel,'' she said automatically. The decision to go with him suddenly became easy. *Let me out of here!* To make her escape, Jane swiftly rescued Angie from her playpen and stepped to the door. "Girls, I'll be back before I go to Grandmother's.''

Cash unsnapped the front of his slicker with a jerk and held up one side like a wing.

With that, she stepped out and under the cover of Cash's arm. Like children just out of school, Jane and Cash ran the block to the Eagle Café, bumping erratically into each other. Jane smelled the clean scent of rain, but also Cash's clothing, which held a mingling of forest scents: pine and cedar and his subtle aftershave. Naturally the running made her heart speed up, but the man beside her brought her senses alive and made them intensely sensitive.

Her shoulder accidentally connected with his chest, and she felt his solid strength. As she ran under his open slicker, with Angie in her arms, she was blindsided by an elemental oneness—man, woman, child.

Entering the half-filled restaurant, Jane found herself grinning in spite of being wet up to her ankles and sprinkled all over. Cash joined in the lighthearted mood by theatrically sweeping off his dripping cloak. Raindrops flew into the air around him. He then held it outside the door and flapped it twice like a scatter rug. Finally he swung it up on one of a row of hooks where other raincoats, swamp jackets and umbrellas already dripped along the wall.

A possessive arm under hers, he escorted her and Angie to a booth near the front. For those few moments she let herself revel in his special courtesy, and she wondered if he had been aware of the fleeting connection between the three of them. They slid in across from each other, still grinning. On Jane's lap, Angie spontaneously clapped her hands, and Jane bent to kiss her forehead.

At this gesture of love, Cash felt a clutch at his heart. Dena must have known how much Jane would love Angie. Covering this sudden rush of poignant emotion, he signaled to the waitress to bring them two coffees.

Cash lifted the heavy white mug. As long as he could recall, this café had used the same style cups. All this summer since he had moved north, he had savored the continuity of the past, present and future here. He felt as though he had come home at last. He had deep roots here from when he was young, and he wondered if Jane felt the same way about Eagle Lake. Was that why she had opened her business and established her life here?

Jane leaned back against the red vinyl and took her first sip, then sighed luxuriously. Dressed in a tan skirt and an ivory short-sleeved sweater, Jane fit in perfectly with the backdrop of the maroon-and-white café.

Jane Everett is a beautiful woman. The thought still had the power to startle him. She wasn't gawky and fourteen— she hadn't been for over a decade. How could he have been so blind? She ran the fingers of her right hand through her burnished hair, coaxing it into its own natural waves. Watching her brought an ache, a lack, an emptiness inside him. Then it became a name, a plea. *Jane.*

The waitress brought over two menus and a high chair, which she placed at the end of their booth. Once Angie was in it, she playfully patted the tray and tapped her heels against its footrest. Reeling with his inner confusion over Red, Cash hid behind the plastic-covered menu.

Jane smelled a mouth-watering mix of aromas in the air, but she conquered her urge to order a second breakfast. She turned her attention to the man across from her. His longish, black hair caught the fluorescent light and shone. Raindrops glistened on the crown of his head. Her fingers longed to tousle his hair and make the raindrops dance then disappear.

Why had she been cursed with the Everett family trait of constancy? Other women fell in and out of love. Why couldn't she—once and for all—get Cash out of her system? Six years ago she had become infatuated or fascinated with him. She knew that there would never be anything but Angie between Cash and her, so why did she still react to him?

Sternly she turned her thoughts to the present. She cleared her throat. "How's your work going? Has the rain held you back much?"

"A little, but fortunately it's so hot between storms that it dries out pretty fast. Today, however, I would have been sitting around just watching the mud ooze till it was time to be at Lucy's."

Before long the waitress set a platter down in front of him and recited, "Two eggs over easy, four slices of bacon, soft, two griddle cakes plate-sized and a hill of hash browns". She grinned and placed a saucer of golden, buttered toast and a small plastic glass of apple juice in front of Angie's tray. Apologetically she eased a towering homemade cinnamon roll in front of Jane. "It's the last one. I thought you might change your mind about not wanting anything."

"Thanks." Jane pointed to Cash's overflowing platter. "You're right. I can't hold out in the face of that!" The waitress grinned and left them. Angie wiggled and babbled for her juice, so Jane held the glass to the baby's mouth and let her take a long swallow.

With a smile Cash speared a combination bite of egg-bacon-pancake. "I'll help you finish that roll."

"I don't think so." She buttered her roll with real butter

and refused to think about cholesterol or calories. An Eagle Café cinnamon roll was a true indulgence and should be enjoyed as such.

"Come on. You'll never finish it," he teased between bites.

"Will to." She gave him a superior smile, then took a bite of her cinnamon roll. A spot of butter slipped off her lower lip and melted its way down her chin.

Before Cash gave it conscious thought, he caught the butter with his index finger, and the tenor of their exchange instantly altered, becoming intimate, charged. Their eyes connected and held. The richness of those moments on July Fourth flooded him, making him long to reach for her hand.

Jane couldn't take her eyes from Cash's face. As he moved his hand away, his fingers brushed the underside of her chin. The touch careened through her, lighting flash fires in her veins.

A burst of laughter from behind them shattered their connection. Cash drew back his hand completely and sat up straighter.

Without invitation, Carmine Vitelli, Mel's dad, slid into the booth beside Cash. He greeted Angie, "Hi, Toots."

Angie giggled. Crumbs from her toast dotted her face and bib, and her chin was slick with butter shine.

"Now that's a breakfast," Carmine said, ogling Cash's platter.

Cash raised his shoulder, blocking Carmine's threat to his breakfast. "Get your own, Vitelli."

"Get your own, Vitelli," Jane mimicked, protecting her cinnamon roll from Carmine. Joining in the gaiety, Angie giggled and clapped again.

"Don't mind if I do." Carmine tipped his hand up as though drinking coffee. Reading his signal, the waitress came over with a fresh mug for him and took his order.

Then he turned to Cash. "So what are you going to do about Hallawell?"

Cash swallowed a long draught of his coffee. "Why should I do anything? This summer's *delightful* weather is the only thing interfering with my construction project."

Carmine teased Angie by acting as if he were going to steal her apple juice. "I've heard he's tried to strong-arm some of the suppliers to slow down your materials deliveries."

"You listen to gossip too much, Carmine." A steely confidence dominated Cash's features.

Suddenly Jane felt very sorry for Roger Hallawell.

After their breakfast Jane checked in at the shop and changed into her portrait dress downstairs in her office. Feeling slightly festive as she always did in her grandmother's peach-toned flowered dress, she slipped into Cash's Jeep, and he drove the three of them out to Lucy's cottage for another sitting.

The memory of Cash's hand against her chin this morning dominated Jane's thoughts as they walked toward Lucy's door. "It's stopped raining. That's something," he said, sounding doubtful.

"Yes, now we'll *steam* for the rest of the day." Jane blew through her mouth and fanned herself with her hand against the humidity and heat which at mid-morning already suffocated them.

Lucy was waiting at the cottage door. "Good morning, sweetheart," Lucy called and waved to Angie.

"We're here, too, you know," Jane scolded.

Ignoring Jane and Cash, Lucy lifted Angie out of Cash's arms and spun around, making the child laugh in delight.

"I feel a bit slighted myself," Cash complained broadly.

"Oh, you two are just spoiled brats. Who would want you?" Lucy laughed at them and carried Angie into the house.

After a few minutes of chatter, Lucy led Jane into the living room and began preparing to paint. Taking up her palette, she said to Jane, "Spread and smooth your skirt a bit more, Jane. And then tilt your chin down and to the right. Show us your best side."

Jane obediently tilted her head. Lucy adjusted it slightly more to the right, then stepped behind the easel and began touching her small, round brush painstakingly to the canvas.

Cash sat on the dark green wicker chair near the large window overlooking the lake. Out of the corner of her eye, Jane watched him hold a blue, circular shape sorter in front of Angie and help the baby find the right slot for each of the red and yellow blocks. Angie pushed and growled, trying to force a square block into a star-shaped opening. Cash slowly rotated the shape sorter till he found the matching square hole. Angie pushed the block in and yelled her approval at conquering the challenge. Jane smiled. Did every mother think her child was brilliant?

Cash's gaze caught Jane's eye. He smiled at her, sharing the joy of Angie's small victory. In that smile Jane read his abundant love for this beautiful child they shared. She felt her eyes misting.

"What is our topic of discussion today?" Lucy asked, invisible behind her easel.

Jane blinked rapidly, holding off tears. She spoke up to divert herself, keeping her voice light, "I'm afraid I have another chapter in the continuing saga of What's Missing at Jane's Shop?"

"The skirt returned?" Cash asked.

Jane caught herself just before she nodded. During posings, she let herself become a puppet with invisible strings connected to Lucy's hand and brush. "The skirt returned and a quilted jacket vanished—"

"And now the jacket returned?" Lucy stepped around the easel.

Jane replied, "It must have, because I think Mel bought it."

"I am having a hard time figuring out what the point of all this is," Cash said.

Jane continued. "At the very least, it means that someone is taking clothes from the store, then returning them for some bizarre reason. In the case of this jacket, it's tempting to assume that, since Mel bought the jacket, she is the one who had taken it out. But why? She could have just asked, couldn't she?"

"Not if she only decided to buy it after taking it out as she had the first two items," Cash commented. "So I can't see where her buying it makes any difference in this mystery."

"If I may," Lucy said, "I would like to offer a bizarre reason for taking and returning clothes."

"Please do, Watson," Jane directed from her seat.

"It's called How to Have a Larger Wardrobe without Spending any Money."

Jane suppressed a frown, maintaining her pose expression. "Ah, I see. I'm selling some slightly used clothing."

Peering at Jane, Lucy nodded and bit her lower lip in concentration. Then she began making very short strokes and alternately eyeing Jane and the portrait.

"This really has you tangled up," Cash said. "Does it matter so much? After all, nothing is actually being stolen...."

"I think you're only playing devil's advocate with me, Mr. Langley." In spite of herself, Jane tingled at the sound of his voice and the knowledge that his attention had turned to her. "I have a reputation for distinctive clothing here. Usually I only carry a few of each item in a very few sizes. In a small town, women count on that. They don't want to see someone at church or at a restaurant in the identical dress they are wearing. And I'm charging healthy retail prices, not thrift shop ones. I have a reputation of honesty to maintain.''

"Go over the events of this weekend again," Cash said softly. "The jacket Mel bought?"

Jane watched Angie in Cash's arms. Fighting her morning nap time, Angie repeatedly fluttered open her eyes, but they drooped lower and lower each time. Finally they closed in sleep, and Cash very gently arranged Angie's neck in a more comfortable position across his arm. The baby stirred, but did not wake. Again the sight of his tender care of Angie in contrast to their separateness nearly moved Jane to tears.

"I was out of the shop the day before yesterday, the Fourth." Jane pushed away her memories of that emotionally draining day. "It could have been returned that day, and then Mel could have bought it yesterday while I was on break. She didn't mention it to me, but we were very busy, and then I didn't go through all of yesterday's receipts till this morning. I'm baffled. If some stranger were shoplifting and returning items, the clothing would not be retagged neatly as though it had never left. It must be Mel or Tish because the items are always repriced and replaced exactly where they should be."

Lucy clucked her tongue over the problem. "And there isn't any reason for either girl to do this. That's what's vexing to me. I'm sure Carmine and Rona are very generous with Mel, and I think Claire's whole income goes on Tish's back. So what's the point?"

"There isn't any." Jane forgot and momentarily pursed her lips. She quickly reshaped her mouth into a half smile.

"I'm sure you'll find out what's going on and why," Cash said. "Whoever is doing it will overlook something and indict herself."

Jane glanced at him. In contrast to his matter-of-fact tone, his eyes were on her, and their intensity made her shiver. After their showdown, she was able to see Cash and their situation more clearly, but a new danger to her peace of mind had moved her to tears twice in the past hour. They were man, woman and child—but not husband, wife and daughter…and they never would be. She must always keep this clearly in mind or she might presume to behave inappropriately to their situation and bring embarrassment down on herself. A tremor of uneasiness quivered through her.

A polite tap on her back door startled Jane from her reading.

"Jane, got a minute?" Rona peered through the screen to where Jane sat on her back porch.

"Sure. Want some iced tea?" Jane put down her magazine.

"Desperately." Rona tugged at the midriff of her thin cotton blouse as though it were stuck to her skin. She followed Jane into the kitchen and took a glass of iced tea.

"I should have worn something cooler," Rona complained.

"Cooler?" Jane looked askance at Rona's neat blouse and shorts outfit.

"It's the color." Rona took a long swallow of the tea.

"That color is called pimento and it looks great on you."

"Yeah, but every time I look down I think of hot peppers and I feel hotter."

Jane shook her head and led Rona back out onto the relative coolness of the porch. They sat down across from each other.

"So what's up?" Rona asked, giving Jane a long assessing look.

"Just trying to stay cool." Jane waited, wondering what Rona had come to find out.

"Yeah, can you believe this heat?"

Jane shook her head. "Just go ahead and ask, Rona."

"What?" Rona asked innocently.

"Rona, you've got to get better at this. Usually you just dive in and say what you want. But if romantic gossip or matchmaking is your mission, you hem and haw. I'm too hot to go the long way around with you. So just ask."

Rona colored to a light shade of pimento. "Well, I hear that Cash spent the Fourth of July with you."

Jane's pulse jerked. "Cash spent the Fourth with me and my family. How did you hear about it?"

"Del Ray Martin saw him on your family's pontoon boat before the fireworks," Rona explained.

"I see. So what? Why shouldn't my family invite Cash to our picnic?"

"Well, Cash told his foreman that *you* had invited him."

"What does it matter if *I* invited him or Lucy did?" Jane couldn't keep a peevish tone out of her voice.

"Well, the whole town has been wondering how long the two of you would keep arguing over the baby before you gave in."

"Rona, I can't believe we're having this discussion!" Jane set her glass down with a thump.

"Well, you told me to just say it. And besides I thought you would have picked up on it by now."

"What exactly are people saying about me?" Jane looked at Rona grimly.

"Don't get so touchy. No one means any harm. It's just that Cash is so good-looking. Angie's such a little doll. And it would just be perfect if you two fell in love. The three of you would make such a great family!"

Jane felt like shouting with frustration. "You mean that people are sitting around actually discussing this?"

"Why, of course."

"There's nothing to it." Folding her arms, Jane flushed warm with embarrassment.

"You two are perfect for each other."

Before Jane could say her next word, the kitchen phone

rang. With an exasperated shrug toward Rona, Jane hurried inside.

"Hello, Jane?"

Leaning against the kitchen wall, Jane gripped the receiver. "Roger?"

"Yeah, I wanted to call you sooner after the Jaycee's dinner, but I've been busy. Hey, how've you been?"

"So-so." She waited, not able to quell the anxiety bubbling up in her stomach over the gossip Rona had revealed. Why would Hallawell be calling her?

"I'm going to the Aquabat Show Friday night. Want to come? I'll take you out for supper after."

Waves of nervous tension surged through her. In her mind Rona's words repeated, and she saw Cash on the night of the Fourth leaning down to kiss her, then she heard his stumbling apology. Maybe a casual date would confound the gossip and blunt her sharpened feeling for Cash as well. "Friday night? Yes, I'll go." Her stomach clenched in a quick spasm.

"Great. Got to go. Pick you up Friday at six-thirty!" In the background over the phone she heard a door slam and voices.

Jane hung up. An emotion, just one step shy of panic, whirled through her. Looking up, she saw Rona, standing in the opposite doorway.

"You didn't just do what I thought you did, did you?"

Jane glanced all around the kitchen, everywhere but Rona's face. Now this would be all over town, too!

"Why would you go out with Hallawell? Carmine is concerned about him. Things might get out of hand."

"What *things* are you talking about?"

"Cash is well liked around here. The Langleys have owned property here for over fifty years. The Shores has given a lot of men work, not only for the summer, but on into the next year." Rona frowned, causing a deep horizontal line to crease her forehead. "I would have thought you'd be on Cash's side. Your families—"

"Rona, you beat everything." Jane frowned, mirroring Rona's expression. "A month ago you were the one who came to my shop, playing matchmaker—"

"I didn't have a crystal ball! I didn't know there would be trouble with Hallawell. I really don't think you should go out with him. The whole town will see you!"

Jane's mouth was dry, and her palms were wet. Cash will see you, Jane's inner voice paraphrased. She knew why she had accepted this date, a date she would never have contemplated otherwise. It was a gesture of cutting loose from her attraction to Cash, and it would supply the meddling gossips with something unexpected to stew about.

"I hope the town will enjoy it," Jane said sarcastically. "I have to do my part and give them some fresh material to work with—"

"Jane! You can't mean that!"

"Why not? It will be an unexpected episode in my story that the whole town can enjoy for several days afterward." Jane heard her own voice becoming shrill. "I'll thrive on walking in on discussions of why the Everett girl—"

Angie's crying announced the end of her nap and cut through Jane's tirade. "Coming, Angie," Jane called, turning to Rona. "I'll be right back."

"I'll be gone. And believe me when I say that no one will hear about this fit of irrational—"

"Then I'll take out an ad in the paper. That will prepare people, so they will remember to bring their cameras—"

"I can't believe this!" Rona called as she escaped through the back door, letting it bang behind her.

Jane marched through the living room and up the stairs to Angie. Finding out that the town had linked Cash romantically with her was too close to her own fear of Cash discovering her true feelings.

* * *

Two nights later Jane opened her door and, with an inward lurch of warning, took in the sight of Roger Hallawell. He was dressed nicely in black jeans and a charcoal-and-gray-striped shirt, open at the neck. But his self-satisfied smile promptly gave Jane the urge to slam the door in his face.

Instead she opened the door wider. "Come in."

He took one step inside and then one more, bringing himself within inches of her, crowding her. Slowly his gaze slid downward. "Like your outfit."

Jane had decided to wear a high-necked, light green blouse and darker green culottes. A more chaste outfit would have been hard to imagine. "Thanks."

"And these," he continued, lightly touching one of her gold teardrop earrings.

She fought the urge to slap his hand away. She stepped back from him. "Glad you like them." Jane turned, picked up two blue rectangular boat cushions and handed them to him. "Angie and I are ready."

He opened his mouth and closed it. Then he said in a slightly strained voice, "Didn't know this would be a double date."

"Oh, I couldn't leave Angie with a sitter. She'll love the Aquabat Show." *And it will keep this from feeling like a real date.*

In the two days since she had accepted this date, Jane had felt more like a traitor every minute. But she had been trapped in a limbo of indecision and inaction. She had not been able to bring herself to the point of picking up the phone to call and cancel till late this afternoon.

"Okay." He pursed his lips in a tight smile. Hanging the cushions over his shoulder, Roger held the front door open for her as she wheeled the stroller out.

They walked the two blocks down to Lake Street and

stopped at the bleachers next to Yosacks's Restaurant. The Aquabat Water Ski Show took place every Wednesday, Friday and Sunday night, June through August. At 6:45 a good-sized crowd had already gathered at the cement waterside bleachers.

Unable to resist the buttery aroma, Jane stopped for popcorn and a large soda at the concession stand. She handed them to Roger and, parking the stroller near the railing along the street, she picked up Angie. "Where do you want to sit?" she asked.

He canvassed the bleachers. A hand waved from the crowd below them. Roger waved back, but he continued looking.

With Angie in her arms, she pointed to the shore where a double row of kids sat, all dressed in orange T-shirts that were emblazoned with "Camp Tomahawk."

"See the campers, Angie. They all want to get soaked, so they are sitting right on the shore. When you get about six years older, I'll let you sit there, too. Won't that be fun?"

Two gray-haired men stood up, and Roger returned their signal by holding up Jane's Coke. Then he hurried Jane and Angie down to them. Roger shook hands vigorously with both men.

"Hey there, don't maim me," one man said jokingly, pulling his hand away.

"Hi, Jane," the other man said. She had, of course, recognized John Banning, village councilman and Lucy's bridge partner, and acknowledged him with a friendly nod. He went on, "You know my wife, but do you know Sam Koch, county board supervisor?"

"Only by name. It's a pleasure to meet you, Mr. Koch," she said with a forced smile. When the introductions were finally complete, Roger lay down the two boat cushions and they sat on them.

Both couples had tried to mask their surprise at seeing Jane with Hallawell, but Jane had noted it, anyway. Already feeling uncomfortable about being with Roger, she had the distinct suspicion that this meeting had been prearranged to further Hallawell's well-known campaign to enter local government. What other reason would he drag them over to sit with two couples that were twice her age?

The two women made much of the baby, and Angie obligingly grinned, giggled and patty-caked for them. "She always loves an audience," Jane said wryly, but with pride.

"Our grandson is skiing in the show this year," Mary Banning said.

"Oh, yes, I remember now," Jane said politely.

The conversation drifted away from Jane, then, in a muddle of names and connections. She was relieved when the microphone squawked to life, welcoming them to "The Oldest Water Ski Show North of Silver Springs, Florida."

She had seen this show at least once a year since she had been an infant. It was a forty-year tradition in Eagle Lake. First, the cast of amateur skiers were introduced. Many of the teens were local, but a few were from other states: Colorado, California, Pennsylvania.

She knew the agenda by heart. Tonight's show began, as they all did, with the bathing beauties in white swimsuits with red sequins, holding American flags while perched on the shoulders of young men on skis. Slalom and ski jumping events followed.

But the clowns, one young man always dressed like a girl in a mismatched, thrift-shop ensemble, and one like a bumpkin with his pants belted up under his armpits and a battered polka-dotted hat were her favorites. The two clowns, who both tried to take over the show, did pratfalls into the water, chased each other in a little round motorboat of bright orange, took the ski jump backward, and thoroughly delighted the crowd.

Angie could not understand the byplay, but she laughed and clapped along with the crowd. Through Angie, Jane enjoyed the show as though she had never seen it before and forgot that Hallawell sat beside her.

Intermission came with its appeal for donations, since the show was free to the public and staffed by volunteers. The junior skiers went through the audience in twos. Jane glanced idly around and caught sight of Tish's tawny head nearby. She was sitting with a handsome boy. Was he the one Tish and Mel had argued over?

"Enjoying yourself?" Roger murmured, his lips much too close to the rim of her ear.

"I always do." The bucket for donations came by then. When Jane saw that Roger let it go by, she placed a wrinkled five-dollar bill inside.

Then she saw him—Cash. At first she thought her eyes were playing tricks on her, but it *was* Cash and he was heading right toward them. "Evening, everyone," Cash said with an easy grin. "How was the first part of the show?"

"The usual," Banning answered, looking uncomfortable.

Cash settled down on the other side of Jane. Her mouth was so dry she couldn't have answered, even if she had known what to say. Angie squealed a welcome to her uncle and broke away from Jane's restraining hands. Cash put down his drink and caught the little girl as she stumbled into his arms.

"She'll be walking soon," Mary Banning said. "Such a little doll."

"Langley, I was impressed by your model home yesterday. Thanks for inviting the village council out to see it firsthand," Banning said. Koch seconded the comment.

Jane observed Hallawell's spine stiffen. Without turning her head, she caught Cash's grim smile as he thanked both men.

"I'm sure Mr. Langley's model is quite impressive. But

he would have been much wiser to build his development in a different location,'' Hallawell said smoothly.

"Where would you suggest, Hallawell?" Cash asked. Angie stood on his lap. As he held her under her arms, she bent and straightened her knees in a bobbing dance. Cash gazed innocently at Hallawell.

"Some location that isn't as highly developed as this one already is," Hallawell continued, his neck reddening.

"The Shores will add an area of distinctive homes and enhance the tax base for Eagle Lake," Banning said firmly.

The announcer spoke up, silencing the debate. The show went on, dominated by the whine of the high-powered ski tow motors, the voice of the announcer, the clapping and cheering of the audience. Repeatedly the tow boat wakes surged up on shore, soaking the orange-shirted campers, who shrilled their appreciation.

All these noises rolled over Jane as she suffered the tension of sitting between Roger and Cash. She was intensely sorry she had come and hoped there would not be any unpleasantness when the show ended. She would never do anything this idiotic again.

Toddling back to Jane, Angie settled down in Jane's lap and drank her evening bottle. In spite of all the commotion and noise around, Angie fell asleep.

As the evening sky evolved from true blue to rose, amethyst, then deep cobalt blue, the show ended with its grand finale. Along the shore the orange-shirted campers squealed with satisfaction at their final drenching.

Jane felt like a canary, watching the barred door of the bird cage opening. At last she could go home and forget this dreadful evening.

"Why don't we all go to Kelly's for a bite?" Hallawell asked as they stood up to file out.

"Thanks, but I'm busy," Cash replied with thick irony.

The Bannings and Kochs made polite excuses.

"Okay, then I guess it's just you and me, Jane," Hallawell said.

Jane flushed. "I have to get Angie home—"

"I'll carry her for you," Cash offered. She let him roll Angie into his arms.

Hallawell's face turned an alarming red. For a few seconds Jane feared a dreadful scene was about to be served up for all the town to see. But the presence of the two older couples seemed to restrain Hallawell. He said stiffly, "Maybe some other time then."

They walked up the steep steps. Without a parting word, Hallawell left Jane with Cash. She whispered a prayer of gratitude and promised never to do anything so stupid again.

Jane put the boat cushions and diaper bag in the seat of the stroller and pushed it home, while Cash, carrying the sleeping Angie, walked beside her.

Around their pocket of silence, the night was full of the summer sounds she knew so well: the laughter of young men and their dates as they walked up and down Main Street, and lonely young men in cars, revving the motors trying to catch the attention of girls who strolled in groups along the sidewalk. The sounds made her feel old and side-lined as though nothing she did would ever alter the way she felt about Cash or how he felt about her.

Now she saw the reason Hallawell had invited her out tonight. He had wanted to use her connection to Cash to lend more support to his campaign against Cash's subdivision. She admitted to herself that she had accepted out of anger toward the gossips as well as a desire to cut the invisible bond that persisted in connecting her emotionally to Cash.

She wanted to thank him for extricating her from an uncomfortable situation, but could not think of a way to say it that wouldn't make her sound like an idiot. And she wondered how he had known she needed to be rescued. Who had told him? Uneasily she waited to see what Cash would say to her when they reached home.

At her back door, he watched while she maneuvered the stroller onto the back porch and unlocked her door. Then he laid the sleeping baby into her arms.

"Jane?"

"Yes?"

"Will you drive to Wausau tomorrow with me?"

"Wausau?" The crickets keened incessantly in the warm night. Jane brushed away a gray moth that had flown toward her eyes.

"Yes, I've been meaning to look at two Frank Lloyd Wright houses there. I thought you'd like to come along."

"I…" She was grateful that he had not said anything to embarrass her more than she already was about this evening, but she couldn't understand what had prompted this invitation.

"I took the liberty of asking Lucy to watch Angie for us."

"Oh?" She still hadn't a clue what was going on.

"See you in the morning then. Early."

She watched him walk away in the glow from the alley's street lamp. Saturday was the day he usually visited Angie. Why would he want to leave Angie behind? She quelled twin rushes of exhilaration and anxiety.

As Cash walked away, he pushed down the panic, still bouncing around in his stomach. Even though he had been forewarned by Rona, the shock of seeing Jane with Angie in her arms, sitting next to another man was still with him. He wouldn't let it happen again. Years of business had taught him that taking the offense was always better than a superb defense. Tomorrow he would launch his offense.

Chapter Eight

Cash helped Jane into his blue Jeep. As he glanced back to Lucy's doorway, he watched Angie in her great-grandmother's arms, waving bye-bye to them. At this gesture of affection, Cash was swept by a fierce tenderness. He wanted to rush back and scoop up the little pink bundle of ruffles and sweetness. But he had something important to accomplish this day, something that he had to do for Angie. He shut Jane's door and took in the dismal sight of the rain streaming down the Jeep's sides, making vertical lines in its coat of mud. The elements were against him in today's campaign.

As he slid behind the steering wheel, he realized Jane had picked up the feeling of the gloomy, wet day. Her expression was closed. She had dressed in a gray blouse, worn jeans and old sneakers. Even her lustrous curls had been covered with a drab green, hooded slicker. He, on the other hand, had dressed with care in crisp, new navy slacks and a maroon shirt. If he couldn't lighten her mood, it would make everything harder for him.

"Think it will be any better in Wausau?" he asked hopefully. Distant rumbling punctuated his words ominously.

"I don't think the sky will be any bluer in Wausau. And the tourists will be flocking to town, and Mel and Tish will be swamped." She stopped and heaved a deep sigh. "But I need a day out of town." Then she looked at him. There was uncertainty in her eyes. Was she wondering why he was taking her away for a day alone?

"I'll second that," he said cautiously. "I need a day away, too."

She nodded glumly.

"At least it's cool, instead of steaming," he pointed out.

"Until the sun burns off the clouds."

"Thank you for that cheery prediction." She was in a "mood" all right. He tried to think of a way to trigger the Everett good humor he knew was waiting only a phrase away. Today he needed to put her in the right mood for his plan to work.

A strained stiffness perched between them as he drove out onto the highway. How could he launch a sustained, friendly conversation with her? In an effort to fill up the emptiness, he switched on the radio. The local station announced that rain was expected all morning, but to look forward to clearing and warmer temperatures for the afternoon.

"Should I assume he's wrong, just because I agree with it?" she said drily.

Cash shrugged and watched her shift in her seat as though she were wearing starched underwear. The station began to play a raucous country-western tune about a cheating man. He snapped off the radio. "Oh, sorry," he said instantly contrite. "Were you listening to it?"

"What was playing?"

He snorted in amusement. "I guess I didn't need to apologize." He paused. "Jane, you've had your size-eight mystery, and I've had my troubles this summer. Can't we try to enjoy getting away for a day?"

Slowly she gave him a half smile. "Why not?"

He smiled broadly in return, relieved he'd chosen the right words. Outside, the rain slowed to a sprinkle. They rode in comfortable quiet until they came upon a lakeside restaurant. "I didn't have time to eat. How about breakfast?" he invited.

At her nod, he pulled into the parking lot. Inside the rustic log cabin restaurant, they sat on a screened-in porch, overlooking a small lake. They ate lumberjack-sized pancakes with warm boysenberry and maple syrups.

"I like to watch the circles rain makes hitting the water," he said, spearing another sausage link with his fork. The temperature still hovered in the low seventies. The fresh-rain scent was clean in his nostrils.

"I know. I like the sound, too. Kind of a restful plunk-plunk. Great breakfast."

He nodded. "We'll have to remember this place."

All night Jane had tossed and turned, trying to figure out why Cash had invited her today. Now she felt her initial apprehensions dissolving. It might be possible for Cash and her to have a pleasant day together without any negative repercussions. She would have to careful, however, to draw the invisible line between her infatuation with Cash and reality. She took a swallow of coffee.

By the time Jane got back into the Jeep, the constraint between them had almost vanished.

Cash asked, "How much do you know about Frank Lloyd Wright?"

"Why don't you ask me how much I want to know about Frank Lloyd Wright?"

"Oh, she's in a sassy mood. I shouldn't have fed her breakfast." Grinning, he slammed her door and went around to his side. "Did you know, Miss Everett, that Frank Lloyd

Wright was born in southwestern Wisconsin? Near Madison there's an organization for architects interested in Wright, called the Talisien Center.''

"I didn't realize Wisconsin was so into architecture."

"It is. Do you enjoy touring old homes?"

She wrinkled her nose at him. "I live in one, remember?"

"You live in a comfortable thirties' house. I'm talking old, older than yours by about fifty to seventy-five years."

"In that case, I must say yes."

The pause in the rainstorm ended. Sheets of water enveloped the Jeep. The windshield wiper dashed the rain back and forth frantically.

Jane watched tensely as the storm devoured all Cash's attention. He drove sitting forward, trying to see the road ahead clearly. The water pounded on the Jeep's fiberglass roof.

"Do you think it would be better if we pulled off?" Her voice was muffled by the din overhead.

"I'm afraid if I pull off just anywhere, I'll make us a target for someone else just pulling off," he raised his voice to be heard. "I can still see the center line—barely."

As suddenly as the downpour began, it ended. Cash whistled in relief.

Jane relaxed in her seat. "You can say that again. I thought we were going to end up swimming all the way to Wausau. So how did you get interested in Wright?"

"Your grandfather was the one who got me started—"

"My grandfather? When?"

"I got the mumps when I was twelve, and he visited me with a thick scrapbook of photos he'd taken of homes all over the Midwest. The ones I liked the best were Wrights."

"I had forgotten Grandpa's scrapbooks. Why were Wright's the most interesting to you?"

Jane, now at ease, let Cash ramble on about his favorite

subject. They sped over the remaining miles. The rain still spotted the front glass, but was no real hindrance.

They stopped at the Marathon County Historical Museum near downtown Wausau to get more information. When Cash led the way back down the steps of the museum, the rain was only lightly falling, but the lady at his side still needed protection. He popped open the large red-and-white-striped golf umbrella he had brought along. Holding the umbrella over them with one hand, he read aloud from the walking-tour brochure in the other. "The most notable architect working here between 1906-1920 was George Washington Maher—"

"Not Wright?"

He glanced at her and watched her push back her hood and shake her head, making her golden-red curls bounce. The vibrancy of the color made the gray sky look grayer. He had to force his eyes away from her brightness.

"No, we'll see his two houses later, okay?"

She grinned at him. "Okay."

He read on, "Of the Chicago-based Prairie School, Maher expounded the 'motif-rhythm theory,' the combination of natural and geometric elements to unify a particular design." He lowered the brochure. "Up for it?"

"Lead on." They were in the heart of the old city. Traffic was light but steady on the one-way, maple-lined street.

Under the dome of the shared umbrella, he took her arm and led her to the corner. "Look across the street. The A. P. Woodson house, 1914, Maher," he read from the guide. "What do you think?"

With obvious deliberation, she studied the two-story, ivy-covered brick house. "The chimney..."

"Yes, quite unique. Three connected, diamond-shaped stacks."

As casually as he could, he draped his free arm around her shoulders. Out of the corner of his eye, he saw her cheeks warm to a pleasant pink. He could make her react to him. He felt a surge of power.

Afraid of reading more into his closeness than he intended, Jane averted her face. Did he consider an arm around her as merely a friendly gesture, unlike a kiss? How should she react?

"Come on." Under the umbrella, he tugged her along. "This is the Underwood-Hagge house, 1894, neoclassical revival. Look at the symmetrical peaks of the roof."

Jane liked the stately home with a full porch across its front. Three peaks dominated the house, like a castle. "It looks like a perfect place to dream away a rainy afternoon. Can we go in?" She imagined an alcove high up in the house and a little girl like Angie, only several years older, reading quietly there.

"No, sorry. All these homes are privately owned except for the museum." He turned and looked directly into her eyes. She had forgotten how devastating the blue "windows of his soul" could be. She suppressed the urge to touch his curly eyelashes but she could not turn from his penetrating gaze.

She felt his fingers ruffle through her hair. Wondering why he had touched her, she looked up at him. Without warning, he brushed his lips over hers in the gentlest of kisses. In a rush, she relived the first kiss he had given her. Once again, he enticed her with his tentativeness. The web his lips spun around her made it impossible to call a halt to his tender encroachment.

Before she could respond in any way, he straightened and nudged her toward the next house on the self-guided tour.

He proceeded to show her the Claire B. Bird, 1910 Tudor revival; the Ely Wright house, an 1881 Italianate; and the Michael Hurly house, 1899 Queen Anne. The umbrella shielded them from the cars, whooshing by on the wet street. She accompanied him slightly dazed, wondering what had triggered his kissing her today. She couldn't believe it was her ridiculous date with Hallawell, but what had changed him? The pause in front of each house was an opportunity for another touch, another kiss. Jane found her blood pulsing at an unusual cadence.

She tried to study each house. The houses truly were beautiful, but his magnetism and her inner confusion robbed her of concentration. Her emotions ran rampant. She asked herself why had he begun kissing her, and why was she letting him, without asking his reasons? Could it be possible that after all these years, he had finally noticed her as a woman? Was his heart beginning to thaw? *Sweet Lord, have my prayers been answered at last?*

"There are more," he said in a husky voice, "but maybe you'd like to see the Wright houses now?"

The red-and-white umbrella over them, the street sounds of cars whizzing by in the distance; closer cars rattling over low manholes and the old brick street; the puddle under their feet—all the calls back to reality—summoned her. "You're the tour guide," she managed to say lightly.

They walked back to the Jeep. He opened the door for her, and when she stepped in front of him, he came closer and wrapped his arms around her from behind. Her head fit just under his chin, and she could feel his breath against her cheek.

"Are all your tours this stimulating?" she asked, drawing on her humor to remind him of their purpose. By way of a reply he nudged her up onto the seat and closed the door with a playful thump.

In silence they drove slowly past the two homes designed by Wright. But since both houses were in quiet residential areas and privately occupied, they didn't stop or get out. She waited in vain for him to tell her what he was thinking and why he had kissed her.

Though Jane's response to him was all that he had hoped

for, Cash refused to identify the sensations he was experiencing. In any negotiations, he had learned he must keep a clear head. Staring straight ahead, he asked, "How would you like to do something unexpected?"

"I think we already have," she replied softly.

He looked at her, then, and smiled. He loved it when she showed her resemblance to her grandmother, especially with her openness and wit. He knew she would be delighted with this side trip because he knew Lucy would have liked it, and Jane was so much like Lucy.

He drove them west of Wausau, out among the hay and cornfields. The rain had stopped, but the clouds hadn't broken yet. Before he'd left home this morning, Cash had tried to plan ahead how to say what he wanted to Jane. The first kiss he had given her had been a trial. He'd hoped she would react to him. But concentrating on what her response to him might have been had left him completely unprepared for his own new desire for Jane. It burst over and through him. Kissing Jane was sweet, unbelievably sweet.

"The hay is an interesting shade of green," she murmured.

He nodded. "The color would look good on you." He was gratified to see her cheeks become rosy at his compliment.

"The Wright houses were hard to see clearly." She looked out the window away from him.

"That fits his idea that the structure should blend with its location and its purpose. Therefore, a house shouldn't stand out from its settings."

"I see."

He made a broad turn off the state highway onto a county road, and she looked at him questioningly.

He grinned. Her warm, golden-red beauty lit up the dim interior of the Jeep. "Our next destination is out of the way."

She raised an eyebrow. "Out in the cornfields?"

He nodded. The Jeep followed the route of the county road that twisted around and rolled up and down the gentle hills left by prehistoric glaciers. At last he turned off the road into a small, mowed and fenced square of lawn. A small marker stood in the middle.

Rolling down her window, Jane read aloud:

"GEOLOGICAL MARKER
This spot in section fourteen, in the town of Rietbrock, Marathon County, is the exact center of the northern half of the Western Hemisphere. It is here that the nine-tieth meridian of longitude bisects the forty-fifth par-allel of latitude, meaning it is exactly half the way around the earth from Greenwich, England. Marathon County Park Commission."

She turned to him with an amused expression.

"It's not every day," he observed laconically, "that one can be at the absolute center of things."

"Shall we put our feet on the exact spot?" Her brows rose with sudden high spirits.

"Thought you'd never ask."

They scrambled out into the mist. As they hurried to the marker, the saturated sod squished underfoot. They both put a foot on the small metal circle that marked the spot, de-noting the exact center of the Northwestern World.

Jane grinned at him, showing her lightened mood. He had been right about her reaction to this. Again he felt that ev-erything he wanted from today would go well.

Two fat raindrops plopped onto his forehead. Then the onslaught of rain came down as though a faucet had been turned on. Cash lifted Jane up and ran, carrying her to the Jeep. He lunged inside, slamming the door behind them.

Still in his arms, she faced him in a convoluted posture,

the steering wheel behind her and her legs over the center gearshift. A bead of rain slid down her forehead and then dripped off her nose. A second one followed the first.

As the third ran down, Cash grinned and kissed her nose. He chuckled. "You're raining on me, Red."

Embarrassed, she moved to the passenger seat. When she watched his face draw nearer to hers, she almost pulled back. Instead, feeling his uneven breathing on her cheek, she tilted her head back slightly, inviting him closer.

The rush of warm breath as he exhaled tipped the balance, making a chill arc through her. His lips roamed over her face, enticing but innocent. They demanded nothing from her, took nothing from her. Instead, she reaped the closeness, his regard for her. Each touch of his lips felt like a gift bestowed.

Her hands found the sides of his head, and she drew his face to hers in a renewed embrace. She pressed her lips to his skin, so warm and masculine.

She felt him kiss the tip of her nose, then her closed eyes, and finally he satisfied her longing by caressing her lips with his. Her heart sighed.

"Jane, Jane, I," he murmured.

A loud bawl interrupted him.

Jane drew back sharply from him. "Oh, for heaven's sake," she said, putting her forehead into her hands.

Two cows had their heads over the fence and were only inches from Cash's window. Their warm breath fogged the Jeep's glass.

Jane hung her head farther and stifled a moan. Just as her mother's phone call had, the night of the Fourth, this intrusion snatched away the intimacy of the moment. She was sure he had been about to tell her why he was kissing her.

Cash's face became a mask. He put the Jeep into reverse. Mud flew up as he backed out onto the county road again.

Jane stared out her window.

The cloudburst slowed and gushed by turns as they drove down the meandering road over the green, rolling hills. At a crossroads, the pink neon sign at Bud and Pearl's Café beckoned them. Jane touched his arm. "Want to try it?"

"Have you been in there before?" He asked with surprise.

"No, but I have found in Wisconsin that these little places always have the best food."

"It looks like a dive." The building appeared to be about fifty years old and to last have been painted the year Jane was born.

"It's not a dive. Pearl wouldn't preside over a dive. I'll grant you it isn't a croissant or quiche type of place. Are you game or not?"

He studied the old restaurant. A number of muddy trucks crowded around the small, roofed entrance.

Jane's stomach rumbled aloud, and she grinned. "Well?" she challenged him.

With a shrug Cash gave in. Under the large umbrella again, he led her inside, past the pinball machines, to a booth along the wall. The interior of Bud and Pearl's did not disappoint his preconception. Its walls were painted with gray enamel. The floor was a speckled, black-and-white, industrial-grade asphalt tile which would probably last far into the next century.

There was no decor to be seen: a few booths, counter and stools in a long, narrow room. The pinball machines near the entrance were the only splashes of color. Two ceiling fans with lights were the only illumination and ventilation. Several local patrons, who were all seated along the counter, watched the newcomers with politely veiled interest.

Jane and Cash sat down in one of the booths and silently read the day's menu, which was on a blackboard behind the counter.

After eyeing them discreetly for about three minutes, a plump woman in jeans and a gray UW sweatshirt came over. "Hi, what'll it be?"

"I'll have the hot plate special," Jane said cheerfully.

Cash pursed his lips. "I'll try the Reuben."

The woman nodded and walked through the curtained doorway that obviously led to the kitchen. Cash heard her clearly tell Pearl their order.

"You should have gotten the hot plate special," Jane said quietly.

"You may regret it." He glanced around once again.

"I don't think so. Use your nose," Jane suggested.

"What?"

"You've been so busy looking the place over that you missed the most important element. Haven't you sniffed the delicious aroma emanating from the kitchen?"

Only then did he become aware of the homey fragrance in the air. "Roast beef," he said.

She nodded, grinning. "I think we hit a good one."

The waitress came back with tableware and beverages. Then she delivered several plates to the men at the counter. After a few minutes she returned to their booth with two overflowing platters.

Cash's plate was covered by a huge pumpernickel Reuben sandwich and a mound of creamy potato salad. Jane's was heaped with a hot roast beef sandwich and mashed potatoes, liberally doused with deep brown gravy. It was obvious that nothing on either plate had come from the contents of a premeasured box.

Jane sighed with satisfaction. "Hold a piece of rhubarb pie for me."

"Make that two," Cash added quickly. The waitress grinned and made a notation on their check. She turned back to the kitchen.

"I don't know why I said that," Jane whispered. "I don't

know how I'll make it through this, much less have room for dessert.''

"Don't worry, Jane. I'll do everything I can to help you in this challenge.''

Protectively Jane covered her plate with both hands. "Don't even try it.''

The food was down-home delicious. It had been a long time since breakfast. The two of them didn't waste eating time with talk. Two pieces of rhubarb pie appeared at their elbows. Though he felt uncomfortably full, he eyed Jane's pie teasingly. When he aimed his greedy fork toward her piece of pie, she—just as she had warned him—slapped his hand away.

When all their plates were clean, Cash sat back. Now as he looked around, he noted the touches that made the long room homey. The sampler over the blue gingham curtains to the kitchen read: "Home is where you hang your heart,'' and some child's drawings were tacked onto the wall behind the counter. Again he was struck by Jane's ability to make the mundane things of life interesting, enjoyable. He settled the modest bill, and they walked out to the Jeep. Outside, the clouds were as thick as they had been at dawn. Cash turned on the ignition and headed for home.

Jane hummed along with the country station on the radio. While she listened to the lyrics about broken hearts, trucking men and true love, she took inventory of this unusual day. She had toured streets adorned by classic homes, then had eaten lunch at Bud and Pearl's. She had been alternately sprinkled and doused by rain and had shared kisses under a red-and-white umbrella. She had stood at the center of the Northwestern World, chaperoned by two cows. What a country-western ballad that would make!

Closing her eyes, she leaned back. The hum of the Jeep's tires lulled her to sleep.

The startling noise of pounding rain over her head woke Jane. She sat up, slightly disoriented.

"It's another cloudburst," Cash muttered.

In spite of the slashing wipers, she couldn't see through the front windshield. She sat up tensely. "Cash, I—"

"I'm going to have to pull off, but I don't want to just pull off on the shoulder, it's too dangerous."

For the next few minutes, the Jeep crawled along the highway till Cash finally glimpsed an exit ramp to their right. He followed the lane cautiously till he pulled into what appeared to be a parking lot. It was impossible to see whether it was a business or a public wayside. He stopped. Jane reached for him.

"We're okay," he said, grasping her hand.

"I don't remember a summer where I've been so frightened by the weather. It makes me worry about Angie and Lucy—"

"They'll be fine. Lucy's cottage is one of the safest places Angie could be."

"I know, but this weather still worries me. Storm after storm. What is it building up to?"

In response to her worried tone, he took her other hand and tugged her toward him.

Jane knew she should—for her own peace of mind—resist this closing of the gap she had tried to maintain between them. Cash leaned closer to her. She smelled the rain in his hair and clothing and bent to claim his mouth.

Their first kisses of the day had been hesitant. This time when their mouths met, she felt like she was being swept away by a flash fire. Once again his lips passed over her brow, eyelids and throat. She whispered his name.

"Jane." He pulled her against him fiercely. He froze.

Feeling the abrupt change in Cash, she surfaced from the sensations that had overwhelmed her. "Cash?"

His arms around her had become protective. "The rain

has slowed. There are two trucks parked near us. They'll be pulling out soon, and they'll be able to see us.''

Jane looked around. The rain had lessened to a steady wash over the windows. She could see that they were parked at the edge of a gas station.

Cash started the Jeep again and they drove back onto the highway in silence. *It's now or never.* Everything he could surmise from her response to him today said, ''green light.'' It was time to put over the deal.

''Jane,'' Cash said.

Momentarily Jane feared he would apologize once again for kissing her. She held her breath.

''Jane, I've been thinking. We should get married.''

For a few trembling moments, she doubted her ears. ''Married?''

''Yes.'' He took a deep breath. The memory of seeing her with Hallawell last night had struck too close to what he feared. It was preposterous to believe that Jane wouldn't marry. And the thought of another man, living with Jane, acting as Angie's father, filled him with an intensity of panic he had never experienced before.

He continued smoothly, ''I've decided that it would be a good idea. Angie needs a family—a mother and a father—not just a guardian and an uncle. We could marry, and I'd build us a home at The Shores. I suppose you could call it a marriage of convenience, but I believe it would work out very well. What do you think?'' His confidence had grown as he had explained his plan. Surely she would agree. Her response to him today had been more positive than he would have predicted.

Jane trembled with a surge of anger stronger than any she had ever felt before. For uncounted moments, she was unable to do anything except hold out against the urge to scream her fury at Cash.

Finally she surfaced from her emotional tempest. She became aware that Cash was driving through another steady rain, going north on the state highway toward Eagle Lake. What had she expected from Cash? He'd never said one word of love. She should have realized by now that only with Angie did he allow emotion. For a few moments she had thought he'd lowered the staunch walls around his heart. *Dear God, how could I have been so wrong?*

She took a deep breath to still her lingering inner chaos. Without looking at Cash, which would only have stoked the flames of her anger all over, she said with deadly calm, "No, thank you. I don't care to be a convenience to anyone."

Chapter Nine

Inside a large tent in the city park, Jane smiled down at little twin girls with identical brown bangs. They shyly looked up. Both wore gold lamé dresses much too large for them, old fox fur boas and pillbox hats with nets askew. "How about lipstick?" Jane asked, the golden tube already poised in her hand.

They nodded and submitted with serious concentration.

"Ready to show your mother?"

Without speaking, they turned and stumbled in their too-large, high-heeled shoes out the door of the tent. Their mother waited outside with a camera. Jane's assistant, Mel, cheerfully posed the duo. When the photo opportunity was exhausted, Mel and Jane helped the girls out of their finery. With shy waves, the twins left for the puppet show, which was already in progress at the far end of Tory Park.

"They're the last." Mel sighed. "Now I have to go sell hot dogs and then help with the cleanup afterward."

"Better you than me," Jane said. "I only have to rebox the clothes for use next year."

Mel hurried away, and Jane, suddenly feeling fatigued

from a very busy morning, stretched her arms over her head and scanned the park. Under the tall oaks and evergreens of the city park were booths, very messy booths. "Art in the Park" was never neat. Wood-block sculptures, Jell-O finger paintings, pinecone-and-peanut-butter bird feeders, necklaces of dyed macaroni, littered the tables and benches and hung from low branches. All these would be claimed by the young artists after the puppet show, the grand finale. The aroma of freshly popped popcorn had taunted her all morning and now her empty stomach growled. She hadn't had time for breakfast.

At the face-painting area across from Jane's tent, Lucy, dressed as a clown in a paint-smeared smock, finished another rainbow on a child's chubby cheek. Lucy waved to Jane over the toddler's head. Jane waved back. Then she went inside her drab green tent and began sorting the clothing into categories.

"Hi."

She turned to see Cash in the tent's entrance. Within seconds she felt her neck and face blazing with her anger. Her heart beat in a dizzy tempo. Stinging words bubbled up, but she tightened her mouth to hold them back. She finally asked brusquely, "Where's Angie?"

"With your dad at the puppet show."

"I see." She wanted to know how Angie had liked her first art fair, but she would ask her father later. She wanted nothing to pass between Cash and her—not even polite conversation.

"Like your outfit."

"Really?" she said without expression. To suit her volunteering job, she had dressed herself as a twenties flapper in a beige dress and matching cloche hat that had belonged to her great-grandmother. She had added many long strands of fake pearls, and gold-sequined garters held up her knee-high hose.

"It's you all right." His words sounded forced, and she noted the dark smudges under his eyes.

But she turned away from him and started to fold dresses into a huge cardboard box.

He persisted. "Are you busy for lunch?"

"I don't have time for lunch. I have to get back to the shop. Saturday is my busiest day."

"How about Sunday brunch, then?"

His voice grated on her nerves. Provoked, she looked up. Their eyes connected and sparred. She knew she would have to see him tomorrow because he would arrive for his visit with Angie, but she wanted to accept nothing from him and give him nothing but the barest politeness. The memory of his proposal washed through her painfully. "I'll leave Angie with my parents. Why don't you stop over there after lunch tomorrow?"

"Jane, I don't understand why a simple proposal—"

She cut him off. "That's right you don't understand, and I don't feel like explaining it to you. My mother is working at the shop for me. I have to get back to relieve her."

He left without saying a word, snapping the flap closed behind himself.

She clenched her teeth. Strong emotions coursed through her in wave after wave. Furious with him, she attacked the piles of clothes, sorting and folding, then taping and labeling the boxes.

When she finished, she walked over to the park's bath house, which was the changing area for volunteers.

Retrieving her clothes from a locker, Jane stepped into one of the curtained cubicles. Carefully she hung her strings of pearls onto the wall hook and then undid the hook and eyes down the side of her flapper dress and slid off her garters.

As she slipped into butterscotch crepe slacks, a taupe silk shell and an ivory jacket for work, she simmered with outrage. Trying to calm herself enough to face customers and her mother's perceptive eyes, she fluffed her hair and outlined her lips with coral lipstick.

Jane hurried down the block to her shop and entered from the rear. Tish was with a customer, but paused to tell Jane that Aunt Marge had driven out of town before the traffic had been unleashed after the puppet show.

Another two women walked in. Jane sighed inwardly. She wanted to get away from everyone, but she went forward to greet the customers. At their question Jane directed them to the racks of the few remaining shorts and blouses, then waited by the register. Within minutes they both picked out several blouses and shorts combinations and returned to Jane.

"My, that was quick," Jane commented as she began the process of tearing off the tags.

"We told our husbands that during vacation this year, they'd have to take a turn doing the laundry at the Laundromat," one of them said.

"Yes, and we may do this every year." The other one chuckled. "They managed to destroy one load completely, so we get to buy a new summer wardrobe!"

"We still haven't figured out how they did it!" her friend explained cheerfully.

"Jane!" Lucy called as she entered by the rear door.

Jane's spirits sank lower. *I can't face Grandmother. She'll know something is dreadfully wrong.*

Jane finished the sale, then walked reluctantly downstairs, closing the door behind her. There was no escaping the inevitable.

At the bottom of the staircase, Lucy, now transformed from a clown to a chic lady in ivory cotton slacks and a blue silk tunic, waited with a large, white paper bag in her hand. The unmistakable scent of ground beef and fries emanated from it. "I was in the mood for saturated fat today. I hope you are, too."

"I didn't expect to see you." Jane, trying to smooth the strain out of her voice, cleared one side of her desk, and Lucy brought out thick hamburgers and fries. They sat down and faced each other.

"So why did you tell Cash he could see Angie at your parents' cottage tomorrow? What's happened?"

Jane tried to deflect her grandmother's words by teasing, "I'm so glad you are capable of subtlety."

"Well?"

Stalling while she thought of her answer, Jane took a bite of her burger. She barely tasted it, and her empty, nervous stomach moved her near nausea.

Under her grandmother's thoughtful scrutiny, Jane suddenly wanted to cry. She battled herself and controlled the urge. Someone had told her once, Be careful what you pray for, you might get it. She had once prayed fervently that Cash would ask her to be his wife. Now he had, and she felt as if she were chewing a mouthful of ashes. She put down her sandwich and wiped her fingertips with a napkin. "I can't seem to get my emotions under control today."

"What happened in Wausau?"

Jane shook her head. "Please let's talk abut something else." Her love was a foolish hope, and not even to her grandmother could she reveal her emotions for Cash.

"About Angie?"

Jane wanted to shout, *No! About Cash. I love him, but he doesn't love me!* Tears did come to Jane's eyes then. They ran freely, and she wiped them away with her hands till Lucy handed her a flowered handkerchief from her pocket.

In a rush of sensation Jane remembered Cash's kisses as the final cloudburst had shielded them from the world. In that private moment she had thought she and Cash had finally come together. But in light of his subsequent proposal, his kisses had only amounted to a test drive of a wife he intended to negotiate for.

"Is there anything I can do for you, dear?"

Jane sucked in a deep breath and resolutely picked up her sandwich. "I just miss Dena so," Jane spoke her only alibi. "I'll be all right."

Lucy gave her a look of heart-rending concern. "Yes, dear, I pray so."

The final evening hours of Crazy Days, Eagle Lake's sidewalk sale came at last. Main Street had been blocked off with wooden barricades. The stores had all moved their sale merchandise out onto the sidewalk and the street itself. Though the month was July, Christmas lights had been wrapped around the city light poles. Shoppers milled around in the street and huddled around the store displays. Two clowns circulated through the crowd, amusing the children and giving away candy. Jane sat at a card table in front of her shop.

"Hi, Tish. Hi, Mel." Three teenage girls stopped to browse. Hearing *Hi, Tish. Hi, Mel* one more time made Jane's jaw muscles clamp together painfully. Recalling the agony of the tension headache she had after the trip to Wausau, she consciously tightened and relaxed her muscles from the top of her head to the end of her spine.

"Miss Everett, is there anything here that my mom would like for her birthday next week?"

Jane opened her eyes. Del Ray Martin's daughter had unhooked herself from her two friends, who were giggling with Tish.

Jane stood up and picked out a few bright scarves that would suit Del Ray's taste. The girl chose a bright-red-and-black scarf from Jane's selection. Jane let Mel take care of the sale.

One more hour, just one more hour and I can close. Shut-

ting her eyes once more against the garish lights and the noisy combination of carnival and lounge music, she leaned back against her display window.

"Hi, I like your jewelry."

Jane opened her eyes. "Hi, Rona. Glad you like it." Rona was referring to the fact that some shop owners were dressed up as though it were Halloween to add more color to Crazy Days. Jane had decided that costuming for the event did not fit the mystique of her or her shop.

But over the past three years, she had collected a fine assortment of junk jewelry. So on this the final day of Crazy Days, she and her two assistants sported a rainbow of gaudy, plastic bracelets, rings, necklaces and earrings. Tish wore all shades of blue and purple. Mel had chosen reds and pinks, while Jane had opted for white, silver and green.

"How do you like my specs?" Jane asked, tapping her frames.

"They really do it. Whatever *it* is." Rona grinned.

This year Jane had added the pièce de résistance, three pairs of fifties-style glasses, without lenses, that she had picked up at a flea market. The pair Jane was wearing was silver and shaped like butterfly wings and encrusted with rhinestones.

"Did you hear?" Rona asked conspiratorially.

"What?"

"The word is that after dark last night Hallawell's crew dumped off trash at the entrance of The Shores."

Jane made a face. "Isn't this getting a little childish?"

"I agree. Carmine says some of Cash's crew have had it."

Jane shook her head. "What will be, will be." Her words were casual, but a tremor of warning shivered through her. She sent up a silent prayer for a peaceful end to these hostilities.

Rona gestured toward the two circular racks and one table

that Jane had moved outside. "Is there anything I should buy now, or should I wait till your Labor Day fifty-percent-off, final-summer-clearance sale?"

"Take a look at the swimsuits. There are a few left you might like." Jane pressed her fingers to her temples.

Rona nodded and began intently going through the rack nearest her daughter.

"Bye, Tish. Bye, Mel." The latest trio of teens departed.

Then two high school boys paused, obviously eyeing Tish and Mel.

I will never again hire teens to work during the summer, Jane vowed silently. "May I help you gentlemen find something?" she asked pointedly.

"Uh, no, just looking." The youngest of the two blushed. They left quickly. Tish gave their backs a look that stated they weren't in her league, anyway.

Carnival music from the nearby park floated to them. The band at the Wildcat 'n' Lace, a lounge restaurant across the street competed with the carnival's taped calliope music. Every time its door swung in or out, rock music with an overpowering bass pounded, giving a throbbing background beat to the evening's atmosphere. The painful pulsing at Jane's temples picked up the same rhythm. She observed a few of the carpenters and a plasterer who worked for Cash go into the lounge.

A sudden gust of wind tossed dust up. Jane sneezed.

"Bless you, my dear," Lucy said.

"Grandmother! Where did you come from?"

"I planned my route carefully, so I could sneak up on you." Lucy had "dressed" for Crazy Days. This annual event always sparked her wearing of an outrageous lime-green-and-white sundress from the seventies.

"How long will this dress last you?" Jane asked, shaking her head.

"I know. It's so delightfully atrocious I look forward to

wearing it every year! I can't help it if I'm still crazy after all these years. And you should talk! Look at those glasses!''

Jane posed artfully. ''I think I should have worn them for the portrait, don't you?''

''What portrait?'' Tish asked, standing at Jane's elbow.

''Never you mind, young lady,'' Lucy said primly. ''Jane, please have someone take a picture of you in those. My cousin Dulcy had a pair just like that in 1953. I'd love to send a photo to her of you wearing them.''

Tish turned her back and walked away.

Jane rolled her eyes. ''I'll try, but I won't promise.''

''All right. But getting back to business, I really came in to settle some of the final arrangements for your parents' party. We only have a little over a week, you know.''

''I know.'' The wind gusted again, and Jane winced at the escalating ache at the top of her skull.

Lucy frowned at the sky. ''If I'm not mistaken, we're going to get another storm tonight.''

''I'd bet money on it,'' Rona said, stepping close to Lucy. ''Here, Jane, I'll take this one. Would you put it on my account?''

In a loud stage whisper to Jane, Lucy said, ''I don't think I would let her charge anything. She looks shifty to me.''

Jane smiled and took the mocha-brown-and-tan swimsuit from Rona. Sitting back down at the card table, she began writing out a receipt.

''What did you decide on for the entrée for Phil and Marge's anniversary party?'' Rona asked Lucy. ''Veal *picotta* or prime rib?''

''I decided on the prime rib. I really wanted crab linguini, but I decided to be traditional. My son would prefer straight steak and potatoes.''

Jane handed Rona her receipt and bagged the suit.

''Jane, you'll be asking Cash to be your escort, won't you?'' Rona asked.

Jane frowned. Her neck tightened another degree.

"Oh!" Rona put a hand to her mouth. "I did it again, didn't I? Stuck my nose into your business. On that note, I'll move on." Rona walked briskly away.

As Jane's gaze followed Rona walking down the street, she saw three men who worked for Hallawell push their way into the lounge across the street.

Voices from behind made her look over her shoulder. Two tall high school boys had stopped to chat with Tish. Mel, with naked envy in her eyes, glared at them. Jane turned back to her grandmother. She told Lucy in an undertone, "I don't know how much more I can stand of 'cruising' teens. There were a few earlier, but tonight since around six, it's been an endless teen parade."

"In the future I suggest you don't hire such pretty girls," Lucy murmured. "A pot of honey can't help attracting bees."

Jane nodded glumly.

"I'm glad you turned Angie over to your parents for the evening. They are enjoying her to the hilt. I think they took her on the merry-go-round five times."

"I'm glad they were able to come up early this weekend. It's so nice they could take a turn with Angie. I always feel like I ask you too often—"

"Tut, tut, my dear. She's an angel and you know it. But I'll be off now. I haven't had my venison burger yet this year and I never miss it. I do so love telling all my vegetarian friends about it. It drives them crazy!" With a wave of her hand, Lucy walked briskly away.

Jane waved in return and sighed.

"Bye." The latest males took their farewell of Tish. Jane watched Mel's eyes crackle dangerously with jealousy and wondered when the next Mel-Tish spat would begin.

Then she looked down the street and saw Uncle Henry

and Aunt Claire, heading straight for her. Jane put her head in her hands, moaning inwardly.

"Hi, Jane," Uncle Henry launched the duet.

"We wanted to stop by—" Aunt Claire put in.

"And warn you that a severe weather watch—"

"Is in effect—"

"Till 10:00 p.m.," Uncle Henry finished triumphantly.

Jane's eyes widened. How did they do it? Did they practice at home in front of a mirror?

Jane swallowed, then replied, "The wind has changed direction, and we've been getting strong gusts, too."

Claire and Henry asked in unison, "Where's Leticia?"

"She had to go to the bathroom," Mel answered. She folded her hands together and a half dozen plastic, bangle bracelets slid down her arms and clanked loudly together at her wrists.

"Your jewelry is quite striking," Claire said.

Jane smiled at the pun her aunt had uttered without realizing it.

"Thanks," Mel said, making the bracelets slide and clack again on her arms.

"Well, we have to be moving on—" Henry began their last comments.

"We haven't bought our Aquarama tickets yet. This might be our—"

"Year to win the boat!" The two hurried away toward the raffle booth.

After they had gone, Mel said, "Tish wanted to try for Aquarama queen this year, and her mom and dad wouldn't let her. That's why she wouldn't stay out here. She's not talking to them."

Jane shook her head.

Mel went on without encouragement. "They said she had to wait till she was a junior at least. Is she ever mad!"

"I'm sure waiting a year won't harm Tish's chances."

"Yeah, but she's still mad."

Tish came outside then. Jane told the girls to check the racks to see if any sizes had been moved into the wrong places. After her uncle's warning, Jane now noticed placards on the racks, windows and tables begin to flap ominously.

Jane scanned the twilight sky. In another half hour it would be dark, and she could close up. At 10:00 p.m. there would be the Aquarama draw, which was the yearly boat raffle, and then the crowning of the Aquarama Queen, the girl who had sold the most raffle tickets. This year, at least, Tish would not be crowned.

At the far end of the block, Jane caught sight of Halla-well, sauntering in her direction. When he turned into the entrance of a men's shop, Jane excused herself and escaped inside the shop for a few moments of peace. Her headache by now was firmly entrenched. She took two aspirin, then reluctantly forced herself back outside.

The wild wind had gotten worse. Along the gutter across the street, an aluminum pop can skittered, making quick, metallic taps against the concrete curb, giving a sound to the wind. A little boy ran after the can, but the wind pushed it faster than he could run. His mother caught up with him. With an eye to the sky, she swung him up in her arms and called to his father.

Thunder rumbled in the distance. A flicker of lightning to the west caught the corner of her eye. "We may be moving in on short notice," she said to Mel and Tish, glancing at her watch. "It's only twenty minutes to closing. We'll see if we can stay open till then."

Mel nodded. Tish sighed and leaned back against the store window.

"Jane!" Lucy walked quickly toward Jane. "That weather looks threatening. The carnival is shutting down. I heard one of the carneys say they'd had too many nights end up with them tying everything down in an electrical storm.''

''Don't worry, Grandmother. It will only take us three minutes to roll this stuff inside.''

Lucy waved farewell and hurried by them.

After her grandmother was out of sight, Jane turned again toward the western horizon. The sunset clouds were deep purple and gray; the final rays of the sun were losing the battle to the surging clouds of the new front.

''Jane!'' Tish said sharply.

She turned to see Cash, hurrying toward the lounge across the street. Tish didn't need to say more. An uneasy acknowledgment niggled in Jane's mind, too. Construction workers from both crews and now Cash were all in the same lounge on a Friday night, and a storm was coming.

Jane looked into her cousin's eyes and saw worry there, too. Tish's concern touched Jane unexpectedly. It was the first time she could remember ever feeling close to Tish. She reached out and took Tish's hand.

Tish pointed with her free hand.

Jane followed the direction just in time to see the back of Roger Hallawell going into the Wildcat 'n' Lace. ''It's as dark as the black hole of Calcutta in there. Maybe they won't even see each other.'' *Dear Lord, make it so.* She squeezed Tish's hand and was surprised to feel Tish return the pressure.

''Jane! I'm closing now!'' the pharmacist across the street called to her. ''I think this one's moving in fast!''

To save herself from shouting over the wind, she waved to him. ''Girls, that does it. If conservative Tim is closing up, we are, too.'' She motioned Tish to roll in the first rack nearest the door.

She went over to get the cash register herself. Carrying it inside, she put it back in its usual spot on the counter. Mel came in with the second rack of clothing. Jane went back out to help Tish carry in the table of scarves and accessories. One scarf fell from the table top, but never reached the sidewalk. It flew up high and away. As the three of them moved quickly, their junk jewelry bracelets clacked together up and down their arms, but now they could barely hear the bracelets above the wind. After the tables were inside, Jane went out to check if anything had been left behind in their rush.

Loud shouts caught her attention, and she turned in time to see a man propelled out the door of the Wildcat. He stumbled backward and fell heavily onto the cement sidewalk. Jane took a few steps forward as though going to his aid.

But immediately on his heels came another two men: one of Hallawell's and one of Cash's carpenters. They were brawling. Jane sucked in her breath.

More fighters poured out of the entrance. The music blared onto the street. The wind picked up the sound and tossed it high. Jane watched as six more men came out, slugging. Some were construction workers, but not all.

"Look! Cash!" Tish exclaimed right next to Jane's ear. Glancing to each side, Jane realized she was flanked by both girls.

"And Mister Hallawell," Mel said with satisfaction.

In horror, Jane watched Hallawell and the plasterer exchanging punches. Cash was hovering beside them yelling at them both.

Jane took another step forward, but was halted by Tish's hand, gripping her elbow. "No, you could be hurt." Again, Jane felt the tie of family to Tish. She put her hand over Tish's and nodded.

Vaguely Jane thought that Tish's and Mel's parents would prefer that their daughters not be witnesses to this brawl on Main Street. But she could think of no way to force them back inside, and she could not make herself go in, either. Her pulse pounded in her ears, making it hard to concentrate. She tried to pray, but all she could whisper was "Cash, Cash…"

The ruckus continued. More and more people streamed out of the lounge, some fighting, some just trying to get clear. Men cradled their arms around dates. Some pushed aside fighting pairs to make way for themselves. Through it all, the pounding beat of the band never faltered.

Though completely ignored, Cash continued yelling at the brawlers and moving around the fighting men, who now filled a good portion of the street in front of the lounge. He returned to the plasterer who was still mauling Hallawell. Cash shouted at his man and dodged a stray punch. "Stop right now!" The words came across to Jane on a violent gust of wind.

The strident sirens of the sheriff's cars came in blasts on the buffeting wind that was tossing up dust and paper refuse. Jane shaded her eyes from the force of the wind, but stood her ground.

The fighters did not slow down till the police cars came around a barricade and pulled up right in the midst of them. The sheriff and two deputies tumbled out of their cars and began shouting at the men. The sirens were off, but the red lights on top of both cars continued rotating, giving a peculiarly wicked cast to the darkening Main Street.

The next blast of wind was like a strong hand, pushing against the three females huddled together in front of the shop. Jane looked up and realized that the red lights were only part of the flashes around her. Lightning crackled in the nearly night sky.

Suddenly the band across the street ceased. But the thunder kept its own beat. Then, in one great wave, the rain sluiced over them. Jane heard herself and her girls shriek in surprise. They turned and ran inside the shop, dripping wet and suddenly chilled.

Once inside, though, they could not help themselves. They all turned back to watch the police cleaning up the brawl. In the end the sheriff left with Cash, Hallawell and about three other men in the two police cars.

Chapter Ten

A half hour after the brawl on Main Street, Jane pulled into the police station parking lot. Outside, the storm center had moved on, but though the wind, thunder and lightning had passed by, rain still fell steadily. Since she was already soaked to the skin, she didn't bother to hurry to the sheriff's office door.

The sheriff wasn't sitting at his desk as he'd been that night over a month ago when she and Cash had come to deal with the would-be vandals. She looked around restlessly. Being here again unsettled her stomach. When she heard Cash and the sheriff coming out, she turned to meet Cash's eyes, but instead encountered Roger Hallawell's flushed face. Jane stiffened uncomfortably.

Then she heard the sheriff's voice from the hallway. "I've had it with both of you."

Hallawell's face reddened a shade darker at these words. The sheriff stepped through the doorway. Cash followed. His disheveled clothing was out of character, and she noted that his lower lip was split and swollen. She tamped down a swell of concern for him. She was here as a friend—nothing more.

"Here to post bail, Miss Everett?" The sheriff grinned.

"Do I need to?" she asked.

"We'll see. It depends."

"On?" She leaned forward against the counter, intrigued by the sheriff's determined tone.

He pointed at Cash and Hallawell. "It's up to these two."

Hallawell interrupted, "If you're not pressing charges, I'm leaving—"

"If I charge you, you'll live to regret it." The sheriff, folding his arms over his chest, braced his back against the wall. "Now, I figured the tension between you two would build till everything came to a head. This brawl is the final episode in this little soap opera. Hallawell, you're here to stay, Langley's here to stay, and I'm out of patience."

Hallawell started to bluster, but the sheriff cut him off. "I'm going to explain how it's going to be. You two are going to shake hands and agree to disagree."

"I'm all in favor," Cash said.

"Yeah, what have you got to lose?" Hallawell asked with a sneer.

The sheriff made eye contact with Hallawell. "Let's talk about what *you've* got to lose."

"So what have I got to lose?" Hallawell demanded.

The sheriff pushed away from the wall. "My cooperation."

A tense silence gripped the quiet room. Desultory traffic sounds from the outside made no impression on the three men.

Finally Cash stepped forward and held out his hand to Hallawell. The other man hesitated, then reluctantly shook Cash's hand. Without a word Hallawell walked out.

Cash nodded to the sheriff, then left with Jane. The night sky still drizzled. Jane unlocked her car. They got in—wet, silent and distant. Keeping her eyes straight ahead, she drove out of the lit parking lot onto the dark county road.

"Is that the end of it?" she asked at last, trying to fill the vacuum of oppressive silence.

"Hallawell would be a fool to cross the sheriff in a town this size." His voice sounded gritty, defeated.

Jane nodded stiffly.

"Why did you come?" he asked gruffly. "Did Lucy call you?"

Jane pressed her lips together, then tried to lighten the unbearable pall which filled the vehicle. "I felt like asking you those same two questions last Friday night at the Aquabat Show."

There was a distinct pause.

Cash frowned. "Rona called me that night."

"Oh. Thanks for coming that night."

"No problem. Thanks for coming tonight," Cash said in a subdued voice.

"No problem."

For a moment a hint of humor trembled in the air. Then it fizzled in the ensuing silence.

Jane sighed. Cash's proposal had erected an even thicker and icier wall between them. She would come if he needed her, but that was all. That day, on their drive home from Wausau, for a few minutes, there had been a chance for them, just a chance.

As she turned a corner to the right, she glanced over at him. In the reflected light from her dashboard, she could make out his grim profile. She couldn't make another effort to relieve their gloom. Finally they pulled up beside Cash's Jeep.

"Thanks again for coming for me." He stared at her for several moments. She nodded but kept her face impassive. Then he got out, closing the door behind him.

Jane watched him amble over to his Jeep. It tugged at her

heart to see him battered and tired. Aching with a devastating loneliness, she blinked back tears and wished she could go after him and put ice on his split lip and give him aspirin for his bruises. Instead, she resolutely turned her car toward home.

The next day Jane took Angie over to Lucy's house. She found her grandmother in the backyard reclining on a lawn chair.

When Lucy spotted them she said, "At last a sunny day that isn't in the nineties!"

Jane joined her grandmother under the tall birches. She glanced over the bluff and for a few seconds she lost herself in the dazzling beauty of the scene below. The rippling lake shimmered, making her think of diamonds dancing on sapphire satin.

"It's such a beautiful day I hate to go inside. Is there anything wrong, Jane?"

"Wrong? What made you ask that?" For the first time she could recall, Jane felt ill at ease in her grandmother's company. Slowly she made eye contact with Lucy.

"Something in your eyes. It doesn't matter I suppose. Let's go in, my dears. I'm all ready to work on that miniature for Cash."

Jane followed her grandmother's instructions on posing the baby. Because of Angie's active age, the miniature of her would be much less ambitious than Jane's portrait. This posing and one more would do it. Which was just as well. Angie wanted to crawl, climb the couch and play with her blocks. Concentrating on keeping the little girl entertained during the sitting took all of Jane's energy.

Lucy asked, "So everything's settled between Hallawell and Cash?"

"Seems to be."

"I'm so glad your parents and I had gotten home with Angie before the brawling last night."

"I've see a few fights before, but nothing like that," Jane said.

"And you've never seen Cash in one."

Jane made no answer. She almost broke down and told her grandmother about Cash's proposal. But some emotion—maybe pride—kept her from revealing it. Cash had shown her how little he respected her, how lightly he regarded the commitment of holy matrimony.

"I just wish this summer would come to an end. Everything's been so—" Dreading Cash's first full-day visit with Angie, that wouldn't include her, was making her miserable. She hated feeling selfish, small. Her prayers seemed to be soap bubbles floating away on an aimless breeze. She needed desperately to feel an assurance that by the time this ordeal arrived, she would have received the grace she needed to accept it. She knew God was able, but how she longed to be rid of this hard lump of dread.

"I understand, my dear. This has been a stressful year for you. Becoming a mother would have been a challenge enough for anyone. But I have faith in Cash to do what is right, not only for Angie, but you, too."

"Your faith in Cash is misplaced." The harsh words flew out of Jane's mouth before she could stop herself. Saying them made her feel sick.

Lucy stepped around her easel and stared at Jane. "What brought that on?"

Jane pressed her lips together, frantically trying to think of ways to deflect her grandmother's curiosity.

"Does this have anything to do with your trip to Wausau last weekend?" Lucy asked shrewdly.

Jane's mouth opened momentarily, then shut.

Lucy, holding her palette and brush, stared at Jane. "You might as well tell me now. I'll find out eventually."

Angie began fretting in Jane's arms. "It's time for her bottle and nap."

"All right. But while you're doing that there's no reason you can't tell me what Cash has done now."

Jane stood up and carried Angie to the kitchen. While she went through the routine of preparing a bottle, she let Angie down to crawl on the floor by her feet.

"Well?" Lucy said, leaning in the kitchen doorway.

Jane felt an echo of her initial fury at Cash bubble up. "Cash proposed to me," she said tersely.

Lucy stood up straight. "Cash proposed? In Wausau? But why haven't you two said anything?"

"It wasn't a real marriage proposal." Jane lifted Angie from the floor and carried her back to the living room. On the way Angie grabbed the bottle, and Jane stuck its nipple in her mouth. Jane sat down in the corner of the sofa and let Angie lie back in her arms.

Lucy followed her and sat in the chair opposite. "How can a man propose marriage without it being a real proposal?"

"He said he thought Angie needed a father and a mother, not an uncle and a guardian."

"Oh," Lucy said quietly. "I suppose he said it just like that?"

"Yes, he did. I was never so insulted in my life. He called it a marriage of convenience. I told him I wasn't interested in being a convenience to anyone. After knowing the kind of marriage my parents have, the one you had, I can't believe he could show so little understanding of how Everetts view marriage."

"You turned him down."

"Of course I turned him down. He insulted the sanctity of marriage. He insulted me and my whole family!"

Lucy sat with her hands folded in her lap. "You still love him."

"Love him! I'd like to strangle him!"

Lucy sighed. "That's a sure sign you still love him."

Her grandmother's words left Jane struggling with a new rush of anger.

"If you didn't love him, you wouldn't be this angry." Lucy glanced toward Jane.

"Grandmother, I told you. I had a schoolgirl crush on him. He never even knew."

Lucy didn't take her eyes off her granddaughter's face. "I know. You fell in love with Cash on your sixteenth birthday and nothing's changed. Unfortunately."

"Unfortunately?" Angie's sucking slowed as she began to fall asleep. Looking down at the angelic face surrounded by the wispy, dark hair, Jane brushed back the little girl's bangs.

"Yes, unfortunately you still love him the way you did when you were sixteen."

"Grandmother—"

"Don't go on denying you love Cash. I know it's the truth."

Jane fell silent. She didn't want to admit it, but she couldn't lie, either.

Lucy said sternly, "It's time your love grew up."

"I don't know what you mean."

"You're still loving Cash, but with an immature love. You've never been allowed to show it, so it's stunted."

"I'm going to stop loving Cash," Jane insisted.

"Oh, how do you propose to do that?" Lucy put one hand on her hip.

Again Jane had no answer.

"It's time you began to love Cash with a love that is patient, kind, keeps no record of wrongs. A love that hopes all things, believes all things. A love that will never fail."

Jane recognized the verses Lucy quoted from First Corinthians 13. Lucy herself had taught them to Jane when she was very young. "But Cash doesn't want my love."

"That has nothing to do with how to love him. Christian love only demands things from the one who loves, never from the one who is loved. You love Cash, so you should love him with the best that's within you!"

"I do. I mean, I did."

Lucy shook her head ruefully. "No, if you did, his cold proposal wouldn't have made you angry, it would have made you sad."

"Why sad?"

"Because it's sad when a grown man knows so little about love."

Jane avoided her grandmother's piercing gaze. Angie slept soundly in her lap now. Tears tried to form in Jane's eyes, but she forced them back. "There isn't any future in loving Cash."

"Then let your heart give up."

"I thought you just said that wasn't possible."

"You have to make a choice. Either love Cash with all that's within you and wait and pray he'll someday return your love, or give up on him. Close the book on loving him. Look for another chance. Start fresh with someone else. It's not that you stop loving Cash. You just stop hoping he'll love you in return."

Jane kept her gaze on Angie. *Close the book.* A sensation like a rock-hard hand pressed down on her, crushing her breast.

Poised over the sweater display, Jane experienced a now-familiar flash of helpless dismay. The sweater, which had been missing at the beginning of the week, was back. Today was Friday afternoon. Yesterday Mel had shared the day with Tish, so either girl could have surreptitiously slipped the sweater back among the others. The cotton sweater was an ivory pullover with a delicate design of leaves and flowers around the neck and wrist. As she examined the band around its neck closely, she stopped. A trace of pink lipstick lingered on the inside.

She turned to Mel who was standing nearby. Keeping her voice casual, she said, "A customer has gotten lipstick on this sweater. Would you take it down to the cleaner?"

"Now?"

"Yes, I can handle things till you get back. Tell Doreen to put it on my account. Let her decide whether it should be dry-cleaned or hand washed and blocked."

"Sure. Be right back." The brunette teen took the folded sweater and walked out.

Jane had detected no alarm or guilt in the girl's eyes. Mel's lipstick was a pink similar to the trace, but so what? It proved nothing. Tish usually didn't wear lipstick at the shop, but she might elsewhere. Jane sighed loudly. Enough was enough. When would she solve this mystery? Or would she ever find the culprit? That thought was too vexing to be tolerated.

The bell jingled. She turned to greet the customer.

"I haven't seen you all summer," Del Ray Martin complained as a greeting.

"I've been awfully busy with Angie," Jane replied, neatening a scarf display on one of her glass cases.

"Are your parents going to be able to spend August up here like usual?"

"They arrive this afternoon."

"Good. Anyway, I'm looking for another new skirt to coordinate with that black sweater I bought here last fall."

Jane was relieved to get down to business. She led Del Ray over to one of the fall skirt racks. "The black sweater with the shawl collar?"

"Yes, my husband told me to get something that will show off my legs." Del Ray giggled like a teenager.

Jane didn't approve of Del Ray's desire to dress younger and flashier than her two teenage daughters. But Jane went carefully through the skirts, trying to find one that would please Del Ray while still flattering her. A size-eight, black gauze skirt almost leaped off its hanger at her. It was the one that had been missing for over a week!

Before Jane could collect her thoughts, Del Ray, who was standing at her elbow, spoke up, "Oh, that's just like the one I saw your cousin, Tish, wear. It's a little longer than I like, but do you have it in my size?"

Your cousin, Tish! Jane wanted to scream it out and hear it echo off the ceiling. Tish! Her heart pounded. At last one knot of this perplexing summer slid apart like satin against satin.

"No, I only have this one left," she heard her own voice, saying calmly. "How about something more seasonal for fall like this one?" Her arm held out a nubby knit in gray and black that would be knee length on Del Ray.

"I'll try it," the customer said reluctantly.

"Good." Jane turned, and through the front window, she saw Tish's long, blond mane. Until that moment Jane had forgotten Tish was due to come in later today for her check. The bell rang as the girl opened the front door.

"Hello, Tish, what are you doing here early?" Was that really her own voice so smooth as though another person were saying the words?

"Is it ready?"

"Of course. I have it at my desk. Come down. We'll get it together." She turned to Mel, who was back and busy rearranging a small display of turquoise-and-silver jewelry done by a local Indian artist. "Would you help Mrs. Martin?"

She ignored Mel's agreement and Del Ray's objection. Without a backward glance, Jane marched to the rear of the store and down the basement steps.

At the bottom she turned and watched Tish descend elegantly. The girl stopped on the bottom step and looked at Jane, tilting her head as though asking a question.

"You've been taking clothing, wearing it and bringing it back," Jane said flatly.

Tish's eyes widened for a fraction of a second. Then she tossed her head. "So?"

The girl's brazenness fanned Jane's indignation. "It is sneaky. It is dishonest. Don't you have any idea what a reputation is? If I told this—in a town this size—no one would ever hire you again."

"You won't tell anyone," Tish answered in a cool voice, and crossed her arms over her breast.

"What makes you so sure?"

"My parents. If you talk about me, they'll be humiliated." Tish stared narrowly into Jane's face, seeming to dare her.

The girl's audacity momentarily robbed Jane of speech.

"You won't hurt my parents," Tish explained in a sickly sweet tone. "So you won't tell them. I didn't steal anything, anyway. It was just a little borrowing."

Jane found her voice. "You're fired."

This time Tish's face did register surprise, but she regained control quickly. "I quit."

"I said you're fired."

"I'm going to tell my parents that I needed to do more reading before the school year, so I decided to quit. May I have my last check please?" Tish held out her hand.

Jane reached back without looking, picked up the lone envelope and threw it at Tish.

Tish smirked, picked it up off the basement floor and exited elegantly up the steps.

When the girl was gone, Jane sank onto the edge of her desk. Several minutes passed while the confrontation played over and over in her mind: "You won't hurt my parents."

How could she tell Uncle Henry and Aunt Claire the kind of emotional extortion their daughter was guilty of? Tish had attended church faithfully all her life. Hadn't anything sunk in?

Jane had wanted the size-eight mystery solved. But where could she go from here?

Chapter Eleven

Jane carefully wiped all inner frustration from her features and lifted her face into position for Lucy. She was still angry with Cash, and Lucy's scolding still stung.

Just a few feet away to Jane's right, Cash played with Angie. Her only success at distancing Cash had been that instead of letting him pick Angie and her up as usual, Jane had arranged to drive to Lucy's on her own. All the progress she had made in sharing Angie with Cash had been reversed. The thought of seeing Cash take Angie away for a day on their own made Jane ill.

Cash's playful teasing made Angie giggle. Jane's neck tightened. She cleared her throat. "I can't believe this is the last sitting and I'm still having a hard time posing."

Lucy nodded, but it was obvious that she was fully involved in finishing the portrait.

"This little girl is unstoppable." Shuffling behind Angie, Cash came into view. He was holding the child's hands above her head, helping her walk.

"She'll be walking by herself soon," Lucy murmured, then paused and stood, gazing at Jane.

Cash said, "One of my carpenters said his little girl walked at nine months—"

"That was *his* little girl," Jane snapped.

Cash looked up at her, showing his surprise. "I didn't mean anything against you—"

"Of course not," Lucy said soothingly. "Jane, let that frown go. I need your face... Yes, that's it."

While Lucy worked intensely on the portrait, Jane could hear her grandmother muttering to herself. Out of the corner of her eye, Jane kept tabs on Cash and Angie as they made their circuit around the room. Angie was endlessly intrigued by all the small sculptures and fine china on the low maple tables and shelves. Jane tried to keep her focus on the toddler.

Cash could feel Jane's attention on him...not on Angie's halting progress. He was also gripped, dominated by an awareness of her. Ever since that day they drove home from Wausau, every time he detected her cinnamon fragrance or saw sunlight touch her hair, he thought of the feel of her skin against his cheek, on his lips.

He knew that her response to him that day had been more warm and enticing than he'd ever imagined. But after his proposal, she had turned into a sharp, abrasive ice maiden. Now every time he encountered her he felt waves of frigid animosity flowing from her, warning him away.

Earlier in the year she had initially sparred with him over joint custody. After their June showdown, he thought she had gradually begun to come around. But this iciness was much worse than either previous phase. What had been so awful about his proposal? Their marrying for Angie's sake only made sense.

"It's done," Lucy announced simply.

Jane felt an unexpected shiver of excitement go through her. "May I see it?"

Lucy nodded, and Jane rose to stand beside her. Warily

she looked at the canvas. There she was, in her grand-mother's peach dress, sitting on the white wicker. But her expression in the portrait was what snagged her attention. Lucy had, of course, painted her granddaughter in a flattering way—Jane had expected that. But Jane's expression was at once winsome, wry and somehow wistful.

She touched her grandmother's shoulder affectionately, feeling Lucy's soft, worn cotton blouse under her fingertips. "Is that how you see me, Grandmother?"

Lucy put her hand over Jane's and whispered into Jane's ear, "Now if only Cash would be smart enough to see it."

Jane experienced a sudden desire to cry. Resolutely she pushed it away. "Mom and Dad will be pleased with it."

"Great job," Cash said, arriving beside Lucy. Angie clapped her hands and leaned forward to Jane. Jane took her into her arms.

"It's only four days away," Jane murmured, keeping her eyes on her grandmother.

"Yes, we cut it a little close," Lucy said. "Jane, why don't you wear the dress to the party? It will make the presentation of the portrait more striking."

Jane pursed her lips. "If you think I should."

"Your parents' party is only four days away, and that means Angie's first birthday is only seven days away," Cash pointed out.

Ice closed around Jane's heart. Twelve days till Angie would leave her for a day.

Jane smiled as cheerfully as she could at Angie, who sat in her car seat in the Blazer. *What's wrong with me tonight? I am delighted that my parents are celebrating thirty-five years together. Angie looks adorable in her new pink dress with ruffles and lace. I know Mom and Dad will love the portrait. It would, all in all, be a festive, joyous evening* with family and old friends. What had caused her emotions to snag together into a tangle of knots?

She knew the answer without voicing it. Cash Langley. Of course he would not dream of staying away tonight. Their two families had been friends for generations. But having Cash near, while she celebrated her parents' long-lasting love, would rub her like salt in an open wound.

She pulled up near her parents' summer home and parked in the crowd of cars at the base of the hill. With Angie in her arms, Jane, wearing heels, walked up carefully. Ahead in the doorway her grandmother waited. In honor of the occasion, Lucy wore one of her vintage Paris originals, a simple bell-shaped dress in pale green.

At the door Lucy greeted Angie. "I'm so happy you could come, little Miss Angie," she cooed to the baby, kissing her cheek. "Hello, my darling." She kissed Jane, also, and gave her a glance filled with love and concern. Jane could only nod in response because she was already forcing back tears.

Next in the informal receiving line were Jane's parents. Her father kissed her and teased Angie. Marge smiled in delight and claimed Angie for a quick hug. Another couple came up the steps behind Jane, so she tried to retrieve Angie from her mother, but the baby refused to leave her grandmother. Immensely pleased, Marge leaned forward to murmur to Jane, "I'll keep her. Cash has your corsage. You look wonderful in Mother's dress."

Jane nodded and entered the hall, then the living room. Her own feeling of tentativeness in these familiar surroundings unnerved her further. Her arms felt empty without Angie's reassuring company. Soft, taped music played in the background. Musicians would come later for the dancing. The large L-shaped dining-living room was already full of cheerful people, talking and eating hors d'oeuvres. Jane tried to shake off her melancholy and behave naturally.

Cash saw Jane enter. Holding the corsage box in front of him like a peace offering, he moved through the crowd to her. She turned and caught sight of him. He froze. For a few seconds he could only stare. Surely he should have gotten used to seeing her in the dress she had posed in. His mouth became dry and his hands trembled slightly like a schoolboy, picking up his date to his first dance. Jane was the most beautiful woman in the room.

As she walked gracefully to him, she moved as effortlessly as an angel hovering near the earth, creating in him a surge of anticipation. In spite of himself, he longed to pull her to him. He would kiss—

"My corsage please?" she asked coolly.

The cold tone of her voice killed his thoughts. A dangerous fire burned in her emerald eyes. He almost retreated a step. She was still angry over his proposal, and he still could not understand her reaction to a perfectly honest suggestion. Weren't flowery declarations of undying affection passé now? Had she expected him to go down on one knee and declare undying love?

She took the white box from him. As though his skin were repulsive to her, she made certain she touched only the box. Irritation bubbled up inside him. But as she walked away, he still couldn't make himself draw his gaze from the sway of her hips.

Jane clutched the box in one hand and went down the hall to her parents' first-floor bedroom. Closing the door behind her, Jane felt the room, decorated in restful blues, was a welcome haven.

But there, in front of the wall mirror was Rona, putting on lipstick. Rona was wearing the informal uniform that she wore to catering jobs, a black tunic over black slacks. But Rona being Rona, she had added color with a russet and gold scarf at her neck.

Inwardly Jane sighed, but made herself walk forward. She

hoped Rona wouldn't be in a prying mood. "Could you help me pin this on?" She held the box out to Rona.

Rona took the delicate confection out of the box and then looked at Jane's dress. "New dress?"

"It's my grandmother's."

Rona carefully pinned the flowers onto the right shoulder of the dress, high above its scooped neckline. "One of her originals?"

"No, but it was purchased in Paris."

"That explains it. I don't know how your grandmother does it. Half the time she dresses wacky, but when she wants to be beautiful, she succeeds every time."

"Grandfather said it was the artist in her. The desire to surprise and delight."

Rona stepped back and looked Jane over critically. "You look lovely, of course, but you're very pale. Aren't you feeling well?"

"I'm fine, thanks. It's just all the getting ready. Angie does make it a challenge." Jane, stepping around Rona, looked into the large mirror and fluffed her hair with her fingers, then smoothed the full skirt of her dress. "You did a good job of pinning the corsage. It feels secure and isn't sideways."

"Vitelli's offers a *full* service catering. Well, I can't hide in here all night. I have work to do. Carmine will be yelling his head off for me any moment now."

They went back to the noise of the party. Cash, holding Angie, was waiting at the entrance of the living room for her. Jane took a firm grip on her emotions.

"Good luck," Rona whispered and left her side.

Jane walked up to Cash. Wordlessly he led her to the kitchen snack bar. Perched on a high stool next to Cash's, she accepted a goblet of sparkling white grape juice and looked around.

Lucy had considered Mylar balloons as too gauche for

this formal occasion. Instead small, artful arrangements of late-summer blossoms: pink asters, dusky gold mums, bright yellow snapdragons graced the end tables and mantel. And a bounty of gladiolus. There were huge floor vases of these tall, regal flowers in bold white, peach and yellow. They filled the spacious room. The abundance of flowers set the festive mood, and Jane focused on the smiles and friendly voices around her. Angie also appeared to be fascinated by her surroundings. As Angie's attention roamed the room, she sat unnaturally still on Cash's lap.

Pivoting in her seat, Jane noted the other party preparations. In Lucy's mind a formal party still meant crystal, silver and bone china for a sit-down dinner. The guests now milled around the long L-shaped living room and dinette. But outside, the large screened-in porch, which encompassed the length of the lake side of her parents' home and then curved around the far end of the house, was prepared for dinner. The porch had been adorned with a rainbow of lanterns and candles. The tables there were ready to seat thirty-eight people. And, of course, Lucy had somehow magically influenced the weather to cooperate this evening, and the summer's storms and heat were blessedly absent.

Cash cleared his throat. Reluctantly she looked up. He touched his glass to hers and leaned forward so she could hear him. "To you."

Automatically she tried to read his mood from the expression on his face and tone of his voice. He seemed merely polite. Why do I continue to look for something in him that had never been there and would never be there? Keeping the occasion in mind, she smiled politely in return and introduced a neutral topic. "I'm happy your conflict with Roger is over."

He lifted his glass in salute. He leaned forward again. "How's your size-eight mystery going?"

Her spine stiffened. She tilted her face nearer him, so he

could hear her over the buzz of voices and tinkling of ice in glasses. "It's ended."

"Which was it? Mel or your cousin?"

"Tish quit and the size eights have stopped vanishing and returning, I'm leaving it at that."

"I see. If it *was* Mel, she would now be forced to stop simply because there is no longer anyone else to muddy the issue."

"Exactly." Knowing the culprit was her own unrepentant cousin made her grit her teeth, but she managed to smile.

"Jane?" an unexpected voice came from behind her.

She turned around. Tom, whom she hadn't seen since the reading of Dena's will at his Chicago office, stood before her. "Tom! I didn't know you were coming up for my parents' party." She jumped down from her stool and gave the lawyer an affectionate hug.

"Well, Lucy called me last week and invited me to come up and stay with her. I decided I could use a week away from court."

"You can forget all about briefs and judges now." She tucked her arm in Tom's, glad of his presence, which would provide a welcome distraction to the tension of being with Cash.

"Angie has really grown." Tom took Angie's small hand and shook it. "She looks so much like Dena."

"Yes," Cash answered woodenly. When would any reference to his sister stop slicing through him like a sharp razor?

"She's a doll. She has your hair, Cash."

Angie unexpectedly stretched out her arms to Tom. He lifted her gingerly as though the little girl were made of cotton candy. "She's so light!"

"Thank goodness," Jane said wryly. "She isn't walking yet."

Tom held Angie close to him and began reciting nursery

rhymes. Angie listened to the chanting cadence with obvious fascination.

Cash felt a whiplash of jealously slice through him. When Jane had arrived, her beauty had rocked him from head to toe. As he had sat next to her, talking about nothing, her icy anger had washed over him in progressive, freezing waves. Then at Tom's innocent mention of Dena he had been stabbed with pain, and now jealousy ricocheted through him like live ammo. Why was everything hitting him so hard tonight? The party had just begun.

Tom nuzzled Angie's cheek and then handed her back to Cash.

Tish appeared at Cash's side. He stood up politely and nodded to her. "Hi, Cash," she said. He noted that her soft tone warred with the barbed glance she gave Jane.

Jane quelled the urge to say something back to her cousin. Tish was wearing a black cotton sheath which, instead of draining her light complexion as it should have, enhanced her pale ivory skin. That style was much too sophisticated for a sixteen-year-old. Why didn't Aunt Claire stand up to her daughter more? "You didn't buy that at my shop," Jane said pointedly.

"No," Tish said airily. "Mother and I drove to Wausau yesterday. Your shop is nice enough, Jane, but it's too small to offer much variety." The girl slipped her arm through Cash's and rubbed noses with Angie in their accustomed greeting.

Jane bit her tongue before she said something she'd regret. Instead of reacting with anger, maybe it was time to start praying over her relationship with her cousin.

"We're going to go again," Tish continued. "To Wausau, I mean, before school starts. I saw some lovely clothes, but I just didn't have to time to try everything on. That's one thing I owe your shop, Jane. Working there gave me such a desire to wear a variety of styles. I hate wearing the same thing over and over, don't you?'' Tish turned innocent eyes to her cousin.

Jane flushed. So far she had been unable to tell her aunt and uncle about their daughter's "borrowing" clothing from her shop. It made her angry to think that Tish considered herself the winner in this situation. But Jane still intended to settle Tish's "hash." She would put the problem before Lucy, and she was confident that their grandmother would know just what to do to teach Tish the lesson she so richly deserved.

At this thought Jane smiled. "No, frankly, Tish, I think I take after Lucy about clothes. What I like, I like, and I don't mind wearing my favorites. I love fashion and its trends, but I hope that you will find and retain your own style. That's the mark of a truly well-dressed woman."

"I must say that I like what you are wearing tonight," Tom said appreciatively.

"It's Lucy's." Jane swayed slightly, letting her full skirt ripple.

Tish sniffed. "It looks like one of those weird square dancing dresses old women wear."

"Not even a little." Lucy's voice came out cold and clear. She stood right beside the suddenly flushed Tish. Over the hubbub, Lucy announced that dinner was ready and please would they all find their places out on the porch.

Tom steered Jane out onto the porch and located their name cards. Reading the other name cards at the main table, Jane found that Aunt Claire, Uncle Henry, Tish, her parents and Lucy were to be joined by Cash and Angie.

Lucy had said nothing to her about inviting Tom north for a week. *Is Grandmother trying to take my mind off Cash?* She told me I could choose to find someone else. Jane glanced at Tom. He had always seemed a little overly serious, but she had no doubt he would make an excellent husband and father.

"Let's sit down." Tom gently guided her into her chair. "I'm happy your grandmother seated me next to you," he whispered into her ear. "I think I am going to enjoy this week off. I had forgotten how lovely the Everett women are." His compliment was balm to her shredded pride. She smiled up at him.

As Cash watched Jane smile at Tom, he numbly put Angie in her high chair. Jane's dad's best man from thirty-five years ago rose and led them all in a toast to many more happy years for Marge and Phil. The glasses clinked. There was applause and the salads were brought out efficiently. The tables hummed with happy conversation.

Cash watched Jane's parents touch glasses again and exchange a look charged with love. He looked away as though he had come upon them kissing. His eyes touched Tish, and she smiled at him. He smiled briefly in reply, then turned to the task of helping Angie with her meal. He was glad feeding Angie gave him something to do. In spite of having to keep up with Angie's demands and his trying to eat enough of the delicious food in front of him to be polite, he still found his attention being drawn in two directions: to Jane's face and to her parents.

All through the meal, Tom kept murmuring into Jane's ear, making her smile, nod, laugh. Cash was possessed by an urge to bump Tom off the chair next to Jane and take it for himself. Why? Tom was a nice guy. In the past, he'd dated both Jane and Dena. So why did Cash want to suddenly do him bodily harm?

The other irresistible draw was Marge and Phil. At every possible opportunity their hands touched; their eyes sought out the other. There seemed to be a warm glow around them, unseen, but still evident. He had always liked the Everetts, but never had Marge looked lovelier and Phil more content, fulfilled.

The meal finally came to a close with a flaming dessert. Another toast was observed for the Everetts.

Then Lucy rose majestically. "Friends and family, tonight is a very happy evening for me. Watching my son live happily with this wonderful woman for the last thirty-five years has been an untold blessing to me.

"I know personally that it has been a happy and successful time for both Marge and Phil. So Jane and I, with Cash's assistance, planned a special gift to honor them. Will you all come into the living room to view its presentation?" She motioned everyone to rise, then led them back into the long room.

In front of the vaulted stone fireplace, an easel, draped in white, had been set up in their absence. Without another word, Lucy marched directly to it and swept the cloth aside.

Cash stared at Jane's likeness. The peach dress, her copper hair and the white wicker were harmonious, sunlit and lovely. Glorious. Spontaneous applause swept the room, and he watched Jane blush at its sound. People came forward, shaking Jane's hand, patting her shoulder and hugging her. Cash's attention alternated between Jane's portrait and Jane herself.

Cash watched Lucy, Marge, Phil and Jane being pushed forward to stand beside the portrait and accept more congratulations. When Tom came up and kissed Jane's cheek, Cash felt a charge of heat flood his face. Electronic flashes from many cameras went off in bursts. Angie, in Cash's arms, cried for Jane, and he had to give the baby to her. Awkwardly he stepped out of camera range.

"If I may have your attention please," Phil raised his voice and the gathered friends became quiet. Jane, holding Angie, stood beside Lucy. "I won't talk a long time, but this is one of those rare opportunities when a man can speak about what really matters in life.

"It goes almost without saying that I am a fortunate man.

You all know my mother and so you will believe me when I tell you that she was not surprised in the least when I came home from the first day of ninth grade and told her I had met the girl I was going to marry. Her name was Marjorie. When I think of all the men who waste years vainly trying to find their true love, I am very grateful. God said, 'It is not good for man to be alone' and He has blessed me with a true helpmeet.'' He smiled broadly and tightened his arm around Marge.

"This portrait is a lovely gift, but Marge and I received another gift this year. Our first grandchild. Jane, bring Angie here please."

Jane walked the few feet to her parents. Her father lifted Angie into his arms. "Of all the gifts we could have received this year, having this little girl become part of our family has been the best. Don't you agree, Marge?"

"Yes, losing dear Dena was sad," Marge spoke softly. "But Angie is a precious trust from Dena. We will do our best to live up to Dena's faith in us—along with Jane and Cash, of course."

"Thank you all for coming to celebrate this occasion tonight." Phil motioned to the musicians, and they began to play a slow dance.

Cash was shaking inside. Phil Everett's simple words of gratitude to God for his wife's love had shaken Cash to his core. As the music began again, the guests moved back to make room for the dancers. Cash looked around and realized that Tish was standing beside him. She had a discontented expression on her face.

Jane approached them, carrying Angie. "Cash, would you hold Angie. Tom has asked me to dance." Without saying a word, Cash took Angie. The little girl yawned.

Cash said, "Tish, would you get Angie's bottle and warm it? It's nearly her bedtime."

"Sure," Tish said.

Cash watched Tom lead Jane out onto the patio, then take her into his arms for a slow dance. Cash's jaw clenched. He turned away and walked down the back hall to the master bedroom. There, a folding crib stood in the corner next to a cushioned, platform rocker.

Cash laid Angie down in the crib, which held diapers and clothing in Angie's size. He murmured softly as he took her out of her fancy dress, changed her diaper and snapped her into her lightweight summer pajamas.

"Here's her bottle," Tish said, still sounding disgruntled.

Cash sat down in the rocker, positioned Angie across his lap, tucked his arm under her and took her bottle from Tish. With a contented sigh, Angie stopped fretting and relaxed in her uncle's arms.

Tish flopped down on the end of the bed. Cash looked up. "You don't need to stay here. You'll miss all the fun."

"Fun!" Tish scowled at him. "A bunch of old people! Mother said if I didn't come tonight, she wouldn't take me shopping to Wausau. I couldn't make her change her mind—"

"Of course you had to come tonight. It's a family event," he said mildly. "You're fortunate to have such a wonderful family—"

"Wonderful!"

"Yes, wonderful. Did you ask your parents if you could bring an escort—"

"No way! I wouldn't bring anyone from school. I have the weirdest family—"

"I don't think they're weird," Cash insisted. "They're just highly individual—"

"Weird! My grandmother's wearing a forty-year-old dress—"

"It's a Balenciaga original—"

"It's forty years old, for crying out loud! And Jane is wearing a thirty-year-old dress—just because it was the dress...'' Tish's voice became dramatic as she imitated her mother's voice. '"The dress Mother bought on her last trip to Paris with Father.'" Her tone hardened abruptly. "Who cares?"

"I do." Lucy's voice startled both of them.

Tish and Cash swiveled to watch Lucy enter. "You are talking nonsense—"

Tish stood up combatively, her chin thrust forward. "I don't care. What do I care about Grandfather? He was dead five years before I was born!"

"He was your mother's father," Lucy said in deadly calm. "You are a part of him. He lives through you. And will live on through your children."

Tish made a sound of disgust.

Lucy's face became scarlet.

Cash suddenly was worried about her. "Lucy, sit down. You're flushed—"

Lucy ignored him, her attention riveted on Tish's face. Her voice came out low and outraged, "I never thought I would hear anything so devoid of true feeling come from a relation of mine."

Tish's face now matched Lucy's shade of red. "You've always hated me! It's always Jane, Jane—"

"I have never hated you," Lucy went on relentlessly. "I've only hated the way your parents have overindulged you. The minute you were born, they let you take over their family—"

"No, that's not true. My parents never let me do anything I want. They didn't let me be Aquarama Queen!"

"You know yourself that only junior and senior girls are expected—"

"I don't care!" Tish stomped her foot. "If you can wear forty-year-old dresses, why can't I be Aquarama Queen a year early?"

"The two situations are completely different. A Paris

original is a work of art. Can a true work of art go out of style? I don't wear my originals to be different. I wear them, so that others can see them and enjoy them."

"I don't care why you wear them. It's stupid!"

Tish glared at Lucy. Lucy stared back, not giving an inch to Tish's defiance.

"Granddaughter, I have only one thing more to say to you. Pride goeth before a fall." Majestically raising her hand, Lucy prevented Tish's retort. "Go wash the tears off your face and go back to the party."

Tish made a face at her grandmother and stomped out.

Lucy shook her head. "How did Angie fall asleep through all that?"

Cash looked down at the sleeping child. "I don't know. I think her ears were effectively muffled by my arm and chest."

"I'll take over now." Lucy held out her arms.

"No, that's all right. You go back. You're the hostess—"

"I am an exhausted hostess. Cash, I'm in my seventies—"

Cash stood up and transferred Angie to Lucy's arms. He didn't want to go back out to the party, but what choice did he have? He couldn't leave the party so early without calling attention to himself.

He stood outside the door at the end of the porch. Against clear instructions to the contrary, his eyes insisted on picking out Jane. She was still dancing with Tom. Cash made himself turn his attention elsewhere, and his gaze caught Phil and Marge just as they kissed lightly. The people around them smiled and nodded. As Phil began talking to another couple, he tucked Marge closer to him.

The song ended. The band took its first break. Once again disobeying him, Cash's eyes roamed over the gathering and picked out Jane.

Tom stood beside her as they talked to another couple.

Tom's arm rested possessively on Jane's shoulder. Cash watched Jane grin up at Tom and playfully punch his chin. Tom laughed and squeezed Jane's arm. Jane moved closer into Tom's embrace.

Cash hurried from the room without a backward glance. He ducked out a side door to the back hall and then outside. Skirting the house he sought cover in the long evening shadows of the trees.

Farther down the bank beside the Everetts' boathouse, the dock projected out into the dusky water. His footsteps thudded rapidly down its length. Waves lapped against the shore and the pontoon boat moored there. He stepped onto the pontoon, knowing the boathouse and canvas cover over the boat would shield him from the house windows above.

Leaning over the railing, he scanned the opposite shoreline automatically. But instead of seeing the scene of the lake and pine trees, he saw faces—Lucy, Dena, Phil, Marge, Jane. Then all the faces faded and one stood out alone—Jane's.

"Cash." His name was murmured from behind.

He turned to face Jane. She took one more step forward. He was instantly aware of her intense concentration on him.

He struggled with himself, but he could not stir himself to speak. He turned sideways from her, keeping his taut face out of the light, not wanting to let her read his confusion. He watched Jane, silhouetted in the ebbing sunlight, continue to stare at him as though nerving herself to say something.

The lowering sun's rays caught the brilliance of her hair, and a shimmering halo lit up her face, her reddish-gold hair, creamy skin, clear green eyes. He allowed his gaze to be drawn down the line of her perfect chin. He wanted to draw her into his arms, press his face into her neck and inhale the cinnamon scent that whispered, "Jane," enticingly.

He reached for her, pulled her close. He let his eyes close

in anticipation as he bent to kiss her. But his lips met her hand, not her lips.

His eyes opened.

"No," Jane said firmly. "No more empty kisses."

"What?" His voice was low and thick with emotion.

"Cash, I have loved you since you kissed me on my sixteenth birthday, but you never even noticed." She repeated, "You never even noticed. No more. Tonight I declare my independence from your hold over me. You don't love me. You never will. I accept this tonight, and I won't let it cripple the rest of my life. No more empty proposals from you. No more foolish hopes from me. You don't love me. And now my heart is closed to you."

With that she turned and walked away slowly and deliberately. He listened numbly to her high heels tap evenly on the wooden pier. Then she was out of sight, the boathouse blocking his view.

He felt as though someone had plunged a needle into his chest and was using it to draw his heart out of him. He winced with the pain.

"I love you, Jane," he gasped. Unspoken, more painful realizations ribboned through his mind: I've loved you for months. How could I have missed how much I need you?

Chapter Twelve

"I took your advice. I told Cash my heart was closed to him." Jane felt her jaw harden on the word, *closed*. In Lucy's sitting room, Jane sat with Angie on her lap while Angie unknowingly posed for the miniature Lucy was painting for Cash.

"Oh, dear." Lucy's brush stilled.

"I can't waste my life—"

"I know, my dear. You don't need to explain to me. It's just that I can't believe Cash can be so mutton-headed or do I mean muddle-headed?"

"Mutton-headed sounds good to me," Jane replied drily.

Angie twisted in Jane's lap, looking up at her. The little girl squirmed onto her knees and rested her head against Jane's breast.

Jane swallowed tears and hugged Angie.

"Now let's turn around for Grandmother," Jane coaxed Angie. Angie obediently slid onto her seat again.

"I'm almost done, sweetheart," Lucy cooed and began painting with careful, intricate strokes.

"Where's Tom this afternoon?" Jane asked.

"He wanted to do some shopping in town. Are you certain, Jane, that you're not—" Lucy stopped her question.

"I'm not misleading Tom," Jane said quietly. "He is a fine man. He and I have known each other almost our whole lives. Wasn't that what you were thinking when you invited him here?" Jane paused.

"Perhaps." Lucy kept her eyes on her work in progress.

"And I have decided that I don't want Angie and me to be alone for the next twenty years—"

At this Lucy stepped around the easel. "You've truly closed your heart to Cash completely?"

Jane pursed her lips. "Yes. I told you."

"I see." Lucy looked at her granddaughter.

"I want to marry. I don't want Angie to be an only child. I want more children, Grandmother."

Lucy nodded solemnly. "I wanted a houseful, but it wasn't to be. I hope you have better luck. The miniature's finished, Jane."

Jane swung Angie into her arms and stood up. On her grandmother's easel was an oval about two inches by three. In such a small oval, there was only room for Angie's round, cheerful face.

"Beautiful. Simply beautiful." Jane kissed her grandmother's cheek.

"Thank you, dear. But really it would have been impossible to make Angie look anything but darling."

The two women stood side by side. Angie clapped her hands.

"Lucy!" They heard Tom call as he came in the back door.

Lucy replied, "Come in, Tom, and see Angie's miniature. I've just finished it."

He came quickly and stood behind the three females. "How delightful. You look great, kid." He ruffled the raven curls on top of Angie's head. "How about a swim, Jane?"

Her eyes connected with his. She let a smile take over her mouth. "Angie, too?"

"Delighted to have her. Did she bring her trunks?" he teased.

"It's a gracious invitation, Tom," Lucy interposed, "but I think Angie should take a long rock on my lap and maybe sleep."

"Still game then?" Tom asked.

Jane kept her smile in place, but the tug of tears caught at the back of her throat. When would she stop teetering on the brink of tears, moment by moment? Giving up a six-year fascination with Cash wasn't going to be easy.

But in only a matter of minutes Tom and Jane were thundering down the end of Lucy's pier. As they had done thousands of times in the summers of their childhood, they both jumped off the end.

Surfacing, Jane smoothed her wet hair back from her face and looked around for Tom. She turned a complete circle and then called, "Tom—"

She squealed. Two hands jerked her ankles and pulled her back under. The two of them thrashed frantically in the water, then began alternately chasing and dunking each other.

Tom finally swam to the side of the pier. On its vertical posts hung black, oversize inner tubes. He tossed out two. Jane swam to the farthest tube, dived and surfaced in the middle of it. She rested her arms around the tube, her feet dangling. Tom paddled his over to face her.

"Jane." He looked into her eyes. The unguarded expression on his face made it impossible for her to speak. "Jane."

Hesitantly Jane let her hand glide over the wet surface till her fingertips touched his inner tube. With a quick smile, he laid his hand over hers. Once again tears caught in the back of her throat.

Quickly she slid back under the water and struck out into deeper water, liberally splashing Tom's face.

"Mister Langley, explain yourself." Lucy glared at Cash. Moments ago when she had entered his office, he had risen hastily, causing the blueprint he had been studying to roll shut with a hushed wap. "Lucy?"

"Explain yourself." She took another step forward, closing the slender gap between her and the cluttered desk in his on-site trailer.

"What? What's wrong? Is Angie—"

"There's nothing wrong with Angie. I am asking you to explain yourself, sir."

Her imperious, irritated manner took him so much by surprise that he couldn't think of how to answer her. Finally after at least five seconds of staring, he gave up trying to figure out what to say. He lifted a mound of paperwork off a chair next to his desk. "Won't you sit down—"

"I prefer to stand. Thank you." Lucy let her large canvas purse settle on the front edge of the desk. She folded her hands on top of it.

Cash straightened his spine. "What am I explaining?"

"Your mutton-headed behavior toward my granddaughter."

"I...I..."

The door behind Lucy opened. "Boss, that load of—"

"Pardon me." Lucy turned to face the man. "I am in conference with Mr. Langley." She pulled the door's knob toward herself, forcing the man to back down the steps behind him. When the door closed, she clicked the lock button and swung back to face Cash.

"What the heck is the bee in your bonnet?" Cash demanded.

"Calling my mood a bee in the bonnet is like calling Hurricane Andrew a thunderstorm."

"Why don't we just get down to business? What's this all about?" His hands found his hips. The vehemence of his voice was overshadowed by the sudden pounding of rain on the metal roof above them. He groaned aloud. "More rain!"

"The fact it's raining one more time this summer should be of no surprise to anyone. Don't try to distract me."

"What is it, Lucy?"

"I believe I informed you that I wanted to know why you had been playing the fool with my granddaughter."

"I don't know what you're referring to." But uneasiness settled in the pit of his stomach.

"Tom would understand what I am referring to—if he knew what had been going on between you and Jane this summer."

"Tom." Cash's voice was hard. "I've been asking myself why he received a special invitation to stay with you."

"Because it was time for Jane to have someone around who appreciated her."

"And I don't appreciate her."

"I believe that was my first point."

They glared at each other.

"You proposed a marriage of convenience to Jane."

"She told you!" Surprise shimmered through him. He hadn't thought Jane would tell her grandmother.

"Who else? Why...how could you have blundered so completely?" Her tone softened, and she spread her hands in a gesture of appeal.

"I thought it made sense." He shrugged helplessly.

"My granddaughter is beautiful, successful, tender-hearted. For the past six years I have waited for you to, hoped you would, wake up and see what a treasure she was—"

"How was I supposed to know she'd been in love with me? She was the best friend of my baby sister. I wasn't a cradle robber!"

"Your past blindness is no excuse. Your proposal was an insult. An insult!"

"I didn't mean it to be." He looked down. "I can see now that it was a mistake, but—"

"You regret it?"

"With all my heart."

A few seconds of silence vibrated between them. Finally Lucy sat down in the chair he had offered her before, and he let himself settle back into his chair.

"What are your feelings for my granddaughter?"

His mouth went dry. "I love her."

Lucy gave an exaggerated sigh. "I take it you realized this after you proposed?"

He nodded glumly.

Lucy went on, "So you've finally come to see what you should have known for ages, but now you can't tell her—"

"Because she'll think I'm saying it to manipulate her into marrying me *just* for Angie's sake. I don't suppose you could talk this over with her?"

"Impossible. If I did, she'd know I've talked to you about her."

"And it would only make me more suspect."

Lucy sighed loudly again. "This is a fine mess you've gotten us into. And it makes no sense. In fact, you haven't made sense for a long, long time."

He looked at her quizzically. "I don't know what you mean."

"That's obvious." She looked into his eyes. "Cash, you've been running from life ever since your mother walked out on you and your father."

"I don't discuss that."

Lucy crossed her legs and folded her arms over each other. "Too bad. We're discussing it today."

"I don't see—"

"Exactly. You've been blind. It's time you shifted your

attention from what was taken from you, to what you were given. Dena did.''

"What are you talking about?" Cash sat back and hunched to one side.

"Dena lost your mother and then your father just like you did. But she never lost hope. Very early she let me introduce her to her Heavenly Father, the author of love, joy and hope. But every time I've tried to give you the same gift you turned away."

"You know I believe in God, Lucy. What has that got to do with—"

"All love proceeds from God. You believe in God, but it's only a cold, dead acknowledgment of His existence. Love Him. Let Him love you! Thank Him for all the love He brought into your life!"

Cash barked an imitation of a laugh. "I've lost everyone I've ever loved."

"No you haven't! You haven't lost me or Angie."

"I lost Dena!"

"You were given her for twenty-two precious years. Can you imagine what your life would have been like if she hadn't been born? Don't you realize your mother had already begun to stray before Dena's birth? God knew you would lose your mother, so he sent you a beautiful sister."

The frightening thought of never having had his sister in his life chilled Cash. "I loved Dena every day of her life. I'll miss her every day for the rest of my life."

"And she loved you, but more important, she turned toward God and life. She lived every day without regret. She didn't give the past any power over her. We've lost her and her husband too soon, but they loved each other with a beautiful, an eternal, love. The same kind of love Jane has in her heart for you."

Cash froze in his chair, feeling as though Lucy's words had turned him into wood.

Lucy leaned forward. "God gave you Jane, and you never even noticed."

"Jane says she doesn't love me anymore."

"Jane loves you. She's loved you for years."

"That's not what she plans to do in the future." The words nearly caught in his throat.

Lucy paused and bent her head in prayer. When she looked up, she said, "Cash, I think it's time I told you the truth."

He looked into her eyes. "The truth?"

"Dena came to see me before she and her husband drew up their will."

A horrible, descending feeling gripped Cash.

"Dena told me that if anything happened to her and John, she planned to give their expected child to Jane."

"Why?" The single word rattled through him like an earth tremor.

"She was afraid that if anything happened to her, you would retreat into your shell completely and take her child with you."

A tear slid down Cash's cheek.

"She paid me the compliment of telling me how much my family had meant to her and how much she loved us." Lucy's voice shook and she had to pause to wipe her eyes. "She said she knew if she gave the child to Jane that it would force you to stay in contact with my family."

Cash felt brittle. Any word or glance might shatter his fragile emotions utterly.

"You're going to have to talk to Jane about this. But before you do, you need to talk to God. Settle matters with Him, then ask Him for help."

"How?" he asked through dry lips.

"Just be honest. He's never let anyone down who asked for help. I'll leave you to it." With that, Lucy stood up and left.

For several minutes, Cash sat alone, listening to the pounding rain on the metal roof overhead. Finally, he bent his head into his hands. *God, I don't know where to begin. Lucy says I've been a fool. I think she may be right. I love Jane. I need her. What do I do?*

The rain came down harder, making an angry din. Cash felt its force echo inside him, in his pulse. Tears, pent up for months and years at great cost, released, pouring from his eyes. Images flashed through his mind. His mother, his father, Dena at different ages, Lucy, Jane, finally Angie. *Help me, Lord. I'm through running things my way. I've made a mess of everything. If I have any chance to win Jane for Angie and me, help me. Please.*"

The shop doorbell jingled. Jane glanced up and was shocked to see Cash walk in. She hadn't seen him since her parents' anniversary party. Her unruly heart thudded once, then settled back to its natural pace.

"Hi," Cash said, trying to look calm. He still felt drained after his encounter with Lucy two days before, but he felt free of the past. Something new, which must be hope, had resulted from his request to God. Jane still might love him. He believed it now.

Maintaining his pose of nonchalance was difficult, but Lucy had suggested an excuse for him to see Jane tonight. In spite of his fledgling faith, his palms were wet from nervousness. What if he opened his stupid mouth and said the wrong thing again?

"Hi, what can I do for you?" Jane answered, masking her displeasure at his invading her shop.

He hooked his thumbs into the waistband of his worn denim jeans, and she could tell by his dusty appearance that he'd probably been working at his site. "Lucy said you needed someone to look at your roof. You've lost some shingles. And there's another storm on the way."

The Eagle Lake Florist delivery boy, Mel's brother, breezed in. "Flowers for Jane Everett."

Chagrined at the boy's untimely arrival, Jane stepped around the counter, her eyes avoiding Cash's.

"Roses," he explained, offering her a long, white box.

She smiled stiffly, feeling Cash's attention on her. "Now that you've told me, should I bother to open them?"

Carmine's son was not embarrassed. "Why not? Roses are nothing to sneeze at—unless you're allergic to them." He grinned and left with an undaunted wave.

She forced herself to open the box on the nearest glass counter. Twelve perfect, dewy red roses and one white one rested on the moist greenery and darker green tissue paper. The prominent note read: "To a charming lady, Tom." Flushing slightly at the memory of Tom's parting kiss, she purposefully ignored Cash and tucked the card into her skirt pocket.

"Lucy told me your roof's been leaking," he prompted.

"What can you do about it now? It's late, and I'm sure it will be raining soon," she rattled off.

"I think I'll have time to take a look at it before the storm starts." Gambling on her natural courtesy and the fact that her roof did need attention, he crossed his arms in front of his chest and waited.

"I suppose you could come home with me. I might as well just close up. No one is going to come out with the sky going dark at 7:00 p.m." He nodded, and she swallowed the last traces of her irritation. She couldn't actually blame Cash for not loving her. There was no cosmic law that obliged him to do so, just because she had been foolish over him for the past six years.

Obviously Lucy had mentioned Jane's damaged roof to Cash in passing, and out of politeness he was following it up. Feeling his unwavering attention on her, she finished up her daily closing-up routine and picked up the flower box.

During the few-block walk to her house, the gusting wind rocked against them and swirled dust into their eyes, keeping them from talking. Its cool edge signaled the new and powerful front which seemed only minutes away. In silence they reached her door.

With his eyes examining the roof above, Cash left Jane's side and edged around the house while she hurried inside. Within minutes she had paid an uncommunicative Tish who, though no longer working at the shop, still sat for Angie. Tish left by the back door to go to her car in the alley. As Angie always did after a separation from Jane, she begged to be held.

With a jolt Jane's stomach rumbled, demanding supper. Outside, thunder rumbled also. Realizing that she would probably be obliged to invite Cash for supper, she grimaced. But resigned to her fate, she carried Angie and the flower box into the kitchen and slid the box onto a lower shelf in the refrigerator. With Angie settled on her hip, Jane went down the steps to her freezer in the basement.

After a hasty search she lifted out a casserole she had made in one of her cooking frenzies. Upstairs she installed Angie in her high chair with miniature crackers on the tray. "Your appetizer, mademoiselle," Jane murmured and tickled Angie under her chin.

She slid the casserole into the microwave on Defrost and began making salad for two. Fortunately her freezer held a half gallon of rainbow sherbet for dessert, and she had cleaned the kitchen the night before. "My imitation of Suzy Homemaker," she said to herself, but it was a cozy feeling to be safe at home in the face of the approaching storm.

She heard Cash let himself in the front door, thud quickly up her front stairs and on up into the attic. He thumped around noisily over her head. The sounds Cash made filled the house in a way she hadn't expected, as though some part of her had been waiting for him to come. She shook her head at herself.

Then Jane heard him exit the same way he had come in. Several minutes later he let himself back in the front door. This time the door got away from him in the wind and banged the outside wall twice before he could latch it. Then without a word he entered the kitchen and sat down at her small table.

Her physical awareness of him jerked all her senses awake. She identified the faint mixing of his scents, a mix that she found compelling as always. The deep timbre of his softly spoken endearment to Angie caught her ear.

Feeling insecure near him, she turned to say something defensive, but instead she bit her lip. His expression was either weary or morose, she couldn't tell which. She took out a pitcher of iced tea and put it on the red-and-white-checked place mat in front of him. "Stay for dinner?" she invited neutrally.

He looked up then. "Thanks. If it's not too much trouble." He eyed her warily.

"Just heating up a casserole."

"Sounds good to me." He gave Angie a tired smile and stroked her head once. Jane noted that it was a much different greeting than the exuberant ones he usually gave his little niece.

Setting the wooden salad bowl at the center of the table, she sat down across from him. He looked so lost. Suddenly she longed to say, "What's wrong, Cash?" But she reminded herself of her resolve. Whatever he was thinking was none of her business and she would have to learn to isolate herself from him emotionally.

Cash was searching his mind, trying to think of what to say to Jane now that he was here with her alone. The only ideas that came to him were mundane comments about her roof. Why did he have to be so completely hopeless when talking to a woman, especially this woman?

After a long swallow of tea, he cleared his throat. "I'll send my roofer over tomorrow. You've lost quite a few shingles on the west side. I'm afraid you'll get some leakage tonight if this storm doesn't pass us by."

"I don't think there's much chance of it passing us. Let's just hope I don't lose any more shingles tonight." As if on cue, the first large raindrops splattered against the kitchen window. At the noise Angie swiveled her head to look at the panes of glass.

"I know it doesn't seem like it, but we've been lucky," Cash said. "Eastern Minnesota got hit with tornadoes the same night your roof was damaged. Two people died."

Jane opened her mouth to reply. The microwave bell rang. Rising, she rotated the glass casserole dish and reset the timer. When she turned back, Cash was again deep in thought, and Angie was staring at him as though even she had noticed her uncle's abstraction. It was unusual for him to sit beside Angie without engaging her in conversation and teasing. Realizing this caused Jane a deep disquiet.

Trying not to call attention to herself and stir Cash's concentration, she quietly finished setting the table for the two of them. The rain dashed against the windowpanes and filled the small room with an intense, relentless rhythm. The microwave bell rang for the second time, and she lifted out the dish.

The aroma of Mexican spices: cumin, chili powder and red pepper, floated over and around the table, bringing her impromptu guest out of his inner concentration. He sniffed broadly and gave her a half smile. "That smells delicious." He looked back to the gale outside the window. "This storm is going to screw up my building schedule one more time."

So that was what was on his mind. She was vaguely unhappy and couldn't put her finger on why. Of course, he wouldn't have been thinking of her. As she set the dish on the table, she motioned toward Angie, whose head already drooped. "She looks like she may fall asleep before she finishes eating."

Jane sat down and began to dish up the cheesy beef, beans and cornmeal for Cash. For Angie to eat, she put down chunks of yellow cheese and some wheat crackers while her dish cooled.

"She likes this stuff?" Cash asked.

"You know she loves people food and hates baby food."

"What's this called?"

"Enchilada bake."

He took another forkful. "It's good."

She murmured her thanks, but turned her attention to the storm again and frowned. The center of the accelerating storm was advancing on them with frightening speed. Lightning flashed outside the darkened kitchen windows, and thunder punctuated their sentences.

"Did Tom head back for Chicago?" Cash asked as innocently as possible.

"Yes." She frowned down at her plate.

"I called here several evenings, and Tish said you were out with him." As soon as the words were out of his mouth, he was irritated with himself. Why bring up the competition—especially when the man's roses were probably in the refrigerator?

"I was." She turned to a drowsy Angie, giving her another mouthful of the casserole. She reached over to the counter and lifted the baby's bottle waiting there. The little girl's eyelids were steadily drifting lower.

"I can't believe it's only three days to her first birthday," he murmured as he watched Angie sucking her bottle.

Jane stiffened visibly.

Again, he felt her cold response to his words as though shards of ice crackling around his ears. How could he have brought up his day alone with Angie? He could easily guess how much it still upset her. Why couldn't he keep his mouth in line?

The three of them finished the meal in silence. They cleared the table and filled the sink with soap and dishes. By now the storm was relentless—flashing, booming.

"This system is not moving away as fast as I thought it would," he said, lifting his voice to be heard. "Do you have a transistor radio—"

Thunder exploded overhead. Angie screamed in fright. Jane leaped to her feet and lifted the shrieking child into her arms.

"That was close," Jane gasped. She held Angie close, trying to soothe her. The room had gone black, but outside, rapid lightning lit the room like artificial strobe lighting.

"That was a direct hit. Where's your flashlight?"

"I only have a small one, but I'll get it." Jane opened a kitchen drawer and found the solid tube of metal by the brilliance of the staccato flashes. She handed it to Cash and he turned it on.

"Let's go downstairs and check your breakers."

With one hand she felt her way around the erratically lit room. Angie had stopped screaming, but sobbed raggedly against Jane's neck. Without speaking, Cash took Jane's arm. By the thin thread of light from the flashlight, they fumbled their way to the rear of the kitchen and down the narrow, back hall steps. The thunder was now a building crescendo. Jane felt herself tensing with each wave of sound.

Cash used the flashlight to locate the circuit breakers on the basement wall. He checked them manually. All the switches had been tripped. But when he turned them all back to On, no lights from above shone in the rippling darkness.

"Double whammy," he said.

Boom! Crack! The metallic clatter of hail struck the basement windows.

"What's happened?" Jane's voice was loud and shrill.

Cash also raised his voice over the rampaging thunder and hail. "It's an outage plus your house was just struck by lightning."

"Struck! That's never happened before!"

"It's not that uncommon in a storm like—"

Angie whimpered loudly. The sound caught Cash's heart. He put his arms completely around Jane, cuddling the baby between them. He murmured softly into Angie's ear.

Jane felt the little body pressed against her slowly relaxing. The baby's periodic sobs ebbed, then ceased. Angie shivered once more and let go of the last of her tension.

Taking two tentative steps backward, Jane encountered the edge of the daybed she stored in the basement. Cash let her go, and she sat down on its edge and, humming close to Angie's ear, rocked gently.

"Can we go upstairs?" Jane whispered.

"Let's wait. That wind sounds dangerous." He shone the flashlight up at one of the small basement windows near the laundry area. The window rattled, straining at its latch.

With the flashlight, he showed her the sheets of wind-driven rain still buffeting the basement window. The slashes of lightning continued. Jane shivered. Angie's now-sleeping body became a deadweight across Jane's tired arms, but she held the child till she was certain Angie wouldn't stir.

At Jane's softly spoken suggestion, Cash went to the nearby dryer and brought back a basket of freshly laundered diapers. The cotton diapers made a cozy mattress and blankets. In a matter of moments, Angie, slumbering deeply, was tucked comfortably into the large, oval wicker basket.

The town's tornado siren blared. Its sudden blast jolted them both. Jane jumped up and collided with Cash. He took her into his arms, tucking her tightly to him. The siren wailed on, competing with the beating rain, pinging hail and roaring thunder.

Another bolt of lightning exploded overhead. Jane clutched Cash as though she were drowning. The thunder detonated overhead again, again, again. Each blast urged Jane closer to him, to his solid strength.

Cash's awareness of her soft, slender body surged at the same pace as the storm. Her cinnamon scent was all around him, filling his head. Though afraid she might push him away, he kissed her.

His lips caressed hers. Quivers of excitement like fragments of the lightning arced through her. She swayed in his arms.

He pulled her snugly to him again. His mouth closed over hers, searching and claiming the eager sweetness there. He moved against her, unconsciously imitating the rhythm of the tumult out of doors. The incessant crashes and flashes continued outside, but they receded in her consciousness.

In a surge of almost unbelieving joy, Cash clutched her shoulders, letting go of the flashlight. It clattered to the floor. He held her close, wrapped in the flickering blackness.

The thunder and lightning blustered unnoticed. Jane let herself stand in the shelter of Cash's arms. She knew she should bring them both back to reality. But this was the only man she'd ever loved. She had intended never again to give in to the attraction of his arms, but this would be the last kiss. One last kiss.

Chapter Thirteen

Angie screeched, breaking the silence of the peaceful morning after the stormy night. Asleep on the daybed, Jane jerked awake. Like a videotape on Fast Forward, images of her kissing Cash while nestled in his arms zipped through Jane's mind. After that bittersweet kiss, she'd lain down on the old daybed while Cash had settled himself nearby on an old reclining chair to wait out the storm.

Angie screeched again. Jane scrambled up, stumbling onto the basement's cold, concrete floor. Angie wailed continuously. Jane lifted her out of the wicker basket.

"Angie, sweetie. Oh, dear," Jane fussed. "I forgot to triple-diaper you for the night. You're completely soaked." She dug down to the bottom of the basket for two dry diapers.

Angie shivered and whimpered against Jane's bare shoulder. Jane hurried up the basement steps, through the back hall into the kitchen.

The back door opened. "Jane, it's me." Cash's voice came to her from the small porch.

"In the kitchen," Jane called back. She cleared the sink

of dishes and began to fill it with fresh water. While Angie leaned against her, Jane stripped the baby of her sodden yellow romper and saturated diaper. Jane swirled a little baby shampoo into Angie's bathwater, then settled the baby into the warm, sudsy water. Angie's good nature instantly restored, she gurgled and splashed at the floating bubbles.

"You bathe her in the kitchen sink?" Cash appeared at her elbow.

"She doesn't like the big tub," Jane said defensively. "She clings to me and cries."

"She looks like she enjoys this." He peered over Jane's shoulder. "Morning, Angie," he greeted the baby. "Jane, I stopped at Lucy's to tell her you and Angie were all right. Her phone lines should be up again sometime this morning."

Suddenly Jane felt Cash's long, muscled arms—one on each side of her—stretch out and surround her. His skin slid against hers. Jane felt her body become charged with an invisible current transmitted from Cash's bare skin to hers.

Grasping one of Angie's hands in each of his, he helped the little girl splash her bathwater. Soapy water sprinkled Jane's face and bare collarbone. She batted her eyelashes to rid herself of the beads of moisture around her eyes. Then she felt Cash's lips press a kiss on the back of her neck. Jane stiffened. She said quickly, "She'll want her breakfast right away. Can you make one-minute oatmeal?"

Cash, releasing Angie's fingers, straightened up. "*Hot* oatmeal?"

"It's her favorite."

"Even in summer?"

"Her stomach doesn't know it's summer. The cereal's on the shelf over the stove, just follow the directions on the box."

"Okay, boss. Oatmeal coming up." Cash turned away and then turned back. He smiled suddenly. This would be the first morning of a lifetime of mornings for Angie, Jane and him in the kitchen for breakfast together. He pressed another kiss on the back of Jane's neck. "Mmm. You taste good. Much better than oatmeal."

Out of the corner of his eye, he saw Jane flush a deep red. He felt like laughing out loud with a teasing joy, and he waited, anticipating her look toward him, either to scold him or kiss him. He didn't really care which, a scold or kiss, because his answer to both would be a thorough Good-morning-I-love-you kiss. He waited.

Instead, Jane kept her attention on Angie. Feeling sharply disappointed that she hadn't responded as he wished, he went to the appointed shelf. His fledgling faith fluttered to life. *What's happening, God? Tell me the words to say.* Taking the box in hand, he read the directions. "Is this oatmeal for two?"

"I usually make enough for two."

"Very well. I'll make it oatmeal for three." He brought the pan over to the sink to measure in the water. As he stood next to Jane, a glance at her trim figure delighted him. He grinned sideways at her. Leaning over, he bent to kiss her shoulder again.

"Don't."

Taken by surprise, he froze. "But—"

"I'll be right back." Scooping Angie out of the water, Jane folded a clean dishcloth around her, then made a wide curve around the other side of the table and out the door.

Her avoidance of him as she left the room had been unmistakable. Cold needles of fear pierced his chest. He went through the motions of measuring the oatmeal and water into the saucepan and setting it on the burner to simmer. Then he found the coffee canister and went to work on Jane's fifties vintage percolator.

A few seconds after the timer bell rang for the oatmeal, Jane walked back into the kitchen, Angie in her arms.

Cash lifted the pan from the burner. He smiled uncertainly. Angie squirmed, and in her private language called for him. Jane ignored this and plunked the baby into her high chair.

"Oatmeal, Angie?" Jane offered.

"Where are the bowls?" Cash, waiting with the saucepan in his hand, asked soberly.

Keeping the table between them, Jane went to the cabinets over the sink and quickly collected bowls, cups and spoons. "Please get the milk." She nodded toward the refrigerator next to him and then sat down beside Angie.

Bringing the plastic jug of milk with him, Cash set the pan of oatmeal on a trivet in the middle of the small table and sat down opposite Jane. He studied her, trying to judge what was causing her agitation. Her outward armor was in place, too. She had put on a high-necked, long-sleeved, floor-length robe.

Pressing her lips tightly, she mixed brown sugar and milk into Angie's bowl of oatmeal.

Feeling a deep uncertainty, Cash went over last night's events. He took a deep breath, said a silent prayer, then forced the issue. "Okay, Jane, what's the problem?"

She flushed.

"What's the problem?" he repeated.

She wouldn't meet his eyes. She spooned up a sugary bit of oatmeal for Angie.

"Do you regret our closeness last night?" he demanded bluntly.

Jane cleared her throat. "I should have shown more restraint."

"I don't think either of us could have shown more restraint. I held you in my arms. We kissed. Nothing more happened. I want you as my wife, Jane. I've made that clear."

"You made that clear with your *convenient* proposal," she said stiffly.

"I've changed. I don't just want you as a mother to Angie. I love you."

"No! Don't say it."

"Why not? You're the woman I love—"

"Don't!" Her sharp tone startled Angie. The baby screwed up her face and began crying. "There, there, sweetheart," Jane murmured. "Angie, here is the spoon. Angie, eat with spoon." Gently she put the spoon into the little girl's chubby hand.

Then Jane looked directly into his eyes. "We both know that you don't love me."

"I've changed. I made a mistake when I made that proposal."

"You made it quite clear that you did not love—"

"A man can change his mind."

Jane snapped, "A man can change his tactics to get what he wants."

"You wanted to be in my arms last night."

"It was that awful storm. I was frightened to be alone with Angie."

"The night of your parents' anniversary you told me you loved me."

"I also told you that night I'd decided to close my heart to you. Last night I was weak. It won't happen again."

Not taking his eyes from her, he fought for control by pouring himself a cup of coffee, then he put down the mug. "I will not let you sweep last night under the rug as though it didn't matter. Your kisses showed your love—"

"I don't want to discuss last night—"

"Too bad. We're going to. Now," he insisted.

"*You're* not in charge here." She glared at him.

He took a swallow of coffee to stop another cutting retort

that nearly jumped from his lips. *God, help me. What should I say?*

Before he could speak, Angie dropped her spoon. Both of them bent to retrieve it. It had fallen on his side. He picked it up, tossed it into the sink, then handed the baby a clean one.

Jane straightened up stiffly and, even though she gave him only her profile, the anger on her features was obvious.

He again swallowed the hot words that rushed to his mouth. He took a slow breath while watching Angie as she tried to spoon oatmeal into her own mouth. A glob of it quivered just below her mouth.

"Jane, I love you and I want to marry you."

He watched her lift her chin, it trembled slightly. "I wish you wouldn't insult my intelligence. We both know you don't love me."

"No, we don't both know that. I love—"

"Stop it!" She turned to him. "I don't want to hear any more!"

He clenched his jaw, holding back another futile declaration of his love. Why hadn't he realized that he needed to talk to her last night, to speak the right words while their closeness was fresh and irresistible? How could he make her believe him now? He felt as though he were sliding down into a black hole.

Angie threw down her spoon and yelled in frustration. Jane took up another spoon, caught the oatmeal blob and slipped it into the baby's mouth.

Cash took in another tasteless mouthful of coffee. "Do you think it's impossible for me to fall in love with you?"

"It's worse than that. I think you've proven it is impossible for you to fall in love with anyone."

Full-blown, complete frustration exploded within him. He wanted to bellow: I love you, Jane! Instead he closed his eyes. For several minutes he kept his eyes shut as he listened to Jane talking to and feeding Angie.

The desire to go to Jane and pull her to him became a physical ache inside him. He craved her touch more than he had ever craved anyone's touch in his whole life. He wanted Jane. Not just sexually, he wanted all of her, for better for worse, for richer for poorer, now and until her physical beauty faded and their passion was a mere glimmer in her eyes. In the past few days he'd just begun adjusting his mind to think of eternity. Now he knew he wanted to be with Jane until death, then beyond. What could he say or do to make her believe he was sincere? He murmured, "I love you, Jane."

Looking up, he stopped, shocked at the pain he saw in her eyes. In that moment he knew she loved him with a love that was so different from any he had known before: a quality of love that he could only imagine. When Jane had come to him the night of her parents' anniversary, she had told him that she loved him. But it had been like explaining sunlight to a man born blind.

From her eyes he now learned much. Jane still loved him, even though she denied it. She loved him in a way he had never dreamed of, in a way he hoped someday he might be capable of returning. Before that day in Wausau when he had opened his mouth and spoiled everything, Jane had wanted to give him a love few people ever imagined. A one-and-only, for-a-lifetime love. She was an Everett, after all. He felt numb. I've been a blind fool.

Two hours had passed since Cash had left Jane's door. Before he left, Jane had been confused by his change of expressions from angry to dumbfounded. She lowered Angie into her playpen in the den. A "Sesame Street" videotape already played cheerfully on the nearby television.

Jane wandered into the kitchen and opened the fridge for

some fruit juice. The white florist box confronted her. Tom.
I forgot all about the roses, she thought.

Lifting the box, she opened it. The blooms looked dry
and neglected. She carried them to the sink and set about
trimming the stems, but her thoughts couldn't be pulled
from Cash. He told her he loved her, but she couldn't believe him. He might even think he really did, but how could
she be sure? He'd ignored her for years. And, after his proposal that they marry only for convenience, she couldn't
overcome her doubts.

Cash wanted her as a convenient wife. But no matter how
she denied it, she still wanted him as the love of her life.
She was cursed with the concept of lifelong love and marriage she'd learned from her parents. Her stomach clenched
and she longed to sit down and cry. Cash had love enough
for Dena, Angie and Lucy. Why couldn't he manage to fall
in love with her? She pulled a glass vase from a cupboard
and began arranging the roses in it.

So it came down to this. She still loved Cash, but she
wouldn't, couldn't settle for less than his heart. To marry
him without his loving her would be a sham, an unbearable
one. Perhaps with time the pain would ebb.

Somehow, some way she was going to have to push this
out of her mind and memory. She must find a way to deal
with her lingering feelings for Cash. Because of Angie she
would be seeing Cash for the rest of her life.

She finished placing the last flower into the cut-glass vase.
She fingered one velvet petal. I'm not being fair to Tom.
Right now, I still care too much for Cash.

She walked to the wall phone and dialed Tom's private
line in his Chicago office. When he answered, Jane nearly
choked on her misery, but she went on, anyway. "Tom, I
need to be honest with you."

Angie's first birthday dawned. Promptly at 4:00 p.m.,
Cash knocked on Phil and Marge's door. It opened quickly.

He could feel the hot sun on his back and the cool rush of air-conditioning on his face.

As Lucy let him in, she offered him a silvery, cone-shaped party hat. "Here's your hat, Cash." The living room was filled with Jane's family, just like on the Fourth of July.

Over Lucy's shoulder he spotted Tish, who was giving him a look that spoke of her excruciating embarrassment over the childish party hats. Attempting to soothe her discomfort, Cash winked at Tish. Trying to be cheerful was costing him. Memories of his lost Dena had haunted him all day. His frustration over Jane had upset his sleep. But with cheerful aplomb, which was in direct opposition to his true feelings, he put the cone on his head at a jaunty angle and snapped its elastic string under his chin.

Tish handed him a metal noisemaker for one hand and a party whistle that would unfold and squeak when he blew it.

"Feels like New Year's Eve," he murmured to Tish.

"Feels like we're at the nuthouse," Tish said to him from the side of her mouth.

"Cash," Marge hailed him from where she sat near the fireplace. "Come here and watch this beautiful child!"

Angie stood on Phil's lap. Phil held her securely under each arm. Angie was trying—with great excitement—to grab the hat from her grandfather's head. Each time she reached up for it, Phil dodged her chubby hands. Instead of squealing with frustration, Angie squealed with enjoyment of the game. Finally Phil let her jerk the hat off his head. Angie crowed and immediately shoved it into her mouth. She was applauded and cheered by one and all—even Tish.

"Now that we're all present," Lucy said formally, "we may begin the activities on this most festive of occasions." Again there was cheering and applause. "Blind Man's Bluff will now commence." Lucy quickly chose Henry as the blind man, tied a handkerchief around his eyes, spun him three times and let him loose in the large living room.

Henry came right at Cash, who jumped backward to avoid being tagged. Tish appeared at Cash's arm and tugged at him to follow her. He let her lead the way down the hall.

"We can hide here," Tish whispered as they arrived in the master bedroom.

"Why do we want to hide?" Cash whispered back.

"You can't tell me that you want to play Blind Man's Bluff. *Kids* don't even play that anymore. When I was ten, I wanted to play it at my after-school birthday party, and none of the kids even knew what it was! Now that shows you how weird—"

"It isn't weird. The Everetts are just…" He groped for the right words.

"The Everetts are just weird." Tish folded her arms across her breast.

"The Everetts are blessed with Lucy—"

Tish snorted derisively and tossed her head like a headstrong filly.

"Your grandmother knows what has lasting value and how to stay young or play young."

"I hate her. I just want to grow up and get away from her and my parents—"

He wanted to shake her then. Tish—who was blessed with a warm and unique family—wanted to run away from it. "I'd give anything to be an Everett."

Tish shook her head at him, opened the door and waved him out. He left, unable to think of what to say to convince her that she was a princess of a royal family, not an unwilling visitor at the state mental institution.

At the end of the hall Henry grabbed him and made him the next blind man. In moments Cash stood with his arms extended for balance, disoriented, reeling from his three turns. He heard muffled footsteps and laughter. He waited till the sensation of being lost left him. Then he caught a whiff of Jane's unmistakable cinnamon fragrance.

No one moved. They waited for him to begin blundering around to mask their movements. He stood still, letting Jane's scent come to him till he felt he knew exactly where she was. Angie giggled.

Cash swung around to his left. His outflung hand caught an arm. "Gotcha!" He tugged off his blindfold. Jane, Angie in her arms, was flushed and glaring at him.

"He got the birthday girl," Lucy sang out. "He wins the medal for this game."

Phil pinned a large paper star on Cash's shirt and stole Angie from Jane's arms, leaving the two of them staring at each other.

"You can let go of me now," she ordered.

Cash dropped her arm as though it were electrified.

The two of them were swept into a rousing game of Musical Chairs. Angie clapped and squealed her pleasure. Tish's absence was obvious, and Cash caught the glances that passed between Henry and Claire. He could read their indecision over what to do about their daughter's mutiny, but in the end they remained silent.

When the last game, Pin the Tail on the Donkey, was done, they all sat in a loose circle in the living room to watch Angie open her gifts.

"Jane, here, you hold Angie and, Cash, you sit next to her and help," Marge suggested, pointing to the love seat.

"Why don't you hold Angie, Mother?" Jane countered. "I want to take some pictures." Giving the child to her mother, Jane went to the corner and lifted her camera from her purse.

Cash understood picture taking wasn't keeping Jane from sitting next to him. Did she have to be so obvious about keeping her distance from him? He cleared his throat.

"That's a great idea. I'd rather watch, anyway." He hoped he had said it with just the right agreeable, unruffled tone.

So Angie sat on Marge's lap while Phil "helped" his granddaughter open her gifts: a rag baby doll from Lucy, a musical teddy bear from the proud grandparents, a pale lavender porcelain angel with a gilded number "1" on her skirt from Uncle Henry and Aunt Claire, a bright red ball from Tish, who had reappeared, and a tiger hand puppet from Jane. Everything was opened, even some uninteresting clothes which Angie pitched out of the boxes in her search for more toys.

While Angie listened to the musical bear, Cash disappeared and returned. Jane saw him first, coming down the hall. Bent over, he pushed a red tricycle ahead of him.

"Angie," Marge cooed, "look what Uncle Cash has for you."

The little girl pushed herself off her grandmother's lap. Momentarily she stood, steadying herself by touching Marge's knees.

"Angie," Cash coaxed, pushing the shiny trike forward.

She chortled and launched herself toward Cash and the trike.

"She's walking!" Tish exclaimed.

"Jane, get her picture!" Lucy shouted as she leaped up from the sofa.

Jane in throes of several conflicting emotions: joy, resentment, awe and guilt, rapidly snapped the camera's button.

Cash lurched forward, catching Angie just as her uneven steps faltered. He spun her around, laughing. "She walked! She walked! To me!"

Jane continued snapping pictures to mask her tangled emotions. Was she really so petty she would resent Angie taking her first steps toward Cash? No, that wasn't it. But why couldn't she stop feeling like an overwound clock, so tight and tense? Jane continued shooting pictures till the film in the camera ran out. Then she went to the table at the end of the room to her camera bag there. She turned and smiled falsely. "I'll have to reload for some more priceless photos."

Phil stood up. "I'm in the mood for cake." He extended his arms to Angie. "Ice cream, Angie?" he invited. She laughed and smiled in agreement, but remained in her uncle's arms.

The party moved to the festively decorated table. The ritual of lighting and blowing out the birthday candles—one for Angie's first year and one for luck—was observed in the traditional way. Jane kept herself busy, taking pictures, serving cake and scooping ice cream. Finally they were all seated around the table, even Jane.

"Marge, that was the best coconut layer cake you have ever made." Phil patted his stomach contentedly.

"Thank you, darling." Marge leaned over and kissed his cheek.

"Angie certainly seems to have enjoyed herself," Claire pointed out. Everyone looked at the little girl and chuckled. In Everett family tradition, the one-year-old had been allowed to eat her cake and ice cream all by herself. Consequently white frosting, ice cream and flakes of coconut liberally decorated Angie's face, hands and hair.

Lucy stood up and folded her hands in front of her. All eyes turned to her. "This has been a special day. And there is one more presentation."

She cleared her throat. "Cash, today is a day of joy, the celebration of the first year of life for our dear Angie. I wanted to give you something to treasure as a remembrance of this day."

Lucy bent down, opened the doors of the pecan sideboard behind her and drew out the small oval miniature of Angie that she had painted. She gave it to Cash. "Jane helped me with the posing, otherwise I couldn't have done it."

Cash could not take his eyes off the small portrait of Angie's bright eyes and chubby smile. Tears knotted in his throat. He couldn't speak, so he took Lucy's hand and squeezed it.

Marge stood up. "We also have something for you, Cash. And you, too, Jane. We know that it will cause you both some pain, but Phil and I decided that we should make some gesture that showed our love for Dena even though she has been taken from us."

Phil rose and returned carrying two antique brass picture frames. "Marge and I were reminiscing over old photographs this summer and we came across this picture which we thought captured Dena and Jane in their childhood exactly as we remember them, so we had two enlargements made and enhanced for you." He handed one frame to Cash and one to Jane.

Jane took hers. She trembled when she saw it. The scene was one which brought back a deluge of memories. They were about eleven years old. She and Dena were fishing on Lucy's pier. They had their heads together over a fish on the end of a fishing line. The undersized fish must have swallowed the hook because the two of them were concentrating on unhooking the stubborn fish to throw it back in.

Dena's dark head and Jane's own carrot top were so close they were nearly touching. The sunny lake behind them appeared as mere flares of light, which focused all attention on the faces of the two girls. From her memory, she could hear Dena's childish voice and the loudly lapping waves behind them caused by boat wakes. Jane began to cry. Her mother pressed a hand on Jane's shoulder in sympathy. "Thank you, Mother, Father. I'll treasure it always."

"Same here." Cash's voice was thick with emotion. "Thank you. Thank you all."

Jane saw his tears and regretted her previous anger toward him. She had a loving family. He had only Angie. She had begrudged sharing Angie with him. *God, forgive me.*

She took a deep breath. *Help me, Lord.* Regardless of her own broken heart and foolish dreams about Cash, tomorrow morning when he came to take Angie for the day, she would let the baby go with him with good grace.

Chapter Fourteen

Hot wind swirled around Cash as he stepped from his Jeep the next morning. Overhead, dark clouds in shades of gray from dove to slate tumbled over and around each other as they rolled on in a swiftly changing skyline. Cash had hoped for sunshine today, his first solo visit with Angie. He had planned to spend the day playing with Angie in the sand and shallows of the lake beyond his parents' cottage. But the high wind and racing, rippling clouds above were clear harbingers of uncertain weather.

Today he would finally achieve his goal of having Angie to himself—if just for a while. But within the past weeks, his ultimate aim had altered completely. Now what he truly desired was several hours alone with Jane, so he could persuade her—somehow—that he loved her. Then he would marry her and have both Jane and Angie with him for the rest of his life.

But today would not be the day. The way to persuade Jane that he loved her still eluded him. He ached to declare the sincerity of his love for her. But as matters stood, it would only push her farther from him. Last night, after a call to Lucy for help, Cash had spent most of the evening reading a new Bible and praying for insight.

He had made a mess of everything. Building high-rise condominiums and subdivisions of beautiful homes wasn't a challenge to him. But why had he never learned how to build a relationship with a woman? Would he ever find the way to win Jane's heart? Saying one more silent prayer, he ran a hand through his hair.

As his foot touched the bottom of her front steps, Jane popped out her door with Angie holding her hand. "Good morning, Cash. Angie's all ready."

Stunned by her cheery tone, he froze, one foot on the walk, one foot on the step. He stared up at her.

Jane smiled brightly. Today she would set the tone for these weekly visitations. She would make Dena proud of her and do unto Cash as she would have him do unto her. Hand in hand, Jane and Angie walked down the steps.

Angie squealed when she reached her uncle. Jane released the little hand—such a small parting, such a wrenching at her heart. Cash lifted Angie into his arms.

"Here's her bag." Jane held out the large denim bag. "It has everything you need. When should I expect you two back?"

"Ah…is six or seven all right?" he stammered.

"That's fine. If I'm not home, just let yourself in."

"Okay. Uh, fine."

"See you later." Jane waved cheerily, turned and walked around the side of her house to where her Blazer was parked.

Her legs trembled as she heard the distinctive sound of Cash's Jeep driving away. By the time she got behind the steering wheel, gloom descended on her, a tremendous weight bearing down on her breast. She forced herself to inhale deeply.

"I am not losing Angie," she told herself sternly. "I have

lost Dena, but Angie will be home tonight in her crib.''
Saying the words out loud helped, even though the oppressive feeling of loss hung around her neck like a thick-linked
steel chain.

She started her Blazer and headed off to a nearby lake
cottage where her seamstress lived. She needed to drop off
some skirts and jackets for alteration. It was the first errand
of the day she had planned, a day full of work, a busy day,
too hectic to allow herself time to think. By the time she
closed up shop at six tonight, she would only have enough
energy to stagger home and put both Angie and herself to
bed.

After a half hour of conversation with her seamstress,
Jane rose from the table and started distancing herself from
the talkative woman. Jane finally made it out onto the back
step.

Outside, the wind snatched and tossed their voices away
from them. Startled, both women looked skyward. Overhead, charcoal clouds blanketed the sky. Below the women,
at the lakeshore, waves surged against the sandy bank and
over the end of the pier.

"This really looks bad," the seamstress shouted, folding
her arms over her breasts.

"Mel is all alone at the store. Got to go!" Jane hurried
to her vehicle. Rain burst over her. Raindrops hit the nearby
lake with such force they splashed up huge plops. She
leaped into her Blazer. Taking a deep breath, she swept her
dripping hair back from her face and started the ignition.

Down the highway she sped, with great waves of water
shooting up from behind her wheels. Sheets of rain rolled
down her windshield; the wipers batting at them furiously.
Storm darkness smothered the daylight. Her impatience to
reach Mel and her anxiety over not knowing where Angie
and Cash were swelled inside her with each mile.

Though praying silently, she fought her panic by shouting

at the elements. "There'll be another outage. And my roof will be leaking gallons! Enough is enough!" Hail pounded the Blazer roof, blotting out her voice. Marble-sized ice balls beat against her hood and window.

As the wind's velocity grew alarmingly, she fought the steering wheel to stay on the rain-slick road. At last, town loomed ahead. The dangerous sky around her lifted from black to a strange, murky yellow-green. The hail stopped. The wind slowed. She sped up, heading straight for her alley entrance. She swung her car into place behind her shop and parked.

Suddenly in the unnatural midmorning stillness, the town siren blared. She shivered at its shrill sound. The wind swooped back. It hit her Blazer from both sides. It felt like a losing boxer in his last round, punched right and left.

When she opened her door, the wind tore it from her hands. It slammed flat against the side of her vehicle. She screamed. But she couldn't hear her voice above the churning sound. The savage wind slashed her hair and clothing. She felt it sucking her out of the car. She grabbed the door handle and clung to it.

For an unreal second the image of Judy Garland in *The Wizard of Oz* fighting the Kansas wind and stomping on the door of the storm cellar paralyzed Jane. In a terror beyond words, her spirit screamed for God's help.

Mighty strength surged through her. She ripped her hand away from the car and fought the few feet to the shop's rear door. Surprisingly it opened with ease. But as the top hinge let go, she screeched in horror and threw herself inside.

There Mel stood, frozen in the center of the shop. As in a surreal dream, Jane watched through the window behind Mel as the parking meter snapped off its base. Like a javelin, it pierced Jane's plate-glass window. Shards of glass, dust and debris sailed everywhere. Jane felt herself screaming, screaming.

Fighting the pull of the howling wind, she launched herself at Mel. She dragged the girl to the basement stairwell, then pushed Mel down the first step. She fought the door shut. At last she tugged the heavy, old bolt into place. The cheated wind shrieked its anger.

Feeling around in the awful blackness, Jane found Mel at her feet, sitting hunched over on the step. Slipping down weakly, Jane wrapped her arms around the girl. With wordless prayers pouring from her trembling lips, Jane clung to Mel, who sobbed and rocked with terror. The roar above them filled their ears. The door vibrated. The screeching wind struggled to break the bolt.

Suddenly Jane heard her own sobbing clearly, then Mel's. She realized the door above her had ceased straining against the lock. Light glowed around the doorjamb. She swallowed deeply and shivered. "Mel, it's over. It's over. Thank God, it's passed us by."

Mel's grip on her didn't loosen. Jane stood up shakily, urging Mel up with her. She drew back the latch and pushed against the door. It opened a few inches, then bumped against something and stuck. She heaved against it and, with much scraping, it opened. A twisted rack of sodden clothing lay propped against the door.

For seconds, minutes, she stared, befuddled, at the crazy disarray around them. Then Mel leaned her face into Jane's shoulder and mumbled something unintelligible. Jane looked down and saw blood. Mel's head oozed crimson blood onto Jane's white blouse. Her hands where she had touched Mel felt wet and sticky, too. With a gasp, she lifted Mel's face in both her hands. She felt nauseated at the sight of blood spattered over Mel's head and shoulders.

She took a deep breath. "I've got to get you to the medical center. It must have been the glass." Even though she said the words aloud, she felt no impetus to move. A sustained moan from Mel finally cracked the ice jam of Jane's shock.

She stumbled around as though drunk, but she managed to get the two of them outside. Her Blazer waited in the back just as she had left it—except that the driver's side door had been blown off. Farther down the alley a delivery van lay on its side. At the sight of this her mind shrieked, *Angie! Cash!* Terror sliced her heart. Where had Cash taken their baby? Had the two of them been in the path of the storm? Panic clutched her breast. She fought for breath. *God, I can't think. Help me. I can't think!*

"Oh," Mel whimpered.

Pushing down her own terror, Jane half lifted, half pushed Mel into her car through the gap where her door had been. Jane climbed in after her. She fumbled around, then realized that she was instinctively searching for her purse on the seat, but it, too, had been carried away on the wind. Then she saw that her keys still dangled from the ignition. She sighed with relief and started the vehicle. Because the van blocked her usual exit, she backed down the length of the alley till she could swing around and head out onto Main Street.

She stopped at the first intersection, not because the traffic signal was red, but because the traffic light itself lay across the road. Making a wide U-turn, she backtracked to take another route to the hospital. The short trip was torture. Downed branches and crackling power lines terrified her. She had to force herself to press on toward her goal. At every corner she wanted to turn her car toward Lucy's cottage. Was Lucy safe? Her parents? Angie? Cash?

When the medical center came into view, Jane felt like bursting into tears of relief. She swung into the lot, parked near the emergency entrance and helped Mel out, then through the automatic emergency room doors. The normally tranquil and efficient small-town hospital buzzed with urgent voices and the sound of crying. The fearful sounds hit Jane, draining her of initiative.

Fortunately a nurse saw them and stepped around the counter quickly. "Come with me." She led them into a curtained area and helped Mel up onto an examining table. Soon she was carefully bathing Mel's face and head. She occasionally contacted a sliver of glass and gently tweezed it out. Jane leaned against the inside wall. The desire to bolt taunted her. She had to find Angie and Cash. But she couldn't leave till Mel had been treated and she took her home.

Glancing up at Jane, the nurse murmured, "Please sit down. It will be a while before I can get to you—"

"I'm not hurt—"

"You are. Just not as much." She pointed to a mirror above a small sink. Leaning over, Jane peered into it and gasped. Her own face was nicked and smeared with blood. Her complexion went white. Her knees lost their strength.

The nurse dropped her basin and grabbed Jane's arms. Without ceremony, she plunked Jane down on a straight chair and shoved Jane's head between her knees. "I guess I shouldn't have told you."

"The window broke—"

"Just keep your head down till it clears."

Nodding slightly, Jane gazed dismally at the gray linoleum floor, feeling light-headed for the first time in her life. She felt so helpless. Her family might be in need of her, and here she sat sick at the sight of her own blood. She tried to pray, but only worrying images flashed in her mind. Finally she sat up and watched the nurse finish treating Mel.

Jane stood up. "Let's get you home, Mel. Thanks. We'll take care of the paperwork on our way out."

The nurse tried to dissuade her from leaving without treatment, but Jane helped Mel down from the high table. They stepped outside the curtain and into the arms of Rona.

"Carmella Stephanie Maria Vitelli! Thank God! I couldn't get you on the phone! I went to the shop. It was awful. I was so worried." Mel wilted into her mother's arms and began sobbing.

Jane longed to throw herself into her own mother's arms—and Cash's. She visualized Angie and Cash as they had looked just hours before on her front steps. A terror beyond any she had known before ripped through her, making her gasp aloud. Where were they? Had they suffered harm? Her mind balked at the possibility that they had been hurt, but she could not stop the fear that they might already be lost to her. She felt a scream welling up inside of her. Not Angie! Not Cash!

Her mind at that moment cut away all but the essential. Angie and Cash were the two most important people in her life. Why had she refused Cash's repeated proposals? Why had she let her foolish pride stand between them? So what if he didn't love her! *Oh, God, are they safe? Help me find them. Let me tell him how much I love him. Let me hold Angie and feel her soft, baby hair once more.*

"Jane! Jane, are you all right?" Rona asked loudly, taking Jane's hands in hers.

"She should stay for treatment," the nurse insisted behind them.

Ignoring the nurse, Jane squeezed Rona's hands, then she moved toward the exit. Her fingers plucked keys from her slacks pocket. As she stepped on the rubber pad that activated the automatic exit doors, an ambulance with blaring siren and flashing lights halted in front of her, blocking her path. Two men in uniform quickly unloaded a wheeled stretcher. Jane barely noticed their activity till she saw her cousin climb out of the back of the ambulance, too.

Tish threw herself at Jane, her arms closing around Jane's shoulders. "Mother's hurt!"

"Tish!" Jane scanned her cousin, noting the girl's disheveled clothing, scrapes and bruises.

"We were driving back to town," Tish explained between sobs. "The wind just pushed us off the road! We rolled down the embankment. Over and over. Mother won't ever wear her seat belt...." She gave in to her sobs, and Jane, her arm around Tish's shoulders, turned back to lead her inside. They followed the stretcher on which Claire lay, white and silent, until it disappeared into another curtained area.

A woman with a clipboard tried to ask Tish the few necessary questions to admit her mother, but Jane had to answer for Tish. Her cousin's eyes never left the curtain, which separated her from her mother.

Tish's arrival caught Jane in a dilemma. Seeing Aunt Claire made her anxiety over Cash and Angie multiply tenfold, but she could not leave Tish. As much as she loved her aunt, it took all her willpower to stay in the chair beside her cousin. She desperately needed to see Angie, her grandmother, her parents and Cash. A yearning ignited within her, a yearning to touch Cash, to see him whole and well. This longing almost swept her into tears. But Tish, sitting next to her, had begun to cry. Jane knew if she also gave in to tears, Tish might become hysterical. Drawing on God's strength through silent prayer, Jane began talking softly, gently to Tish.

Finally she calmed Tish enough so that she could leave her side and go as far as the desk phone. She tried to call each in turn: Cash, Uncle Henry, Lucy, her parents. Downed lines prevented her from reaching any of them, except for Tish's home, but Uncle Henry was not there. She left a message on their answering machine.

Still unconscious, Aunt Claire was wheeled from the curtained area. The doctor explained that one of her lungs may have been punctured and there was a possibility of other internal injuries. Aunt Claire was being taken to X ray immediately, then probably surgery.

Tish clung to Jane. "I'm so afraid."

"I am, too, but the Lord is here. I know we don't feel like it right now, but He is here whether it feels that way to us or not. We only have to ask."

"I don't think He will help me...." Tish began crying harder.

"Of course He will," Jane whispered. "He loves us. No matter what." She swallowed her own tears, held Tish close and smoothed her cousin's long hair back from her tear-stained face over and over.

Then Jane saw Roger Hallawell hustle in. He barked orders at the lone nurse still in sight. Jane caught only the word *injured*. The nurse followed him outside. Within minutes, the woman was back frantically paging staff. Roger returned carrying a girl about ten, who lay limp in his arms.

A rush of staff with wheeled stretchers and chairs passed Jane and Tish. Before Jane could call his name aloud, Roger was back out the door, shouting information to the nurses.

Jane and Tish watched as another four children and one woman were brought in. All five looked battered. Their clothing was ripped and embedded with mud, leaves and pebbles. Jane waited impatiently till Hallawell emerged from seeing the last of his charges receive treatment. "Roger!"

He hurried to her. "What happened to you?" His shocked expression reminded her of her own disheveled appearance.

"Just some nicks from flying glass," she said with a shrug. She didn't mention he was dirty and blood smeared just like she was. His hands were encrusted with mud as though he had been digging earth with his fingers. "What happened to you? Who were those children?"

"They were attending a woodcraft class at the park near

my office. An oak took down the roof. Do you need a ride home or anything?''

"I have my Blazer, minus one door.'' Then she directed his attention to Tish, who sat pitifully drawn and pale, huddled on the molded plastic chair. Jane lowered her voice. "I have to stay. My aunt is in surgery. We can't locate my uncle and I can't get my family on the phone.''

"What do you want me to do? I've got to get going. We're checking damaged areas with rangers and civil defense.'' As he spoke he looked as though he was about to leave her.

Jane gripped his sleeve, stopping him. "I need to have someone check on my parents and my grandmother.''

"Okay. I'll be out that way. If they need help, I'll radio the police. If they're okay, I'll give them your news.'' Even as he spoke, he pulled away from her.

She nodded, biting her lower lip against tears. He waved to her and left at a jog. Jane slipped back down beside Tish and shivered.

Tish looked up. "How much longer can they keep her up there? It's been over an hour.''

She put her arm around her cousin again. "The doctor will be down soon to tell us how she is.''

Tish's face trembled. "I've been awful to Mother this week. Yesterday when I was with one of my friends, I even mocked the way she talks. How could I?''

Jane hugged Tish to her, feeling her cousin's tears on her own cheek.

"Just because she and Father talk so much. I love them. I really do—''

"Of course you do.''

"Then why do I say and do such terrible things all the time?''

"This is the real world. Just because we love someone doesn't mean we do and say everything we should.'' Jane's own words stabbed her. She'd been harsh to Cash because of his proposal. "Your parents love you, and they know you love them, too."

At last the doctor, still in green surgical garb, came down the long corridor to them. "Tish, your mother is in post-op. As soon as she is able, we will move her to IC—"

Tish stood up shakily. "That means she's really bad, doesn't it?"

"I wouldn't say that," the doctor hedged. "But we will have to watch her carefully for another day or two. Have you been able to reach your father yet?" Tish, looking down, shook her head. He patted her arm. "Keep trying, then." He turned away. A nurse immediately called him into one of the curtained areas which were all now filled with new patients. Jane and Tish sat back down, side by side.

"I'm so glad you were here, Jane," Tish murmured, looking away. "I acted so awful that day you fired me—"

"Don't talk about it now."

"But I was awful. I lied—"

"Tish, we all do and say things we regret. Grandmother always told me, 'Just don't repeat the same mistake.'"

"I won't. I prom—"

Jane touched two fingers to Tish's lips to silence her. "I have faith your mother is going to be fine. I'll stay till your father comes." She pulled Tish close again.

Father, I'll let you take care of Grandmother, Mom, Dad and even Cash and Angie. But only because I must. This is the hardest day of my life, staying here when I want to go to them. But I have faith that I am where you want me to be. Tish needs me.

Jane shut her eyes, willing away the haunting pain of not knowing where those she loved best were and if they needed help. Heaven would have to take care of them. If only she had the chance to hold Angie in her arms again and tell Cash she loved him and that she would be honored to be his wife. She sighed and rubbed her hand across her fore-head.

Another few hours crawled by. The phone lines were still down, and the sheriff sent out word that everyone but rescue workers were to stay off the roads while the utility companies worked to clean up broken power and telephone lines. Jane's eyes burned with fatigue and, for Tish's sake, she had to suppress tears of frustration.

She felt her faith was a rock she was clinging to in the midst of a storm. She hadn't felt that way since Dena's funeral. Soothing Tish took all her strength. She felt beaten, drained of energy.

Finally evening darkened the sky outside the double doors of the ER. The number of people seeking medical attention slowed to a trickle. Another nurse tried to take Jane into a treatment area, but Jane waved her away. Jane's face and hands stung where she had been nicked by glass, but she wasn't in the mood to be poked and prodded by a stranger.

As they waited together, she and Tish held hands. Giving in to fatigue, Jane bent her head into her free hand.

"Tish. Jane."

Jane sat up straight. Uncle Henry stood in front of them. He was mud spattered and rumpled like both of them. "The police finally tracked me down. I was helping our neighbors," he said wearily as Tish flung herself into his arms. "I thought you and your mother were safely in Wausau—"

"It's all my fault. I started a fight with her," Tish sobbed, "so we started home early."

"I'm here now, child." He hugged Tish to him.

Jane rose stiffly. "I'll get going then. Have you heard from Mom or Lucy?"

"No, but I think the twister missed them completely. It swung west of them." He pulled Jane into his embrace, hugging both of them to him.

She rested her head against his arm momentarily. Then she straightened up.

"I should take you home, Jane." He tightened his arm around her.

"Claire and Tish need you here. I'll be all right."

Henry nodded and let her go. "Send word when you can. We'll be here."

She nodded and patted Tish's arm.

Outside, twilight was spent. Jane shivered in the cool evening air. The sweltering temperatures of the morning had been swept away by the storm. She fumbled in her pocket for her keys. Her head throbbed, and she was aware of every cut on her face, neck, arms and hands. In the dim light of the parking lot, she felt totally abandoned.

A blue Jeep careened around the corner and swooped down on her. She turned her head. "Cash!"

The brakes screeched. He leaped out and he was there, in front of her. Before she could speak, he began shouting at her, "Hallawell said you were just scratched. Is this what he calls scratched! If I'd known you were this bad, I would have come right away. How could they let you leave like this? I'm taking you right back in there—"

Suddenly feeling like a fretful child, she whimpered, "No, I want to go home. I want Angie." She tried to describe all the worries of the whole long, torturous day, but her words were garbled by gasps and tears. "Angie?"

"Angie's fine. She's with Lucy at your parents' place." His strong arms went around her, and he hugged her close. He placed fervent kisses on her forehead and mussed hair. "I'm here now. Hush. God's been good. Everyone's fine." His lips and gentle words soothed her.

She rubbed her face against his dirty, wrinkled shirtfront. He was so real she was comforted at last. She heaved several deep sobs, then she released a sigh. The tension left her so suddenly that she leaned limply against him.

"I'll take you home now." He swung her up into his arms, carried her to the passenger seat of his Jeep and hooked her seat belt for her. Then he drove smoothly through almost-empty, darkened streets. Large branches, and in some place trees and light poles, lay beside the road. Fortunately the nearly full moon was out.

Jane insisted as strongly as she was able, "I want to see Angie."

"She's fine."

Jane said, "I want—"

"I had to give in to Lucy and your mother. I tried to bring Angie, but they wouldn't let me out of the door with her."

"Are you sure she doesn't need me?" Jane leaned her head into her hand.

"It's dangerous to be out. There are lines down all over, and, as if this weren't enough, more storms are heading this way tonight. Lucy said Angie was already asleep and would be better off with them, but that I was to *get you home*." He inflected the words to mimic her grandmother's emphatic way of speaking. This persuaded Jane as nothing else might have. She slumped back against her seat. Everyone was safe.

She asked, "Where were you and Angie when the storm hit?"

"At Lucy's. After the all-clear was sounded, the three of us went straight to your parents. Then I headed into town to check on you, but Hallawell flagged me down—"

"Roger did find you then?"

"He told me where you and Tish were and that you were scratched up, but okay. I was going to come for you right then, but he asked me to help him—"

"Help Roger?"

"There was a lot of territory to cover. The rangers, sheriff's deputies, civil defense, all of us were stretched pretty thin. So after I stopped back to tell your family about you and Tish, I cruised two camping areas, then met Hallawell, and we patrolled together. He's still out there, but he sent me to get you. I stopped to get Angie before coming for you. After losing the argument with your family over bringing Angie with me, I came right to the medical center for you.''

"I love you. I'll marry you." Her declaration slipped out naturally.

At first the man beside her did not react to it. Moments passed. Then he stopped the Jeep. He tugged her face to his and kissed her.

Cash's kiss had an effervescent effect on Jane. Inside her, an unseen current bubbled up from her toes, lifting her, making her feel as though she floated near him, weightless. He ended the kiss, murmured, ''Jane, God knows how much I love you, but I have to get you home now.'' He gave her a heartening embrace before he turned to the wheel.

Soon he drove down her drive. After parking, he led her to the back door. A cold rain began falling, dampening and chilling them. But when she saw by the light of the veiled moon that her snug house was unscathed, warmth filled her heart. Inside her house the floating sensation, which had carried her in, abruptly deserted her. She slumped against Cash.

"Don't fade out on me now," he whispered. He touched the light switch on the kitchen wall out of habit. When no light flashed on, he grumbled, then swung her into his arms again and cautiously made his way through the dark house to her bedroom. He left her sitting on the edge of her bed.

She heard him making rustling noises in the dark, but she did not feel compelled to make sense of them. Her family was safe, she was in her bedroom, and Cash was with her. Gratitude filled her.

Cash said quietly, ''I know we may not need this, but it will give us some light and warmth.''

She saw Cash starting a modest fire in her bedroom fireplace. Watching the kindling flare made her shiver in anticipation. The cool evening air, cold rain and damp clothing made the fire very welcome. She stumbled to Cash and dropped to her knees in front of the flames flickering to life.

Cash returned the screen to its place and dropped a kiss on her forehead. "You need a hot bath. Hope you have enough water stored in your hot water heater for one."

From across the hall she heard the creak of her bath faucets being turned on and the gush of water pounding the tub. Cash came back in, pulled her to her feet, snatched a white terry cloth robe off a hook on the back of the door and led her to the warm and steamy bathroom. He sat her down on the edge of the tub.

He rested his hands reassuringly on her shoulders. "I'm going to wash your face and put some antiseptic on those cuts and nicks." He opened the medicine chest over the sink.

Jane closed her eyes, letting Cash smooth saturated cotton over her face and dabbing here and there. Even the stinging of the alcohol did not rouse her completely. Dreamily she trailed her fingers in the water, making more frothy bubbles.

Cash said quietly, "I was so worried about you. We will never let things come between us again."

She smiled and nodded. She wanted to answer him and tell him again that she loved him, but a day of panic and fear had exhausted her. Cash left the room, and she undressed and slipped into the hot water.

From that moment on, her contact with reality became more and more muted. Sustained, conscious thought eluded her, but as she went through the motions of a bath, she was aware of the intense physical sensations: the cinnamon fragrance of her bath soap, the warm water, the touch of terry cloth robe as she covered her bare skin, the gurgling of the water as it drained from the tub. She walked barefoot across the hall. Cash turned back her comforter for her and she slid between cool percale sheets.

"Don't go," she murmured.

"Don't worry. Go to sleep." While the small fire crackled with the pine tar in the logs, he sat down on the bedside rocker.

In the dancing shadows he watched Jane fall asleep. The woman he loved had been spared. She had said, "I love you. I'll marry you." She was his at last. Intense gratitude consumed him. He felt so many emotions he couldn't name them all.

When she was completely asleep, he drew close to her. Her natural scent and the fragrance of her soap had cast their power over him. Just gazing at her brought him intense pleasure. As she breathed evenly, he bent and kissed her cheek. *Thank you, Lord. Please make me worthy of this precious woman.* At last he sat back down, propping his feet on the padded ottoman and fell asleep, deeply satisfied, content.

Chapter Fifteen

At first Jane's eyes merely registered light, filtering through her lashes, but the warm, morning sunlight gently tugged her into consciousness. Then she heard the noisy, chattering sparrows on the boughs of the maple tree outside her window. She yawned. She stretched. She sighed. Rolling over, she buried her head into her fluffy down pillow.

Cash, her mind formed the name. Cash is here with me. She sat up.

She was alone. "Cash," she called softly, then louder, "Cash!" His name drew no response. Her face felt tight, dry. She touched it gingerly.

Rising, she walked into her bathroom. A note taped on the medicine cabinet mirror read: "Jane, I had to go out to the site to assess damage." She pulled the note off and read it again. All the fear and frustration she had struggled with the day before cascaded through her like white water surging over a rocky riverbed. Cash, I want you. I need you—here.

Warm tears slid down her cheeks. "How can I go to Angie?" she asked aloud. The ache of loss stunned her with its force. She needed to drive with Cash to her parents' house to see Angie and the rest of her family, to see them safe and whole. She needed to feel their arms around her, smell Angie's fresh-from-the-bath, baby-powder fragrance when she hugged the chubby little body close.

As Jane wiped her fingertips over her cheeks, she felt the scratches on her face. She looked into the mirror at her reflection and drew in a sharp breath. Dried blood starkly delineated each small nick on her forehead, cheeks and chin. A few deeper cuts were perilously close to her left eye.

A vision from the day before of the parking meter piercing her display window sent a chill down her back. For less than a moment she felt the savage wind, the flying glass, heard the wind's roar. She felt weak, and rested her elbows on the sink's rim. "Dear Lord, anything might have happened to us. Anything! Thank You. Thank You for Your protection. Dear Lord—"

Again, images of the ones she loved most came before her, tugging at her heart. Oh, Cash, why didn't you wake me?

Finally she forced herself to straighten up. Reaching into the medicine cabinet behind the mirror, she selected a tube of antibiotic cream. She applied it to her whole face, and it eased the tightness of her abraded skin.

Then, with a sigh, she walked across the hall and into her room again. Letting her clothes match her mood, she tugged on old jeans and a faded, navy T-shirt. She made herself walk downstairs to her kitchen for breakfast, just as if it were any morning.

Another note lay on the table: "Coffee is on the stove, Cash." She had already smelled the coffee as she walked down the steps. Lifting the pot, she felt it was still hot. I just missed you, Cash! Why didn't you wake me?

For a few fleeting seconds she visualized herself bathing Angie in the sink on the morning after they'd slept in the basement during the storm. She remembered the sleek texture of Cash's skin as he had surrounded her with his arms while he had splashed his hands in the water with Angie. She shivered. She almost believed she could still sense his distinctive sandalwood scent in the empty kitchen.

Her longing for Cash, Angie, everyone, gripped her. But she couldn't go to them. Cash had driven off in his Jeep, and her Blazer was at the medical center. She lifted the receiver of the wall phone. It was dead.

She poured herself a cup of coffee, but after a few sips she made her decision. Clattering her cup onto the countertop, she jotted a quick note: "At my shop" and slammed out the front door.

Outside, evidence of the storm's destruction slowed her steps and brought a deep soberness to her. Downed branches and large limbs were scattered over the sidewalk and streets. Windows had been boarded up against the night's rain. Two cars on Main Street lay "beached" on their sides.

In spite of this, her arrival at the shop jolted her. Someone had boarded up the front display window. Touching her face, she thought of Mel and unlocked the front door. Inside, she propped the door open on its catch.

The bizarre wreckage inside the shop halted her. Clothing racks were down and scattered. What remained of her current inventory was sodden, twisted and already beginning to smell of mildew. Fighting tears, she took deep breaths and passed a hand over her eyes. "It's only things, Jane," she said aloud to herself. "Only things, and to quote Grandmother, 'Hard work is good for the soul,' so don't just stand there, get busy." She marched briskly to the rear.

To encourage a cross breeze through the shop, she propped the back entrance open with a broken chair. With a flourish, she flipped on all the switches by the back door. Electric lights and a ceiling fan whirred to life. "Excellent," she said with a sigh. Ever so slightly her spirits lifted.

Stepping carefully over the littered floor, she opened the

utility closet, whose latch had held against the wind. From it, she pulled trash bags, a broom, mop and bucket. She paused momentarily to survey the task before her. Then she vigorously slapped open a large, brown plastic bag and began picking up trash blown in after the window broke.

Roger Hallawell found her bent over, carefully picking up a large pieces of glass. "Jane?"

She stood up. "How are all the children you brought in yesterday?"

"I just came from seeing them at the medical center. They were bruised up pretty bad. A few had broken bones, but they're doing okay. Except for the girl I carried in, they'll all be going home by eleven."

"Oh, I'm glad to hear none of them were seriously hurt." She smiled at him.

"I'm off to take stock of damage to my site."

"I'm doing a similar operation here." She motioned around her shop and put her hands on her hips.

"I stopped here on purpose." He paused and scanned the littered floor. She waited, still looking up at him.

"I was in the wrong about Eagle Shores, about Langley," he started hesitantly. "I was dishonest and I didn't play it very smart." He halted.

She remained silent, not knowing how to respond to him politely.

He started again. "Yesterday when I watched a tree take that shelter down, I suddenly realized there was more to life than beating the competition. People were counting on me. They needed me."

Before she could reply, Uncle Henry and Tish bustled in the back door. "Jane!" Henry called.

"How's Aunt Claire?" Jane asked.

"Out of intensive care," Henry answered. "We were there when she was moved this morning. She's feeling better, but so tired. I thought we should let her rest. Tish suggested that we come and give you a helping hand. Jane, you were a godsend yesterday.''

With a rueful smile, Tish shyly kissed Jane's cheek, and Jane pulled her close for a quick hug.

''I'm glad you came,'' Jane said.

Tish nodded, then began picking up branches, leaves and unrecognizable debris.

''While I have you two men here, would you lift a few of the heavier racks and see if we can get them to stand up?'' Jane pointed to a couple of racks that had clumped together in a convoluted mass.

Henry came over to help Roger. They hoisted up a long metal pole and held it while Jane unwrapped coils of skirts that were tangled around them. She said, ''This reminds me of trying to unravel a twisted necklace from my jewelry case.''

Cash strode in the back door and came to her. ''Here let me help with that.''

At the sound of his voice, Jane's pulse raced. But the presence of the others forced her to abandon her first impulse—to rush into his arms.

Cash supported the middle of the metal bar and found that part of another rack had become enmeshed in the overall tangle.

Jane's eyes kept drifting to Cash's face, looking for a lingering spark of the concern he had shown so fully the night before. But all she read was deep concentration on the task at hand. The skirts from the twisted racks were finally separated into individual lumps on the floor. The three men carried the mangled metal tubes out to the alley and stacked them near the overturned Dumpster.

Hallawell and Cash talked briefly about yesterday's search. Then Hallawell excused himself to go to his own site. Cash walked him to the back entrance. ''Call if you need any more help.''

Jane felt a surge of pride in the man she loved. After shaking hands with Cash, Hallawell left.

"It's amazing, isn't it, Cash," Henry said, "how two of the display cases shattered, but one remained intact? Was there much damage at your site?"

Cash shrugged. "Not much. Just a lot of limbs down in a sea of mud. Let's get this rack up."

Jane listened and waited. Still, Cash made no effort to approach her for a welcome kiss or personal comment. Had she misunderstood last night or dreamed it?

Cash hadn't realized Jane might not be alone when he came. How could he speak to her about their future with Henry and Tish hanging on every word? He gritted his teeth in frustration, but went to help Henry.

Silently unhappy, Jane again unwound each pair of slacks from around the bent circular rack. As Cash talked her through some of the worst tangles, she recalled her anxiety yesterday morning, when Cash had come to take Angie. Earlier in the year she had equated losing Angie with losing Dena. Now she saw clearly that Angie, Cash, Dena were tangled together in her heart like the twisted clothing that she held in her hands.

After last night she could not bear to go backward in her relationship with Cash. *God, help me. Tell me what to say or do. I love him. Does he want me, too?*

Her mind ached with doubt, and she needed a few minutes of solitude. She finished unwinding the last pair of slacks. "I have to go downstairs," she said over her shoulder. "It just occurred to me that I left the place wide open last night. I have a cash box and a lot of new fall inventory downstairs."

"The sheriff had his men out patrolling all night," Henry said.

In the basement not a thing had been moved out of place. Her newest shipment of wool skirts and blazers, awaiting tags, hung against the unfinished concrete wall. Jane shook her head over the contrast above and below the top step.

She used the quiet to try to get her emotions under control. Cash had proposed twice, but she had refused him twice. What if he didn't propose again? She racked her memory of last night. After her words of love, he had kissed her, but had he in any distinct way made his proposal again?

Momentarily she pressed her fingers to her temples, willing away the headache that was trying to come. She wanted to have a time alone to talk with Cash. But in another sense, she wished to hide from him, afraid of what he might say if she hinted at marriage. She sighed in exasperation.

She still had trouble believing Cash loved her. So much had happened yesterday. And he hadn't come in and approached her like a man in love.

Standing in the middle of the basement, she pulled up her reserves of strength and cast her concerns on God's broad shoulders. Cash might not love her yet, but he had not failed her. He had come for her the night before, and he was here now working hard to restore her shop. She was determined to make him love her or at least to make him happy if he married her. In any case hiding in the basement was no good. She had to go upstairs.

She started resolutely up the flight of steps. Pausing on the top step, she touched the old-fashioned bolt lock. She didn't want to think about what would have happened to Mel and her if this bolt had not held yesterday's wild wind at bay.

As she emerged from the stairwell, she came face-to-face with Cash. She looked up in surprise, nearly blurting out her musings to him.

Cash spoke first, "Jane, I—"

"Cash," Henry called. "Help me get this parking meter out of here. How did this thing get in here, anyway?"

Cash grimaced, but stepped back to let Jane pass in front of him.

She watched her uncle and Cash hefting the pole which had pierced the window. Tish helped direct the two men as they carried it out to the alley and laid it down.

"Sweetheart!" Jane's mother called to her.

Jane looked up to see her mother hurrying in with Angie in her arms. Close behind her came Phil and Lucy.

Jane met them and scooped up the baby. "Angie, sweetheart." She spun around hugging Angie while she crooned all her love to the plump little girl. Jane's family surrounded her, capturing her in a group hug. Tish and Henry joined the cluster, and kisses began. There was a crescendo of half-asked questions, answers and endearments.

Cash watched and felt his throat tighten with emotion. Staring at the floor, he stuck his hands into the pockets of his jeans.

Lucy looked up. "Cash!" She swooped to him, gathering him to her breast. The swarm of Everetts followed Lucy. Marge embraced Cash, and Phil thumped his back. Cash grinned, slightly abashed.

Finally Lucy exclaimed, "Everything's ruined, Jane! Your lovely shop!"

"Everything's not ruined, but it is a mess," Jane agreed. "But now that you're all here and Aunt Claire's going to be all right...everything's really okay." Jane shrugged, then kissed Angie's nose.

Cash approached Jane and put his arm around Angie, grazing Jane's arm. She shivered at his touch. Being near him without giving in to the desire to throw her arms around him tortured her. She moved away from him.

Tish answered Angie's greeting and as always gave the little girl an Eskimo kiss. Then Henry quietly brought everyone up-to-date on Claire's condition.

Marge nodded. "We'll go to see her this afternoon. We wanted to help Jane get started here."

Phil scanned the room. "Looks like we've got a lot of work."

Lucy pantomimed looking into a crystal ball. In a mysterious voice she said, "I see a sale in Jane's future. Jane's Super-Dooper, Wash and Wear Clearance Sale." Everyone chuckled.

Suddenly feeling fatigued, Jane sat down on a nearby stool with Angie in her lap.

Henry spoke up, "Only a half mile from here one twister touched down along Highway 51 for about a mile, and a second one destroyed a swath along Bass Lake's southern shore. We were so fortunate neither of the two touched down in a populated area." A sober stillness settled over them.

"Thank you, Lord," Lucy said softly.

Cash recalled yesterday's stark terror when he thought he and Angie might have lost Jane forever. He'd bungled his first proposal to Jane and hadn't done much better since. She deserved the best and he'd begin by giving her a proposal of marriage.

He stepped closer to her and, so he could see her eye to eye, knelt on one knee. "Jane?" he said, his voice sounding gruff to himself. "Will you marry me, Jane Everett? I love you. I can't stand the thought of living without you. I've tried to think of ways to convince you—"

"Cash, dear boy, just kiss her," Lucy said.

He looked into Jane's eyes. "May I kiss you?"

Jane felt a thrill go through her. "Please." Leaning forward, she let her lips meet his.

He pulled back an inch. "Will you marry me, Jane?"

She smiled almost shyly. "Yes."

They kissed again. The Everetts all beamed at the couple. Pressed snugly between Cash and Jane, Angie clapped her hands and squealed with joy.

Epilogue

Late spring, nearly two years later

The blue Jeep came up the final rise smoothly. Jane stepped out first and turned toward the back seat. Cash waved her away and came over to her side. He reached back to the rear seat and undid the hooks of the two car seats. Angie scrambled out under her own steam, but Cash swung their year-old baby, Storme, up into his arms. Storme grinned around her pacifier at him.

Angie rushed toward the crest of the gentle rise, but Jane caught the little girl's hand and slowed her to a walk. Angie and Jane mounted the slope while Cash and Storme brought up the rear. At the top they stopped to take in the view.

Held securely in her father's arms, Storme spit out her pacifier and twisted, trying to look everywhere at once. Then she patted her daddy's chin. He responded by rubbing his face in her belly. After giggling appreciatively over this, she found the pink ribbon that attached her pacifier to her powder blue blouse. With her tiny hand, she lifted the pacifier, sucked it into her mouth. Then she rested her head on her father's shoulder.

Cash swept his free arm eastward. "This will be the view from your kitchen window—east to catch the morning sun."

Jane studied the expanse of the pine and birch forest that she would look at every morning after their house was built.

Cash continued. "I'm putting the great room and screened-in porch on the lake side as we agreed—"

"Mama." Angie stretched her arms up to Jane who lifted the three-year-old and held her close.

Cash put his free arm around his wife's shoulders. They stood, side by side with their daughters facing Lake Elizabeth. Beneath them, on gentle rises up from the lake, other homes were in the process of being built.

"I can't believe we're ready to break ground," Cash murmured.

Jane smiled at him. Then, still holding Angie, she turned toward him and rested her head on her husband's chest, almost eye-to-eye with Storme. Cash and Jane continued standing silently, listening to Storme's rhythmic sucking.

Angie squirmed restlessly, and Jane set the little girl down. Cash and Jane trailed Angie as she walked forward a few feet to a patch of wild daisies. Angie began picking the yellow-and-white top off of each tall stem. Jane soaked in the sun's warmth, the buzz of the boats on the water and the steady beat of nails being hammered into wood.

Smiling with satisfaction, Cash closed his eyes. Storme reached up and touched her father's chin again. Without opening his eyes, he kissed the small, open palm. "We're so lucky. God has been so good." He sighed deeply and kissed the top of Jane's head. "I love you."

Jane nodded her head against him. "Love you, too," she whispered.

"Love you, three," he whispered in return.

* * * * *

Dear Reader,

Thanks for picking out my book! I believe being able to write fiction is a wonderful gift from God. And writing romance is a special treat for me. God so often uses our conflicts with others to change our hearts, especially as a man and woman work out their differences, marry and establish a new home. Cash didn't know he was incomplete and lost. Jane thought her love for Cash was hopeless. But as it is written, "a little child shall lead them," little Angie drew them together, and in the end a new family was born. Cash will never be alone again. His sister's last wish for him was fulfilled.

Never Alone is my first published novel and is close to my heart for that and another, deeper reason. A few years ago I lost one of my special friends, a former college roommate, to cancer. As I wrote about Jane's grieving over Dena, I was able to work through my own deep sorrow and sense of loss. I named baby Angie after my friend. I know I will see my friend Angie again. But for now, this book is a tribute to her vivacious, loving spirit and a testament to God's unfailing love in the most difficult of circumstances.

Lyn Cote

Welcome to *Love Inspired*™

A brand-new series of contemporary inspirational love stories.

Join men and women as they learn valuable lessons about facing the challenges of today's world and about life, love and faith.

Look for the following June 1998
Love Inspired™ titles:

SUDDENLY DADDY
by Loree Lough

IN GOD'S OWN TIME
by Ruth Scofield

NEVER ALONE
by Lyn Cote

Available in retail outlets in May 1998.

LIFT YOUR SPIRITS AND GLADDEN YOUR HEART
with *Love Inspired!*™

Steeple
Hill™

1698

Continuing in July from
Love Inspired ™...

FAITH, HOPE & CHARITY

a series by

LOIS RICHER

**Faith, Hope & Charity: Three close friends
who find joy in doing the Lord's work...and
playing matchmaker to members of this
close-knit North Dakota town.**

You enjoyed the romantic surprises in:
FAITHFULLY YOURS
January '98

A HOPEFUL HEART
April '98

And the matchmaking fun continues in:
SWEET CHARITY
July '98

Can a small town's dedicated nurse learn to let go of
her past hurts and accept a future with the new
doctor—a man who must soon return to his life
in the big city?

Available at your favorite retail outlet.

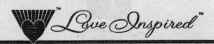

Welcome to *Love Inspired*™

A brand-new series of contemporary inspirational love stories.

Join men and women as they learn valuable lessons about facing the challenges of today's world and about life, love and faith.

**Look for the following July 1998
Love Inspired™ titles:**

SHELTER OF HIS ARMS
by Sara Mitchell

SWEET CHARITY
by Lois Richer

EVER FAITHFUL
by Carolyne Aarsen

Available in retail outlets in June 1998.

LIFT YOUR SPIRITS AND GLADDEN YOUR HEART
with *Love Inspired!*™

**Steeple
Hill**™

I798

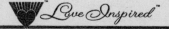